THE LOST CHILD

AN ELA OF SALISBURY MEDIEVAL MYSTERY

J. G. LEWIS

For my son, Jordan Lewis, artist and storyteller extraordinaire.

ACKNOWLEDGMENTS

Once again I am deeply in debt to Betsy van der Hoek, Anne MacFarlane and Judith Tilden for their careful readings and excellent suggestions. Many thanks also to my wonderful editor, Lynn Messina. All remaining errors are mine.

CHAPTER 1

*S*eptember 1226

The familiar tap of chisels on stone rang in the air as Ela Longespée rode into New Salisbury. She glanced up at the massive new cathedral that had emerged from sheep-grazed meadows to dominate the landscape in just a few years. It shone in the morning sun, a testament to God's glory and the grace he'd bestowed on Salisbury and its people.

She'd come here ostensibly to buy a new basket for gathering herbs, but her real intent was to call on her former lady's maid, Sibel, who had recently married the local basket seller. Their shop lay in a side street near the cathedral close, which made for easy visiting. Ela had barely turned onto the street when Sibel spotted her and hurried over, face bright with pleasure.

"Good day to you, Mistress Warren." Ela enjoyed greeting Sibel with her new name.

"And to you, my lady." Sibel bowed her head. "May God be with you."

Ela climbed down from her horse, Freya, and passed the reins to her attendant. "Marriage agrees with you."

"It's only been a few weeks," protested Sibel with a slight flush of her cheeks. "But my good husband is kind and I'm most content."

"I'm so glad—" A shout from a nearby street drew Ela's attention. She'd heard raised voices mingled with the chisel blows as they rode up this street—hardly unusual in the bustling new town—but now they grew too loud to ignore. "What's this clamor?"

"I don't know, my lady." They headed to the corner of the street to peer around toward the source of the noise. A crowd had gathered in the small square where the farmers set up stalls to sell their vegetables. Jeers and shouts rose from the throng. As they moved closer, Ela saw their attention focused on one woman who stood in their midst, her face wet with tears.

Ela glanced back, glad to see her guard close behind her. She strode into the crowd. "What's amiss?"

The yelling and jeering subsided as people turned to stare at Ela. Most of them knew she was their countess. No one offered an explanation. "Why are you yelling at this woman?" Sullen faces greeted her. "Have you all been struck dumb?" She turned to the woman, who was about thirty, in a faded green dress and clean kerchief. "Please tell me what's going on."

"My daughter is missing," the woman choked out, in a voice so small Ela could barely hear it.

"A chit born in sin!" called out a woman behind Ela.

"Silence!" Ela commanded in a voice as loud as she could muster. Then she turned back to the terrified woman. "What do you mean, she's missing?"

"She went outside to feed the chickens this morning, like

she does every day—" The woman's lip quivered. "But she never came back. I've searched for hours."

"The devil came and took his spawn back!" growled a man.

Ela turned to glare. "Silence or you'll spend time in the stocks!"

"You're not the sheriff," mumbled someone. A murmur of assent rose.

Ela's back stiffened. True enough, she was not the sheriff, though not for lack of trying. The king had seen fit to slight her ambition thus far. But God had charged her with protecting and defending the people of Salisbury, and she served him before she served even the king. "I am the Countess of Salisbury," she retorted. "And I command you to hold your fool tongues." Again, she turned to the woman, who shook visibly. "How old is your daughter?"

"Not yet nine, and small for her age."

Ela waited for some nasty remark from the crowd, but nothing rose beyond a general grumbling. "And why are these people attacking you instead of helping you search for her, like a good Christian should do?" She cast a cold glance over the assembled townspeople.

The woman's lip twitched again, and her gaze fell to the ground.

"She's a defrocked nun!" burst a shrill female voice. Ela sought out a fleshy face she recognized as a local alewife. "Living in sin with a fallen priest. They're cursed in the eyes of God."

"Our Heavenly Father himself decides who holds favor in his eyes," said Ela coldly. "Even if what you say is true, this woman's child is innocent of her parents' sin." She moved toward the woman and placed a hand on her arm. "Where do you think your daughter has gone?"

"I don't know, my lady, but she wouldn't leave the cottage yard by herself. She knows better than that. I've searched the woods and the river and all around and there's no sign of her. Then someone said they'd seen her bundled into a cart."

"Who saw it?" Alys turned to the man who'd made the rude crack about the Devil coming for his spawn.

"Whose cart was it?" Ela demanded of him.

He shrugged. "Couldn't say. Maybe it wasn't her." His derisive expression made Ela unsure he was even telling the truth. He might have made up the story to upset Alys. Still, if there was a chance the child had been stolen—

She turned back to the distraught mother. "Where is your cottage?"

"A half mile outside town along the Fugglestone road. She's not there. I ran back to check before I came here."

"Too close to decent people!" rose a shrill female voice.

"Silence!" Ela held her trembling arm. "Has the hue and cry been raised?"

"That's why I came into town, my lady, but the people here—" Her voice tailed off and fresh tears sprang to her red-rimmed eyes.

"We must raise it immediately." She turned to her attendant. "Mount her on your horse with you. We'll ride to the castle."

Fortunately, her guard was an experienced man in middle age and knew better than to look shocked or put out. He dismounted and helped the poor, anxious woman up onto the horse. Her gown wouldn't allow her to ride astride so he sat her sideways, sitting her almost on his lap in the saddle and holding her around her waist.

Ela bid adieu to Sibel and mounted her own horse, then they rode toward the castle. "How long has your daughter been missing?"

"Since before the bells rang for Tierce." The woman

4

looked miserable, perched perilously on the front of the saddle with the man's big arm around her waist. "She likes to stay outside and play with the chickens after she feeds them. But when I called her in to help me with my baking she was gone. I searched the lanes and woods all around the cottage, in case she went out after a stray hen, but she was nowhere to be found."

"Sometimes my children play hide-and-seek. Could she be secreted away somewhere thinking it's a game?" Ela steered Freya around a peddler's cart as they left the town behind them.

"Not Edyth. She's not disobedient. And she knows to beware of strangers because they aren't always kind to us. I called her name the whole way along the road into town."

"Where's your husband?"

"He went to Bishopstone at first light to glean their fields. He doesn't even know she's missing. But it's five miles away and I thought I'd find help quicker in the town—" She broke off into a sob.

"Help is on its way, mistress." At least she hoped it would be, if the new sheriff didn't shirk his duties. "In the meantime can you think of other places we might look for her? Is there anyone—friend or enemy—who might have taken her into their home?"

She shook her head, tears wet on her cheeks. "We have no friends here. We only live here because my mother gave us sanctuary in her cottage and left it to us when she died."

"You didn't grow up here?"

"No. We're from Suffolk. My father came here six years ago to work on the cathedral. He was a stonemason, but he's been dead nigh on four years. They both perished of a fever."

"My condolences." She hesitated, not wanting to upset the woman further but feeling that she needed to know why she was so hated. "You were once a nun?"

She cast her eyes to the ground. "Aye, at Bungay Priory. I felt a calling and my parents paid to send me there." She glanced around, as if she were looking for someone about to hurl a stone at her. "John came to the manor as a novice to manage the oxen. Neither of us wanted to betray our calling but—" A violent shudder shook her from head to toe.

"Never mind that now." Clearly, what the townspeople had accused her of was true. It was hardly unheard of for men and women to leave the cloister, but it was certainly frowned upon. "We must focus on finding your daughter. What does she look like?"

"She's about yea tall." She held her hand up level with her ribs. "She has blonde hair and bright blue eyes. She's shy and always has been."

Their movement was so slow, the town barely behind them and the castle still far ahead through the fields. Ela looked at the guard. "Master Raymond, are you able to hold her tight enough for a trot?"

"Aye, my lady," he said, with only a slight quaver of doubt in his gruff voice.

Ela squeezed Freya into a slow trot that covered the ground a little faster. She realized she hadn't even asked the woman's name. "What do you call yourself, mistress?"

"Alys Wheaton, my lady." Her voice emerged in bumpy hiccups as she jolted and jostled with the horse's movement. "My husband is John Wheaton. He's skilled in the management of cattle and oxen, but the townspeople won't trust him with their beasts so he hires himself out as a laborer."

"Why don't they trust him?" They rode over a fresh carpet of bright oak leaves. "Because he gave up his calling?"

"Yes. But he's industrious and supports us on the small plot of land my mother left us. We have a cow and chickens and grow much of our own food. I make some extra coin selling eggs and dried herbs in the town. The people aren't always so cruel as today."

"Fear can bring out the worst in people." Ela had noticed that some people became bold and brave under threat, while others became defensive and hostile.

"Mistress Hargreaves said it was a punishment for my sins." Her voice broke into a sob on the last word. "What if she's right?"

"Our Father wouldn't punish a child for his parents' sin." At least she hoped he wouldn't. A horrible thought occurred to her. What if no priest had agreed to baptize their daughter and she carried the burden of original sin and might die unsaved? "Has your daughter been christened?"

"Oh, yes. Father Daniel of St. Peter's baptized her. He moaned and grumbled about it, but he said it was his duty to save her soul."

Ela breathed out a sigh of relief, though she certainly hoped the poor child wasn't about to meet her maker. If she'd been taken, there was no time to waste.

THE HORSES' hooves clattered on the hard, dry road that rose toward the castle mound. Ela hoped the sheriff was at home and in a mood to help them. "Dry your tears so you can speak plainly to the sheriff."

She announced their purpose to the guards—her own guards just a few short, painful months ago—and they let them pass. Stable hands took their horses and Ela hurried Alys Wheaton into the hall past all the garrison soldiers thronging the courtyard and entrance to the castle.

Albert, the old porter, smiled and greeted Ela until she told him their purpose. Then he shook his head with distress and hurried in to announce them.

"Raise the hue and cry!" Albert called, with practiced drama. "Ela, Countess of Salisbury, requests an audience with the sheriff!"

Ela spotted Simon de Hal, the new sheriff, seated in his chair on the dais. Surrounded by his foppish hangers-on, his fingers around an engraved goblet, he barely glanced up as she entered. She could almost hear his thoughts aloud—*not you again.*

She approached briskly. "Good morrow, my lord sheriff." She kept her chin high. "We are here to report a young girl missing. Her name is Edyth Wheaton and she is but eight years old. She vanished from her cottage yard and there's been no sign of her since Tierce."

"The bells have not yet rung midday, my lady," he said casually. He handed his goblet to a young man with ermine cuffs. "She is likely lost in a game."

"Or fallen down a well," suggested a tall youth nearby.

Alys Wheaton let out a whimper.

"Or in the river," offered De Hal. "Children do fall in rivers and drown."

Frustration surged inside Ela. "If she's down a well or in a river, then all the more urgency to find her. But she's not one to leave her home and we have reason to believe that someone might have snatched her and made off with her. Can you send out men to search the houses and stop people on the road?"

De Hal stretched and leaned back in his chair as if the suggestion pained him. "You seriously expect me to knock on every door and search every cart traveling through Wiltshire?"

"This is a child." Ela struggled not to raise her voice and sound shrill. "Not a stray lamb."

De Hal glanced at Alys, in her faded gown and worn kerchief. He could see she wasn't rich or influential. Then he looked back at Ela. "Diverting the king's soldiers from their business and the jurors from their trades is a disruption we can ill afford. No doubt the child will come home in due course. She might be at a neighbor's house."

Ela wanted to scream. "Do you not have children of your own, sir? If one of them were to vanish from the garden would you not want to raise the hue and cry and turn every stone in Wiltshire looking for them?"

De Hal took his cup back and enjoyed a swig before responding. "My children are grown."

An idea seized her. "I'd be happy to command a group of men to search for the child. Then your attention wouldn't have to be engaged when you have more pressing matters."

He stared at her for a moment, then had the cruelty to laugh. "No doubt you would. I hear you imagined yourself as high sheriff of Wiltshire!" He let out a guffaw and was joined in his merriment by the soulless ghouls clustered around him.

Ela schooled herself to remain calm. "I come here to raise the hue and cry. Will you do nothing?"

He looked bored. For a moment she felt like a mouse in his bedding that he'd like to smash beneath his fist. Then he sighed. "I shall send a posse of men to stop wagons on the London road. Will that satisfy you?"

If she said no, he might do nothing. He'd say that he'd tried to help and been turned down. And his suggestion made her curious. "Why do you think she would be on the London road?"

He hesitated for a moment, an odd expression in his eyes. "Stolen goods are often transported to London, the better to hide them in the melee."

"True," said Ela, her mind racing. Did del Hal know something? "Searching traffic to London would be a good start."

With soldiers out searching for Edyth, anyone local who held the girl would likely release her to avoid trouble.

Poor Alys was trembling again, her eyes filled with tears. Ela wanted to put an arm around the desperate mother but knew that De Hal would view that as a sign of feminine weakness. "We shall go join the search."

She strode out of the hall. Her horse was being held outside, and she mounted and had her guard mount Alys again. She cursed herself for not bringing more than one attendant so she could send one home to raise her household into action.

"We must go into the town here and spread the word that the sheriff's men are searching." Instead of riding back to New Salisbury, they rode into the village within the castle walls. Ela headed straight for Giles Haughton's house. He was the coroner and an honest man who actually cared a whit for justice, unlike their new sheriff.

As they rode through the town, Ela called out to each person they passed that a child was missing: a girl of eight named Edyth with blonde hair and blue eyes. People looked concerned, especially when they saw poor desperate Alys behind her, but Ela wasn't sure they'd interrupt their daily routine even to save a life.

When they reached Haughton's house, Ela dismounted and knocked on the door. His housekeeper answered, sleeves rolled up and hands wet as if she were in the middle of scrubbing something. "Oh, my lady countess. Master Haughton is…abroad."

"Do you know where he is? It's an urgent matter."

"He's…" she hesitated, and Ela knew instinctively that she didn't want to tell her his whereabouts. She glanced at Alys's tear-streaked face. "He's at the tavern."

Ela tried not to look shocked. The bell had barely rung for Nones. Surely he wasn't diving into his cups this early. "The Bull and Bear?"

"Aye, my lady. His wife is away visiting her mother so he went there to dine. He says it's no reflection on my cooking but he enjoys the company of—"

"Of course, mistress. Many men prefer to dine in company. We'll find him there. I thank you."

THE BULL and Bear was barely two streets away. Ela and Alys left the horses outside with her attendant and opened the scarred wood door under the tavern's brightly painted sign.

The interior was dark as a cave, and the smell assaulted her as soon as she stepped over the threshold—a thick haze of burned meat and unwashed bodies and spilled ale. There was so little light from the small, smoke-blackened window that she couldn't make out any individual faces.

"I seek Giles Haughton," she managed, trying not to cough from the cooking smoke. She could just make out a pig roasting on a spit over a fire in the center of the room, the smoke rising to blacken the ceiling.

"At your service, my lady." A figure rose from the gloom. "I'll attend you outside."

Ela exited the gloomy, malodorous tavern with relief, Giles Haughton right behind her. "This woman's child is missing since this morning. I've tried to raise the hue and cry, but the sheriff won't do more than search the carts on the London road." If he'd even really do that.

Giles Haughton squinted in the bright outdoor light, his salt-and-pepper eyebrows drawn low. "Is someone dead?"

"Dead? No, we certainly hope not." She placed a quick hand on Alys's arm.

"I don't mean to offend, my lady, but I am the coroner. My office is to investigate murders and to secure any funds due to the crown."

Ela's heart sank. "Can you not engage the jurors in helping us search?"

"It's outside my purview, my lady." His manner was formal to the point of rudeness considering the confidences she'd shared with him in the past. Was he afraid of offending the new sheriff by helping her?

Why had God—in his wisdom—chosen to deprive her of the office of sheriff when she was sure she could execute the sheriff's duties better than any of these men? No doubt she had lessons to learn about humility. But her heart ached for Alys and her poor daughter, who must be frightened out of her wits, wherever she was.

"The girl is only eight." She spoke urgently. "What if she's been stolen? Who might take her?"

Haughton rubbed his stubbled jaw. "You're sure she's not with a friend?"

"We have no friends, sir!" cried Alys, her exasperation bubbling over. "We live as outcasts among the villagers. My daughter is my greatest treasure and I feel sure she's been stolen."

Haughton frowned. "You have good reason to be afraid for her. I've heard of other cases of children disappearing."

"Here?" Ela asked, startled. "In Wiltshire?"

"Aye."

"How did I not know this?"

Because you're not the sheriff. His unspoken answer rang in her ears. "The ones I've heard of weren't formally reported, and no one raised the hue and cry that I know of. They were orphans, or the children of vagrants or prostitutes, or others

12

whose disappearance might go unmarked. I've only heard of them anecdotally."

Alys pressed a hand to her mouth and looked like she was about to faint. Ela put an arm on her back to support her. "Who do you suspect of taking them? Why would someone steal a child too young to have knowledge of a trade or to be of use in a household?" Villagers paid good money to have their children apprenticed in a trade. An unskilled child was considered a burden, not an asset.

Haughton rubbed a hand over his face. "A child that young might be taken to serve a rich man's...proclivities." He looked at her meaningfully.

"Proclivities?" Ela peered at him. "I don't understand. What would a rich man do with an untrained child?"

"Your innocence is a credit to you, my lady."

"I doubt that." She worked to keep her voice calm. "Apparently it puts me at a disadvantage. Could you please explain your meaning in plain speech?"

"For sex, my lady."

Ela stared at him. She crossed herself. "Jesus preserve us. We must find her at once."

"She might be halfway to London by now. Or Portsmouth, on her way to the Continent."

Alys let out a wail and fell to her knees before Ela could catch her. Haughton leapt forward and helped Ela raise her up. "We must get you home, mistress," said Ela. "God willing, little Edyth will come home safe and sound."

Ela gestured to her attendant, who mounted Alys on his horse and heaved himself up behind her.

"I wish I could help more, my lady," said Haughton apologetically.

"I'm sure that you can," said Ela curtly, before mounting Freya. "I thank you for your time and candor. May God be with you."

She'd probably regret snapping at the man who'd been her closest ally thus far, but his refusal to help had both hurt and unnerved her. Was there truly no justice for the poor and voiceless? Were they not subjects of the king as much as she or Giles Haughton or Sheriff de Hal?

CHAPTER 2

*E*la rode steadily through a light drizzle until they reached Alys Wheaton's small cottage. It sat hard by the road just outside the new town. The much-repaired thatched roof looked like a stiff wind could blow it apart. Crudely woven willow fencing held their few ducks and hens in a small enclosure.

"Anyone riding past could see your daughter here in the yard," observed Ela. She couldn't imagine being so hated by the townspeople but living right here on the road where they could look down on the family with disgust each time they passed.

"Aye, 'tis true." Alys had barely spoken the whole way back. On arrival she'd called Edyth's name and heard no answer. Her eyes were still red with weeping. "Do you think I'll ever see her again?"

"God willing, you shall, mistress. You must pray for her safe return. In the meantime I promise you that I'll do what I can to find her."

Ela tore herself away from Alys's desperate, tear-filled gaze. She couldn't imagine the pain of one of her own dear

15

children missing, likely in the hands of cruel strangers planning a fate worse than death for her.

"To the bishop's palace!" she called to her attendant, before breaking into a brisk trot.

ELA APPROACHED the cathedral close with some trepidation, sweaty under her cloak after so much riding and fretting. She prayed that she could keep a calm head and a cool voice and enlist the bishop's aid to her cause.

As a man who heard the confessions of the townspeople, Bishop Poore might be privy to knowledge of crimes that she could only guess at. Of course, he'd never breach the trust of the confessional, but perhaps he could point her in the right direction.

She rode up to the bishop's grand new palace in the shadow of the new cathedral. Workmen bustled about, carrying cartloads of stone and wood scaffolding, and carrying out baskets piled high with fresh stone chips hewn from the new stonework. On this dry, windless day there was enough fresh stone dust on the ground for her horse to leave prints in it as she rode past.

Ela sat on her horse while her attendant dismounted and rapped on the door. A cassocked monk answered. "Ela of Salisbury requests attendance with his grace, the bishop."

The monk nodded assent and turned to the dark interior, closing the door. Ela took this as an encouraging sign that the bishop was home, or surely they'd have turned her away. She dismounted her horse with some relief, her legs chafed and sore from so much riding in clothing not fully intended for the purpose. She wished she still had Sibel to prepare and apply a poultice tonight.

But her pains were nothing compared to the terror

inflicted on little Edyth and her helpless parents. Her father likely didn't even know his daughter was missing unless the hue and cry had somehow reached him where he worked.

A male servant opened the door and invited Ela in. "Thank you and God be with you," she replied. "Might my attendant and our horses take some water? We've done much riding and the noonday sun is hot." She didn't want them all standing out there in the sun, then having to ride home again without refreshment.

"Certainly, my lady. I'll see to it right away." He ushered her in and seated her in a chair with embroidered cushions in Bishop Poore's luxurious sitting room. She tried to convince herself that the carved oak furnishings and sparkling silver candlesticks were a testament to God's glory rather than the bishop's avarice.

Ela wanted the bishop on her side. His authority was not equal to the sheriff's in civil matters, but the church had influence at even the highest levels of society. His support and involvement in the matter would make it harder for Sheriff de Hal to ignore her concerns.

"Ela, my dear!" Bishop Poore emerged through a heavily carved doorway, his face alight with what appeared to be joy. "To what do I owe such a welcome visit?"

Ela blinked. His effusive friendliness was unnerving. Did he want something from her? "God's blessings, your grace."

He reached out both his hands and she put hers into them, grateful that he hadn't simply offered her his enormous ruby ring to kiss. His hands were warm and soft—the softest hands she'd ever felt on a man—and she felt a burst of hope that he would help her.

"Bishop Poore, a young girl has vanished from her home here in Salisbury. An eight-year-old child. It's possible that she's been deliberately abducted." She blurted it out before he could interrupt her with his own business.

"Do I know this child?" His pale blue eyes shone like sapphires in his plump pink face.

Ela's stomach tightened. Would the parents' situation poison his mind against the innocent girl? "Her name is Edyth Wheaton." She paused to see what effect the name had on him.

A look of mild perplexity clouded his smooth, pale brow and disturbed his silver eyebrows. "Wheaton? The name strikes a bell, but I can't place..." He looked at her curiously. She had an eerie feeling that he knew exactly who they were.

"Her parents are unpopular with the villagers, I'm afraid." Ela spoke with some trepidation. "Her father was once a man of the cloth and her mother of the cloister, but the Lord called them to create a family." She hoped that by framing their life change as the Lord's work it would seem less distasteful.

"Ah." He twisted his ring. "The Lord moves in mysterious ways."

"Indeed he does. And no matter what one might think of her parents, the child is innocent and in grave danger. She needs our help."

"And how do you anticipate that I might help in this situation? Surely it's a matter for the sheriff?"

"I've alerted the sheriff and raised the hue and cry, but I know your influence extends far beyond the civil borders of Salisbury or even of Wiltshire." Flattery always helped, at least with Bishop Poore. "It's possible that the girl has been spirited to London or even abroad."

She drew in a steadying breath. Her next request bordered on audacity. "Could you alert your fellow bishops and men of the church that this child is missing, and that others are too, and enlist them in our efforts to recover these poor lost souls and return them to their families?"

He blinked and for a terrible moment she thought he was

going to laugh. "What have men of the church to do with children? As a group we have less contact with children than anyone in England." His eyes twinkled with something between amusement and indignation.

Ela lifted her chin. "You've provided generously for the young boys of Salisbury, that they might learn their letters and read God's word in your school. Most children here and throughout England attend services with their parents and guardians. The monks and nuns provide alms and succor for the poor of the parish, including their children. Men and women of the cloth are perhaps more likely than anyone to encounter a stray waif or orphan and offer them refuge."

His smooth forehead had crumpled considerably. "I do understand what you're saying. But if this child has been... abducted, surely she will be held in secret?"

"Who knows the secrets of the people better than a priest?"

Bishop Poore looked more than a little alarmed. "The secrets of the confessional are a sacred trust."

"Even where the life of an innocent child is at stake?"

"Even then." He worked his ring fully around his finger two times. "However, I shall write to my fellow bishops and inform them of your search." He pushed a smile to his lips. "And you shall be the first to hear of any news they send."

Ela's heart crumpled. He was dismissing her concerns. She doubted he would write to anyone. "Innocent children's lives are at stake. It seems they are disappearing all around us, drawn into a dark underworld like lost souls to hell." She hoped to appeal to his spiritual side. "If we can save this one girl, perhaps we can save more."

"Indeed. Your concern is a credit to you, my lady. Now, if you'll excuse me I must prepare for Mass."

Now he was patronizing her. No doubt he felt, like Sheriff de Hal, that she should confine her interests to her herb garden and her needlework. "Thank you for your time, Bishop Poore." She reached into her purse and drew out a small gold coin. "Please accept this offering to buy prayers for the poor lost child and her fellow sufferers."

She intended to stay for the Sext services in the cathedral to hear the prayer. If she was present, her valuable coin would buy a mention of the missing girl that would alert anyone there who didn't already know.

"Your generosity will be noted in Heaven, my lady." He took the coin and pressed it between his thumb and finger.

She said her goodbyes and asked his servant to inform her attendant of her plan to stay for services. The Mass would give her time to catch her breath and offer up some prayers. There was no point in running about Salisbury like a chicken with her head cut off if no one was listening to her.

THE TAP of hammers on chisels stilled as the bells rang for Mass. Sweet relief from the constant banging. Workers climbed carefully down from the scaffolding that rose into the vaults, and most went outside to eat their bread and cheese.

Ela sat in her accustomed seat at the front of the nave near the altar. The other attendees were mostly monks and students from Bishop Poore's new school. A handful of townswomen sat in the rear and muttered among themselves —possibly about her—until Bishop Poore ascended toward the altar.

Ela willed away her worries and cares—all the little day-to-day concerns that cluttered her mind—and gave herself over to the service, listening carefully to the words of the psalms that formed the core of each daily Sext service.

· · ·

BEHOLD, I was shapen in iniquity; and in sin did my mother conceive me.

...O remember not against us former iniquities: let thy tender mercies speedily prevent us: for we are brought very low.

...Let the sighing of the prisoner come before thee; according to the greatness of thy power preserve thou those that are appointed to die—

...Help us, O God of our salvation, for the glory of thy name: and deliver us, and purge away our sins, for thy name's sake.

THE FAMILIAR WORDS struck a fresh chord in her heart and reaffirmed her conviction that Alys had committed no crime in God's eyes that had not already been absolved through her own prayers. She prayed that God would hear the sighing of this tender young prisoner.

The world lately seemed so filled with iniquity: her own husband's cruel and untimely death, the murders she'd investigated during her brief spell as acting sheriff, not to mention the scourge of illegal trade and criminal mischief in their midst.

Ela had a violent urge to run for the door, to mount Freya and gallop somewhere—anywhere—to raise the people to hunt for Edyth and her fellow sufferers.

But she schooled herself to sit still. Bishop Poore glanced at her as he mentioned that there was a young girl missing from Salisbury and that all should be alert for word of her whereabouts.

God willing, they must find Edyth Wheaton before she suffered too much.

BACK HOME THAT afternoon at her manor, Ela paced the

21

floors worrying about Edyth. Bill Talbot, the brave and kind knight who'd been in her family's service since she was a girl, listened sympathetically and attempted helpful suggestions.

"Perhaps you might write to the king and alert him that children are disappearing in his kingdom."

Ela sighed. "The king is consumed with his ambitions overseas and the intrigues of his barons. He won't trouble himself with the loss of one village girl." She also didn't want the king to see her as a nuisance like a buzzing fly. She'd already plied him with requests that she should be sheriff of Wiltshire, and he'd given her reason to hope it could happen —if enough coin was applied.

"Perhaps the sheriff's men will find her."

"Sheriff de Hal cares nothing for this girl. Her disappearance offers no way for him to line his purse. From what I've seen he cares little for anything but feasting with his cronies and exacting fines. But let him neglect his duties and harass the farmers and burghers with his fines. In doing so he paves the path for me to replace him."

Bill stood awkwardly in the corner. No doubt he would have liked to sit, but he was too much of a gentleman to sit when she stood. And she was too agitated to sit.

"Who is this Edyth?" Petronella's voice piped up from the hallway. "I've never heard you mention her before."

Ela glanced at Bill. She didn't want to frighten her own children, but at almost seventeen Petronella was old enough to know the truth. "Don't tell the younger ones—" She beckoned for Petronella to come closer. "But she's a village girl who's been snatched from her home."

Petronella frowned. "But why?"

"We don't know." She didn't want her sheltered, pious daughter to be haunted by nightmares of what might happen to a young girl in the clutches of greedy and lascivious men. "But she's likely in danger and we must find her."

"Perhaps she ran away? Richard told me that Sarah from the bakery tried to run off with a shepherd boy when her parents betrothed her to old Master Whipple the cobbler."

"Don't believe such nonsense. Master Whipple is old enough to be her grandfather. I'm sure it's just scurrilous gossip. Even if it wasn't she'd never be so foolish as to run off. Besides, this missing girl's only eight—where would she go?"

"Why would anyone snatch an eight-year-old child?" Petronella picked up one of the little black kittens stretching itself by the unlit hearth. "She'd be no use except as a mouth to feed. Though I suppose they might train her to be a beggar or a cutpurse, poor lamb."

Ela hoped that was all they planned to do with her. But she doubted it. A pretty young girl...she shuddered. "I shall hire Master Spicewell to employ his network of contacts to find her."

Spicewell was a lawyer friend of her mother's who'd proved his ability to send tendrils into the London under-world the last time she hired him.

"A messenger on a good horse could be there by midday tomorrow," said Bill.

"My mother is in London through the end of the month," said Ela. "I had a letter from her this morning. I shall go visit her."

Bill's expression looked doubtful.

"What? Do you think I'm running too much up and down to London when I should look to my hearth here?"

He stayed silent.

"My true hearth is at the castle and you know that. Until I settle myself by that hearth again my heart will be unquiet."

He still said nothing.

"You think it wrong of me to leave my children? It's true that Will and Isabella, who I trusted to guide their younger siblings, are now married and gone, but Petronella is now almost a woman and quite capable of taking charge of my brood. And they're in the care of their tutors."

Bill Talbot hadn't moved. She tilted her chin at him. "You shall stay here to watch over them."

"Nay, my lady. If you go to London to search for this child you'll need me at your side."

"Ah, he speaks at last!" She turned and crossed the room again. "Are you sure I need your ministrations more than my innocent babes?"

"You have the courage of a man but lack a knight's training. That is a dangerous combination without a squire at your side."

Ela stopped, startled that he would be so bold. She glanced at Petronella to see if he'd shocked her. She was easily scandalized.

"I can mind the little ones, Mama." Petronella straightened her shoulders under her plain green gown. "I'll make sure they mind their books and that the boys don't play outside after dark."

"Well, it seems as if the decision has been made." She looked at Bill. "You and Hilda shall come to attend me."

"Are you sure that's wise, Mama?" asked Petronella. "Hilda's pregnant and should rest."

"She's still in the early stages of her pregnancy." Thank goodness she'd stopped vomiting several times an hour. "She'll be fine. I survived all my pregnancies, as you and your siblings bear witness. We mothers are stronger than we look." She shot a glance at Bill. Truth be told she didn't want to leave Hilda unattended. Her new maid had already demonstrated her foolishness by getting entangled with a much older and thoroughly unsuitable man and finding herself pregnant and alone after he was murdered.

Hilda was emotional from her pregnancy—vulnerable—

and cursed with an excess of beauty. The last thing Ela needed was Hilda, left unattended, falling into the clutches of another man. Better the girl stay by her side.

"I shall write to my mother that we're coming, and we'll leave first thing tomorrow. Please call for the messenger."

When Bill had left the room, Ela drew Petronella close. "I do wish our beloved Sibel was still here to mind the household in my place, especially with Will and Isabella gone, but I trust you to keep the peace."

"It will be good practice for when I become an abbess."

"Indeed it will." Ela squeezed her arm. It wouldn't be long before Petronella flew the nest into either marriage or a convent. Her children were scattering across the country, and it felt like her heart was being torn into pieces to go with them.

She thought again of Alys Wheaton and how desperate she must be feeling right now, her daughter snatched from her home. The very thought of her loss stole the breath from Ela's lungs.

"Petronella, please gather your brothers and sisters that I may speak to them before Compline."

Now where was Hilda? It was time to teach her how to pack in a hurry.

CHAPTER 3

*T*he journey to London was no longer and no shorter than usual. They stayed overnight in an inn that allowed them to attend early-morning services at St. Mary's church in Egham, which buoyed their spirits before they resumed the final leg of their journey. Ela's carriage arrived at her mother's house, with Bill and the attendants trotting behind it, not long after midday the following day.

Her mother's house was large, with three gables and decorative black timbering in stark contrast to the fresh white plaster. It put Ela's rustic manor at Gomeldon to shame. Her mother must have some poor soul up on a ladder spreading fresh lime on it once a month. The black ironwork on the door gleamed as Bill clanged the bell next to it.

Crespin, the porter, welcomed Ela effusively and brought her into the comfortable parlor before going to summon her mother. Hilda removed her cloak and took it away to shake it out and hang it.

Ela expected to see Alianore's face wreathed with smiles at her daughter's unexpected visit. Instead, her mother swept into the room with a stern gaze, her high brow creased with concern.

"Hello, Mama." Ela greeted her brightly and kissed her cheeks. Her mother's poodles barked at her ankles. "Don't look so overjoyed to see me."

Her mother took her hands. "I would be, but I know that you're not here for a social visit."

"What makes you say that?"

"Your letter with its inquiry after Master Spicewell."

"I know he's a close friend of yours, and he's looking into a legal matter for me."

Alianore looked doubtful. "You had him investigating that nasty opium trade for you."

"Indeed. He has many useful contacts that can be of service."

Alianore's eyes narrowed. "Why are you really here?"

Ela sighed. "A child has gone missing from Salisbury. A girl of eight from the village. Apparently it's not an isolated incident. Children are being taken from their homes and sold or traded as if they were chattels or brute beasts."

"And you're here to save them all." It wasn't a question.

"Would you have me leave this little girl to suffer at the cruel hands of her captors when I might lead a search to find her?"

"Is there not a sheriff in Salisbury appointed to do this tiresome and potentially dangerous work?"

"Simon de Hal doesn't do anything unless it can put coin in his purse. This girl's parents have no wealth or social standing. And I strongly suspect that these unfortunate children are being brought to London."

Alianore's chest rose as she inhaled a deep breath as if to steady her nerves. "What makes you suspect they're here?"

Ela hesitated. "I've heard rumors of a criminal organization that operates here to steal and sell children.""

27

"And on this rumor you've uprooted your household and abandoned your own young children to fly to London." Her mother bent to pick up one of her poodles. She held it to her chest and peered at Ela.

"My children are in good hands."

"You're bored at Gomeldon." Alianore's tone was accusatory.

Ela blinked. "I have plenty to do. I've engaged an architect to design the monastery to be built in William's memory."

Her mother lifted a brow. "So he's busy, and you're harrying the sheriff of Salisbury for not taking the position as seriously as you would have."

"It's a child, Mother! A small child as young as little Ellie. If you'd seen her weeping mother—"

"Well, now that you're here in London, how do you propose to find her? Shall we go pace the streets hoping for a glimpse? What are her hair and eye color?"

Ela ignored her mother's snide tone. "Blonde and blue."

"Oh, I'm sure we'll spot her immediately. Shall we head for the market?"

Ela crossed her hands over her chest. "Spicewell has a network of informants that he employs to help him build his legal cases. I hope that they can inquire in the right places to seek information about anyone running an illegal network that trades in children."

"Something so despicable would be cloaked in secrecy."

"Indeed, which is why we won't stumble across it in the marketplace. Do you think it's too late for me to call on Master Spicewell at his chambers?"

"Undoubtedly, but you will have no need to as I've sent a messenger for him and he's on his way here right now." Her mother's expression had softened.

Ela smiled. "Thank you! I do appreciate your help and your hospitality."

"It's not as if I had a choice." Her mother's mouth twisted as if she was trying to fight a smile. "With such a force of nature for a daughter."

"You have no idea how much restraint I show, Mother." She wished she could turn England upside down seeking justice for her husband's untimely death. "But clearly there is urgency to this matter. The child might be spirited out of the country or abused in some way that will destroy her as surely as death." She'd had nightmares of what might happen to this innocent girl.

"Hilda, will you fetch some water for me to wash my hands and face?" Ela asked. Hilda hurried away.

Ela turned to her mother. "Poor Hilda attracts all the wrong kinds of male attention. Please tell me there isn't some handsome young man in your household to turn her head."

Alianore's eyes widened. "How am I supposed to notice if my pot boys are handsome or not? Can you not lock the girl up in a chastity belt?"

"If such a thing existed I doubt it could accommodate a girl who's already pregnant." Ela sighed. Hilda was already more of a burden than all her own daughters put together. But she was her beloved Sibel's niece and had been cast out by her parents, so Ela had taken on the responsibility of trying to see her safely settled in life.

"I'm sure the ironmonger who made the fine metalwork for my front door could put something together for her." Alianore's lips flattened.

"That won't be necessary. And please don't be unkind to her. She's suffering enough already. She cries daily for her lost lover and her fatherless child."

"No doubt that scoundrel would have abandoned her anyway if he was alive."

"We'll never know, because he's dead."

"Killed for the manor he stood to inherit."

"Yes, but his killer was convicted and hanged, and—" Ela glanced at the door. Hilda hadn't returned. She lowered her voice. "And I hired Master Spicewell to try to gain control of the manor for Hilda's child, since it will be the only surviving heir."

A knock on the door heralded Spicewell's arrival. Hilda returned with water and a soft cloth, and Ela quickly washed her hands and face before the lawyer was shown into the parlor. She rose and greeted him.

Walter Spicewell was about her mother's age, his hair full silver but his pale blue eyes full of interest and intelligence. Ela asked Hilda to take her clothes upstairs to the bedroom and air them. When Hilda had left the room, she turned to Spicewell. "Any news of Fernlees?" Fernlees was the manor she hoped to secure for Hilda and her child.

"De Hal has hired a lawyer in an attempt to gain control of the property."

Ela was shocked. Why would the new sheriff think he had a claim to Fernlees? "On what pretext?"

"Expenses and trouble sustained during the trial to convict the man who killed the property's owner. However, he has very little ground to stand on, him so lately being sheriff. He may try to claim it for the king, to curry favor."

"The new sheriff played only a small role in getting the murderer convicted," said Ela. Her blood boiled at de Hal's audacity. He should never have become sheriff. The role should have gone to her after her husband's death. "What of his chances?"

"Well," Spicewell followed Ela's example by seating himself in one of the handsome wood chairs. "I've always viewed attack as the best form of defense, so I've taken the liberty of investigating de Hal's record as both sheriff and deputy sheriff up north. It appears that he was not well liked." His pale eyes glimmered with mischief.

"Do tell!" said Alianore.

"All in good time, my lady. My case is a work in progress," said Spicewell. "A combination of ancient documents safeguarding the manor for the Blount heirs, including Hilda's unborn child, and a release of information that reveals the true nature of our opponent and thus undermines his claim to the property."

"Good." Ela's brain was still working too fast to respond properly. "But I unfortunately need your help now on an even more urgent matter."

Spicewell looked skeptical. "After your last investigation into the shadowy bowels of the opium trade, I'm more than a little apprehensive."

Ela drew in a steadying breath. "We need to find a girl of eight who's been stolen from her home in Salisbury. I've heard there's a gang of sorts that steals children and trades in them." She studied his face.

"I've heard of such. There's a trade in everything in London."

Ela's eyes widened. "This cruel trade seems to be common knowledge. How can people go about their business when children are being bought and sold in our midst?"

Spicewell looked sheepish. "In my line of business I'm privy to news of horrific crimes every day. Not all of them fall within my purview."

"I want urgently to find this girl, and if we can free other stolen children and destroy this group that exploits them, that would be even better."

He inhaled deeply. "As you know, I do have a network of associates who can put their ears to the ground."

"Can they do it today? This girl is in imminent danger."

She waited for him to reply that—for all they knew—the girl was nowhere near London, his people were already occupied, and that it was nearing dinner time...

Spicewell turned and called for the boy who attended him. "Jim, please summon Dalziel and Bray to my chambers. I'll attend them there directly."

"But Spicy dear, we're soon to eat!" protested Alianore.

"These are not men I wish to bring to your doorstep, my dearest Alianore. I shall set them on the trail, then return."

"May I come with you to meet them?" Ela knew it was a bold request.

He hesitated for a minute, probably dying to tell her it wasn't a suitable situation for a woman, especially a great lady. "Please do."

ELA HAD ATTENDED Spicewell's luxuriously appointed chambers near the law courts before, so she was surprised when his carriage turned in another direction and led them to an entirely different building deep inside the city—a low structure of blackened wood, close enough to the docks that she could smell the river.

"What is this place?"

"In addition to my legal interests I sometimes buy and sell a few items. I find it suits me to keep a separate premises." He smiled as if this were the most normal thing in the world, then instructed Bill Talbot to join his carriage driver in a courtyard where they'd be close enough but hidden from sight.

Ela looked at the low, unimpressive doorway. "Do you meet with your business associates here?"

"I do. It's not necessary to excite feelings of envy among those less fortunate." He assisted her in climbing down from the carriage. A servant opened the door, and he took her into a dim interior lit by one small diamond-paned window. Once inside his servant removed his plum-colored, gold-edged tunic and replaced it with a plainer dark gray one.

Ela was grateful that her clothing was simple and plain. She despised ostentation except when entirely necessary and wore a simple blue gown with white embroidery at the neck and cuffs.

He offered her a seat on a plain wood chair. The afternoon was warm for September so there was no fire in the hearth. The room had an air of studied neglect, with dust in the corners and a pile of scuffed ledgers on a well-worn table. It was a stark contrast to his richly decorated chambers near Westminster Hall. Clearly Master Spicewell led something of a double life.

A sharp rap on the door made her jump. The servant—a raw-boned young man barely older than her son Will—opened the door and two men entered. Despite the warm afternoon, they both wore dark cloaks.

"Good morrow, Master Dalziel and Master Bray. I thank you for attending at such short notice. My client here has a matter that needs swift attention." He gestured to Ela. She waited for him to introduce her, but he forged on. "She brings news of a young child missing from Salisbury in Wiltshire. A girl of only eight who was snatched from her home." He poured two cups of wine from a carafe that his servant had brought, then handed a cup to each of them. "I seek your knowledge of the trade in children."

Neither man had spoken, and Ela observed them as they each took a bracing swig of wine. They were close to her own age—two score years or maybe more. One stood taller than the other, with flat gray eyes and oily light brown hair escaping from a plain cap. The other had pale, glassy blue eyes and a dark, dense beard that obscured his jaw. He wore a crudely wrought wooden cross on a hank of string about his neck. Ela should have found the holy iconography reassuring but instead it was oddly unsettling.

The taller man drained his cup and set it down. "One pound for information leading you to those engaging in this trade—" He had a thick London accent. "And ten pounds for the return of the missing girl." It wasn't a question. Spicewell glanced at Ela.

She nodded. The price was dear by any standard. No doubt many would think her mad for pouring her own coin into the search, but it wasn't entirely altruistic. She wanted to buy a reputation as one who could uphold law and order in Salisbury. Nothing came cheap in this age and since she was blessed with the funds to buy justice, then she was ready to pay for it.

She reached into her purse and pulled out a gold coin. "Can you provide us with any information from your existing store of knowledge."

The man's eyes fixed on the coin for a moment. When he lifted them they shone with what looked like amusement and she wondered which was the gaffe—the foreign gold coin or her formal manner of addressing him.

He reached out a grimy finger and thumb and almost snatched the coin from her hand. "I'll need to make inquiries." He spoke slowly, in a tone that might be seen as mocking. "But Master Spicewell knows I'm as honest as the sun is bright."

Ela resisted the urge to gauge Spicewell's expression. She trusted him to choose his associates wisely.

The shorter, bearded man was slower to drain and lower his cup, which he placed back on the tray with a thump. "We'll bring news by tomorrow."

"News?" A surge of anxiety rushed Ela. "We seek the girl

herself, alive and well. If you can find her before sundown that would be ideal."

"Before sundown?" The tall man blinked his dead gray eyes. "That's unlikely. She won't be found idling on a street corner. Such a trade—in living humans—will be tightly bound by secrecy and we'll have to pry the bands off the barrel slowly and carefully so as not to explode it and destroy the contents."

Ela blinked. His metaphor chilled her. Could the search itself lead to the girl's death?

"We'll meet here tomorrow morning after the bells for Tierce, and you shall tell us what you've learned," said Spicewell. "God go with you."

Ela breathed a silent sigh of relief after the men left. Their presence had put her on edge, and she wasn't sure why.

"They are rough-hewn, to be sure," said Spicewell. "But their connections reach into the darkest corners of London. If the girl can be found, they'll find her."

Ela wasn't so sure but didn't want to doubt him. His servant removed the cups and took them into a back room. Ela wondered if their lips had previously touched the cup she used and exactly what method had been used to clean it in between. She didn't hear any splashing of water. Spicewell's young servant likely just wiped them out with a grimy rag.

Spicewell ushered her outside, where she took a deep breath of the air, smoke polluted and river rotten as it was. The sight of Bill Talbot astride his gray palfrey cheered her, and she climbed back into Spicewell's carriage with relief.

Spicewell returned her to her mother's house, where they all ate a lavish dinner and her mother shared the latest gossip about which baron was falling deeper in debt and which lady had become pregnant while her husband was on a pilgrimage in Spain.

Ela was exhausted by the time they snuffed out the

candles and Hilda undressed her for bed. As she said her prayers she wondered where poor little Edyth Wheaton lay right now and what terrors she might be enduring. She prayed that Bray and Dalziel would earn the coin she'd parted with and that tomorrow they could send the sheriff's men in to save Edyth from her captors.

CHAPTER 4

*T*he next morning Ela rose early, restless, missing her old morning rounds at the castle and even her more modest routine at Gomeldon. While the household slept, she attended Prime services at a nearby church with Hilda and one of her mother's manservants in tow. She arrived home to find the household stirring and her mother fussing over her absence.

"This is London, not sleepy Salisbury!" Alianore bustled about the parlor impatiently brushing imaginary dust off the polished surfaces. "You should never go out without Bill Talbot. Anything could happen!"

"I took Hilda and Rufus with me."

"Rufus isn't a knight. What would he do if cutpurses set upon you? I don't leave my house without an armed guard. You can't be too careful these days."

"It's less than three hundred steps from here to the church, Mother." Ela hated feeling like a scolded child. "And here we are, alive and well, thanks be to God." She took an oatcake from a platter on the table and bit into it.

Her mother ordered a serving girl to fetch her a plate and

a cup of freshly pressed almond milk. "People will talk," she muttered. She strode past the hanging tapestry fast enough to send its woven trees swaying. "You're a woman alone. Without protection."

"If they talk about me rising early to worship my Lord, then let them."

"I think it's more likely they'll ask themselves why you're here in London, and going to and fro at all hours of the day and night."

"I'm here to visit my beloved mother." Ela took the plate and added some fresh berries to it from a bowl on the table. She sat and took a sip of almond milk. "Surely no one could find fault with that?"

Alianore shot her an arch expression. "Be careful. There's no good reason for a woman's name to be on people's lips."

"I'm far less concerned about people's flapping lips than you are. I'm here to right a wrong, and I grow more impatient with each passing second." She turned to Bill. "I thought we might go down to the docks on our way to Spicewell's and visit our old haunt."

"Pinchbeck's shop?" asked Talbot.

"The very same. I'd like to see if the opium trade is still being plied there." Her slimy neighbor Osbert Pinchbeck had disappeared in the middle of her investigations into his business—which had turned out to be a trade in opium cunningly disguised as a business importing and selling cheap trinkets. Spicewell suspected Pinchbeck was dead but a body had never been found.

A disreputable stranger with the odd name of Vicus Morhees had first taken over Pinchbeck's manor, then disappeared into the mist when they pursued him as a suspect. If she could find even one of them it would be most satisfying.

"Bill, darling, do tell her not to be silly." Alianore crossed her arms over her chest. "What good can come of poking your nose in where it doesn't belong? The opium trade is not illegal, but it's most certainly distasteful and attracts a dangerous sort of man."

Bill sat quietly, far too sensible to insert himself into a mother-daughter disagreement.

"Bill will keep me safe," said Ela, after chewing her oatcake. "It's on the way to Spicewell's place of business, so why not stop there and see if it's still in operation?"

Her mother gave a dramatic sigh. "I don't know why dear Spicy insists on keeping that place down by the water. I'm quite sure he doesn't need the money so why would he dabble in trade?"

"Probably the same reason he still practices law when he's supposedly retired," replied Ela. "He enjoys it. Not everyone is satisfied by an endless round of banquets and board games."

"Spicy is a dab hand at games of chance. He always wins." Alianore picked up a plump blackberry and placed it in her mouth. "Especially when there's a large pot of coins on the table."

ELA AND BILL TALBOT traveled to Pinchbeck's shop on foot, with an attendant following behind them to hold their horses while they went about their business. The building's worn exterior looked much the same, and the small, discolored sign advertising "necessaries" still hung crookedly near the scuffed door.

Bill's firm rap on the door pushed it open a few inches, so he pressed it further and they peered in. The interior of the shop made even less pretense of a place of business than it had before. Three barrels were the only occupants of the dark storefront, and on inspection one was half filled with the same cheap flutes she'd seen there before. The shelves, which had held a couple of empty birdcages on her prior visit, were now empty, with a layer of dust.

Ela startled to see a man sat at the back of the store, near the door to what she now knew was the real business— rooms upstairs where men gave themselves over to the pleasures of the poppy juice. He was no longer the old blind man of before but a much younger one, with pocked cheeks and oily curls about his forehead. He glanced up, and his gaze fixed into her like an arrow.

Her nerves jangled. "Good morrow, is Osbert Pinchbeck within?"

"Nay." His curt answer was delivered with a sneer. "Never heard of him."

"He owned this shop not four months ago."

"I wasn't here then, was I?" His thick London accent had a mocking tone.

Ela could feel Bill's anxiety from behind her. She knew that he would snatch her and remove her from this place if he could. "May I speak with Vicus Morhees?" Morhees was a wanted man.

Bill's hand on her arm made her jump. The pocked youth rose from his stool and took a step toward her. "Never heard of him." His cold eyes looked directly into hers and Ela felt the chill of his gaze like a dagger to the heart. "And you need to leave."

"My lady," said Bill. His hand tightened on her arm. He sensed danger, as did she. But what would they do? Kill her in cold blood in broad daylight?

"Who operates this establishment?" Ela forged ahead, hoping to glean any information she could.

"The devil himself, *my lady*." He slurred the last words, derisive, and took another step forward.

Does the devil pay taxes to King Henry III for the goods he sells here? She knew they were still secretly trading in opium and evading taxes by hiding the true nature of the business. The criminality of it galled her. She resolved to report this to the local sheriff so that at least some action could be taken.

He raised his hand and placed it on the long, curved dagger at his belt.

Bill tugged Ela, and she finally turned and let him guide her toward the door. Blood boiling, she couldn't resist turning in the doorway and facing the boy one more time. "Tell your master that Ela, Countess of Salisbury, came to call upon him."

She waited a moment to gauge his reaction and was rewarded when his eyes darkened with shock. He looked like he wanted to say something—maybe beg her forgiveness for the insult—but she turned and headed out the door before he could utter another word.

Once out in the street she looked at Bill, who didn't even look back at her. He could apparently think of nothing but getting them back on their horses and on their way to Spicewell's office. She felt grateful that at least she hadn't crept away like a scared mouse, and had left the insolent youth with something to chew on.

As they mounted and rode away she heard a couple of piercing birdcalls, which struck her as odd. London had little birdsong, probably due to the dearth of trees or plants of any kind.

Bill's face had an oddly grim look she hadn't seen before, his jaw set hard as if his teeth were clenched.

"I could hardly let him invoke the devil and then turn and walk away," said Ela, by way of explanation for her behavior.

"You just told him exactly who you are!" said Bill finally.

"That's the point. He insulted a countess of the realm."

Are you mad? His expression thoughts he was too polite to utter. "These people are dangerous criminals, my lady."

"My rank protects me. My husband was the son of one king, the brother of another, and uncle to the present monarch."

"You think these lowlifes care one whit for rank? They care for nothing but silver and would gladly slit a throat for it."

Now that they were a couple of streets away, Ela felt her blood cool slightly. The heat of the encounter had perhaps made her a little bolder than necessary. "I'm sure they're still trading in opium there."

"Yes." His polite response said a lot less than his angry gaze. "A highly profitable trade they will stop at nothing to protect."

"Bill, you act like you expect them to charge after us and grab us from our horses." They'd started trotting, and the exercise further relaxed her. "They'd never dare."

Bill's mouth tightened again. No doubt he felt he couldn't argue with her. She was Ela, Countess of Salisbury—as she'd just bragged.

Perhaps she'd let her pride get the better of her. She'd have to pray for humility. But that could wait.

THEY TROTTED the rest of the way to Spicewell's dockland haunt. Bill remained tight lipped as they dismounted again and muttered some instructions to the attendant to stay out of sight and to be sure to call loudly for help if needed.

"Those criminals are hardly going to follow us into my lawyer's office. And if they do, then we can congratulate ourselves for drawing these villains out in to the light, where the king's men can see them." She wanted to reassure herself that her actions weren't entirely foolish.

Bill blinked, exasperation clear in his face and slightly

labored breath. "Your bravery rivals that of your husband, my lady. No doubt he'd have said the same."

Ela felt a tiny flush of pride. "Yet I hear censure in your voice."

"Bravery has its place on the battlefield, my lady."

"And a lady's place is at home in her parlor," she retorted softly. They were approaching Spicewell's door.

"Have I ever said that?"

"No, but I suspect you'd rather be guarding me there. I value your caution, but I do not seek the role of sheriff so I can turn a blind eye to crime because those committing it happen to be dangerous."

"When you're sheriff, you'll be surrounded by the king's garrison again and will be less vulnerable to the actions of evil men."

She appreciated that he'd said *when* you are sheriff, not *if*. "For now I have you to protect me and I trust you with my life."

Bill didn't say anything, but she got the sense that he thought her trust was misplaced. She didn't want to patronize him by arguing with something he hadn't said. Besides, they were at Spicewell's door and no one had tried to kill them yet.

Bill knocked and the lad admitted them. Spicewell rose from his chair and greeted Ela warmly. "My associates have sent word that they have some information that may lead to the missing children. They'll be here soon."

The wood-paneled interior was so dark that a candle burned even in the daytime. Ela sat in the hard wood chair at the plain table, impatient for his rather sinister cohorts to arrive.

Bill stood rigid opposite the door, refusing both the offered seat and cup of wine. Ela felt sorry that she must have offended him somehow, but he could hardly expect her to shrink from the evil she was trying hard to uproot.

"This wine is excellent," she exclaimed. It was hard to get good wine this year. Something about the weather on the Continent had made it bitter.

"I thank you, my lady." Spicewell beamed. "One of the benefits of importing goods is that you have your pick of them."

"I don't know how you find the time to run a business and practice the law, all while in retirement."

"Ah, but I don't have the sweet distraction of a lady wife, since mine died nigh on eight years ago."

"And you've never thought to remarry?" A lawyer of great wealth and wit and intelligence could surely have his pick of pretty widows half his age.

"I've thought about it but not yet made the leap." His slow, appraising smile stirred an uneasy feeling in her gut. Hopefully he wasn't suggesting her as quarry.

Another rap on the door broke the awkward moment. Dalziel and Bray entered, and Ela fought the urge to rise from her chair out of sheer impatience.

"Good morrow, sirs." Spicewell rose to greet them. "We eagerly await your intelligence."

The boy poured them both cups of wine. The taller one, who she now knew to be Dalziel, looked at Ela.

"What did you learn?" She couldn't stop herself from asking. She couldn't bear to hear a discussion of the weather or some other nonsense while a child suffered.

Dalziel cleared his throat. "We learned of a house where children are taken into service."

"What do you mean, 'service'?"

"To be servants, maids, pages and the like. Or at least that's what they say." He cleared his throat. "But no one seems to know where they come from. They aren't brought there by their parents, and they often seem to turn up under cover of night."

Ela's pulse quickened. "Where is this place?"

"Hard by Westcheap. A three-story house with no windows on the first floor."

"And who did you learn this from."

He hesitated for a moment. "Acquaintances."

"My associates bring information to me with the reassurance that no connection will be made between them and the information," said Spicewell. "They keep the names of their sources private much as we keep their names private in our dealings with the authorities."

"I see." Ela looked at Bray, who stood there silently. "Do you know the names of the people who run this...establishment?"

"Nay," said Bray quickly. "But we've determined that there are children passing through there and then on to other places. None of them is over twelve or so. Some are barely more than infants."

Ela's heart clenched, and she found herself gripping the arm of her chair. "Can you give us the exact address?" She glanced at Spicewell, hoping he wasn't going to explain that was impossible.

"On Westcheap turn right at the Hog and Hound and walk down the street. Three houses down on the left there's an alley, and the house is at the end of the alley."

"No windows on the first floor. Are there other distinguishing features?"

"Nay." Bray didn't elaborate.

"Plain wood door?"

"Aye. Looks like every house in London," said Dalziel. "But the upper windows are shuttered from the outside." He glanced at Spicewell, looking uneasy. "Have we earned our coin?"

"I believe so." Spicewell looked at Ela. "Do you have further questions?"

"Have you seen the children yourself?" She was disappointed they hadn't brought the girl to claim the ten pounds she'd promised.

"Nay, we didn't want to raise suspicion by hanging around. But we have it from a reliable source that they've been coming and going."

"For how long?"

Dalziel's brows lowered over his flat gray eyes. "For years."

Ela's heart pounded with longing to ride there right away. "Thank you. I presume we can be in touch if we need your help again?"

Dalziel glanced nervously at Spicewell. She got the distinct impression they wanted no more to do with this matter. Spicewell excused them, and they left in a hurry.

"We must alert the sheriff," said Ela. "He can storm the house with his men."

Spicewell's face didn't move. She could feel Bill Talbot's nervous energy from across the room.

"What then? Do you have a better idea?" Their reticence irked her. She rose to her feet and moved toward the door. "A child's life is at stake. And not just one child. Imagine those terrified babes locked up in that windowless building in the alley." Her blood boiled just thinking about them. Little girls and boys like her own Ellie and Nicky—innocent and trusting and utterly dependent on the adults around her. "We must ride to the White Tower at once."

CHAPTER 5

*E*la and Bill rode toward the great stone tower that loomed over the city. Ferries and small rowboats jostled up against great merchant ships on the heaving gray river as they rode along near its banks. They had to proceed slowly through crowds of people shopping, hawking their wares, or carrying bundles to market. And, of course, the usual hordes of beggars, vagrants and cutpurses.

One little girl approached Ela and tugged at her skirts, brown eyes wide and tangled curls hanging about her dirty face. "Spare a farthing, ma'am! My baby brother is hungry."

Ela's heart clenched. She knew that most of these urchins were in gangs of youths organized by hardened criminals looking to prey on the soft hearts of wealthy citizens. But now she could see the girl's plight from the other side—she was a victim as much as the citizens she targeted with her plaintive pleas.

"If you give her a coin it'll line the pocket of her master," warned Bill as if he could read her mind.

Ela frowned. She slowed her horse to a halt and reached

into her purse. The girl's eyes widened. Ela pinched a silver penny between her thumb and finger. "Where do you live, little girl?"

The girl reached up to snatch the coin, but Ela held it just out reach.

"Do you live nearby?"

"My brother's hungry!" She lunged at the coin, eyes not leaving it.

"Are you hungry?" Ela's horse stamped impatiently, but Ela held the coin steady. "Would you like me to buy you a hot pie?"

The girl's eyes finally left the coin and met hers, dark with suspicion.

"It's not a trick. I shall buy you a pie." Ela scanned the street. Vendors were all around them, filling the bellies of the sailors and hawkers and clerks that thronged the streets. She glanced at Bill. "Can you buy her a pie? And one for her brother."

Bill jumped from his horse and handed it to the attendant.

"Can I have it?" The girl reached for the coin.

"Is a hot pie not better than coin?" Ela smiled at her, but that was a miscalculation, as the girl suddenly darted forward, under the legs of her horse and out the other side, and disappeared into the crowd.

Ela was still holding the single penny in her hand when Bill returned with two hot meat pies.

"Poor mite didn't trust me." She tucked the coin back in her purse. "I'm sure she was hungry."

"Perhaps she feared a beating more than her hunger. Her master must be watching her."

Ela scanned the faces around them. Everyone looked odd or sinister in one way or another on the streets of London.

Probably even her. Strangers in a crowd of strangers, so unlike comfortable Salisbury, where she knew almost every face in the crowd.

"What shall I do with these pies?"

Ela glanced at another ragged waif, busy begging for coin from an older gentleman walking nearby.

"Here lad," called Bill after the boy. "Would you care for a pie?" The urchin glanced up at him, pale eyes shining in his dirty face. He looked at the pie, then at Bill, then at the pie... then he turned and ran.

Bill raised his brows at Ela.

"They're scared of us." Ela shifted in her saddle. "I wonder why?"

"Scared of everyone, I'd imagine. Poor things."

Bill gave one of the pies to an old blind woman begging for alms alongside a wharf and the other to a ragged young man on crutches who was dragging one foot. Even they seemed suspicious rather than grateful.

BILL ANNOUNCED them at the gate to the White Tower and asked for an audience with the sheriff. The guard seemed unimpressed by Ela's rank but admitted them and pointed them toward a black-painted door on the far side of the courtyard.

They dismounted and Bill knocked on the door, which was ornamented with wide bands and studs of wrought iron. It opened slowly and a harried looking man with thick black brows said that the sheriff was abroad and asked if they'd like to leave a message.

Ela wanted to cry with frustration. The ride here had seemed so long and tortuous despite the relatively short distance. Every step in London was like thirty steps in peaceful Wiltshire. "When will le Duc return? It's an urgent matter."

The man shrugged. "He's abroad on the king's business."

"Abroad where?" It would be just her luck for him to have sailed for Normandy this morning.

"Westminster."

Ela wanted to retort that he was hardly abroad on the king's business if he was waiting on the king at his palace, but there was no point in getting on the wrong side of his clerk or whoever this man was.

"We shall seek him there."

CALLING on the king himself was no small matter and required preparation, even if there was only a chance of seeing him. They returned to Alianore's house to refresh their dress. Alianore fussed over Ela's attire, lending her a heavy belt of wrought-gold links and pinching her cheeks to give them color.

"We might not even see the king, Mama."

"Not see the king at Westminster? Why else would you go there? It's the perfect excuse to get him involved in your endeavors. He's but a boy of eighteen himself. How could his heart not be moved by the plight of innocent children?"

"But he always has that odious Hubert de Burgh at his elbow." Ela hated the man with an unholy passion.

"Unfortunately, De Burgh will manage the affairs of the kingdom until Henry reaches his majority."

"That can't come soon enough for me."

"Why do you despise de Burgh so? He's quite charming when he's in his cups."

Ela's pulse quickened, and she schooled herself to stay quiet. Her mother knew nothing of her suspicion that de Burgh had poisoned her husband. Such knowledge was a liability to anyone who heard it, and she didn't want to put her mother in danger.

"He's officious and arrogant, and I always get the feeling that he thinks I should be at home working my embroidery."

"I've said the same thing to you myself," said Alianore with an arched brow. "Why would you want to meddle in the affairs of the kingdom when you could be enjoying the comfort of your own hearth?"

Ela decided not to dignify her jibe with a response.

"You shall ride in my carriage. The ostler is readying it right now." Her mother turned to the lad standing in the doorway. "Let us know as soon as it's ready."

"But the distance is so short. And Bill hates to travel in a carriage." Ela would much preferred to be nimble on her own horse. What if they needed to follow the sheriff to Westcheap in a hurry?

"Bill can ride behind it." Alianore fluffed her veil and surveyed her with satisfaction. "Now what can you give him as a gift?"

"I don't need a gift. It's not a social visit."

"A gift never goes amiss, my darling. Especially an expensive one. And the new tapestry that Jean brought back from Picardy for our bedroom gives me a headache. The colors are too bright." She commanded a servant to roll it up and tie it well.

"What is the king going to want with your too-bright tapestry?"

"He can hang it in a too-dark room. Or give it away to one of his lackeys. It's the gesture that counts."

Ela sighed. She'd prefer to get right down to their urgent

business and not waste time on pomp and circumstance. "We're going there to find the sheriff."

"Forget about the sheriff. Visit your kin, the king. He shall command the sheriff to do whatever you wish."

Ela wasn't so sure about that but didn't wish to argue. Finally, outfitted with gifts and raiment fit for royalty, they headed out into the cloudy afternoon just in time to catch a sudden downpour of rain.

ELA COULD SEE the wisdom of her mother's advice of going straight to the king. He was at home, as evidenced by the flag hanging soggily above the battlements as they approached. Bill announced them to the guards at the gate and they were ushered in with appropriate fanfare.

Bill explained that they were there on urgent business, and to Ela's delight they were led right past the halls of simpering courtiers and hangers-on, directly to the king's private parlor.

King Henry III sat in a carved and ornamented chair, which perched on a small platform that lifted him almost to eye level with the men—de Burgh among them—who stood around him.

"Ela, my dear." He rose from his seat and stepped down to kiss her on the cheek. Ela was impressed with the maturity and grace that belied his tender years, and heartened by the familiar greeting. "To what do I owe this unexpected pleasure?"

He sat back in his chair and Ela murmured the usual pleasantries as quickly as possible, then launched into her true purpose. She explained about the girl missing from Salisbury and that she'd learned it was not a rare occurrence for children to vanish. Then she shared the information she'd received about the house near Westcheap. She did not say she'd come here to find the sheriff, and she tried to forget that she'd originally decided not to trouble the king with this matter.

The king listened intently. "Children being stolen, you say? But for what purpose? Servants are available for hire in every part of the country. And why would someone want to snare a child so young that they'd have to train it like a weanling?"

"I'm not really sure, your majesty. But I suspect the purpose might be more than simple servitude. I hesitate to pour foul words in your ear, but it's possible that these men are using young girls for…"

She couldn't form the words. Truth be told she didn't even have the words in her vocabulary. "For sinful acts."

"Sinful acts?" Henry looked confused. An unmarried boy of eighteen who'd lived the most sheltered of lives—despite the iniquity no doubt taking place daily between the courtiers under his many roofs—he might have no idea of the kinds of acts that were possible even between consenting adults.

"Do you mean that the children are taken to be sexual playthings?" asked de Burgh.

Ela swallowed. He spoke the cruel words with a casual ease that chilled her. "Yes. It's possible, at least." She turned back to the king. "Tender children in the clutches of…monsters."

"Come now, don't be so dramatic." De Burgh's sharp features took on a mocking humor. "The streets of London are teeming with vagrants and urchins."

Ela's bile rose. "The girl I seek is neither of those things. She was stolen from her parents' cottage just outside Salisbury."

53

"This isn't Salisbury. Surely Simon de Hal should take charge of this matter."

Ela tried hard to keep her expression neutral. She suspected de Burgh was behind the decision to install de Hal as sheriff instead of her, after she'd explicitly requested the role. "From what we've learned, it seems likely that the children are brought to London right away, where it's easier to lose them in the crowd and prevent them from escaping to find their way home." She was inventing as she spoke, but it did make sense. "I've heard they're often sold overseas, so they can't make their way home and no one can find them."

De Burgh lifted a slim salt-and-pepper brow. "And who are your mysterious sources of this information?"

"My lawyer, Walter Spicewell, has men he hires that can slip into the shadows of London's underworld. They've identified a house in an alley near Westcheap—a building with no windows on the first floor—where they say some of these children are being held." She turned and spoke directly to the king. "I request that men be sent to liberate the children so they can be returned to their rightful homes."

"This sounds like a task for the sheriff." The young king looked at de Burgh as if for confirmation.

"Indeed it does," said de Burgh. "I'll be sure to notify him personally." His cold smile didn't reach his eyes. Ela had a feeling her request would die in this room.

"Bill Talbot and I just rode to the Tower in search of the sheriff and were told he was here at Westminster. I hoped to discuss the problem with you and then find him myself. Is he within the palace?" If she approached le Duc with the king's blessing he could hardly ignore her concerns.

The king looked at de Burgh again. Ela prayed that Henry would exhibit more self-confidence once he gained his majority. He was a sensible enough young man—as well he might be with the weight of the kingdom resting on his shoulders since he was a small boy.

De Burgh held up his hands in a gesture of mock helplessness. "I don't have a map to his whereabouts. The palace and grounds are extensive."

"Could a messenger find him?" Ela didn't want to beat about the bush. "An eight-year-old girl is in grave danger right this moment."

She wanted to conjure the image of her mother's desperation and share her dread at facing young Edyth's parents without good news. But she knew revealing her heart would just give them an excuse to dismiss her as too emotional.

"I share your concern, my lady." De Burgh took a step forward as if to insert himself between her and the king. "We shall seek out the sheriff at once—wherever he may be—and pass on your message."

Frustration welled inside her. Could she pace the halls and gardens of Westminster in search of Roger le Duc? For all she knew he was back at the tower by now.

"I'm sure your majesty and my lord justiciar are as appalled as I am by the news that tender babes are being abducted and sold into slavery right under our noses. That they're being held here—imprisoned—in the greatest city in this kingdom." She kept her voice steady and grave, while emotion rose inside her. "I consider it my duty to help return them to their parents."

"God bless you for your generous heart," said de Burgh. "That you care so much for the orphans and strangers of our country when your true duty is to your own tender babes, my lady." His cold gaze belied his words. "Surely they must miss you when you are abroad in London?"

Ela felt a snappy retort hover at her lips, but she schooled herself to remain silent. Nothing good could come of angering the king's justiciar, who still effectively ruled the country. Look what had happened to her husband after he'd raged against de Burgh? No sooner had they sealed their truce with a feast at de Burgh's home than her husband sickened and died.

She was sure de Burgh had poisoned him. But again—what good could come of accusing a man who was unassailable? De Burgh was too powerful an enemy to challenge, much as it pained her. Hopefully that would all change once the king gained his majority and de Burgh no longer held the reins of the nation in his scheming hands. Until then she'd be wise to treat him like a dangerous animal that must be handled with care.

"My children are not so young that they must cling to their mother's skirts," she finally replied, as graciously as she could. "Two of them married this summer with the king's kind permission." She smiled at Henry. "Such a joy to see them safely settled in life."

This opening allowed Henry to ask about the weddings and steered the conversation in a direction that should remind de Burgh that the king was a member of her family as well as the head of state. She'd already given up hoping that either the king or de Burgh would send guards out for the girl. Now all she wanted to do was exit gracefully and come up with another plan to rescue Edyth.

"You must stay to dine with us." The king rose from his chair with a smile. "Sir Thomas Fitzwilliam is here with his lady wife and their eldest son."

No! These evening feasts were always interminable. With no further responsibilities for the day, the men would drink until they slid under the table. The prospect of sitting there making small talk while poor Edyth was possibly being loaded onto a ship sailing for Venice or even Constantinople made her want to scream. Agnes Fitzwilliam had no interests outside of gossip about her neighbors and her husband was dull as a bog. And no doubt there'd be a crowd of other royal hangers-on offering condolences for William's death and maybe even scheming to marry her and her fortune into their family.

But this was the king.

She couldn't say no.

"How delightful." She tried hard to smile and likely wasn't successful. She glanced at de Burgh. At least his displeasure at her company should warm her impatient heart.

But it didn't. He now smiled with what looked like genuine enthusiasm.

Probably he was happy that she couldn't now pursue the girl as she wanted. She'd thwarted his plans to marry her to his nephew, and now he intended to thwart every plan she made for the rest of her life.

Ela glanced at Bill with her fake smile, and he returned a sympathetic glance and made some enthusiastic noises, before they shuffled off—in the king's company—to the dining hall, where the smell of roasted peacock was already filling the air.

IT WAS full dark by the time she finally managed to make her excuses and leave. Bursting with impatience and fury, she knew it was too late to do anything to help Edyth tonight. She'd brought up the issue of the sheriff with de Burgh somewhere in between the candied quails eggs and the truffled plums and had dismissively been told that he was being informed and that she should focus on enjoying the king's hospitality.

The carriage had been sent home due to its inconvenient size in the busy confines of the palace stable yards, and two attendants had returned with horses for them to ride home.

Once fresh, those horses were now sleepy and irritable after waiting several hours in the royal stables for them to be released from ceremonial bondage.

A thick bank of black clouds covered the moon. Their two attendants now walked on foot, carrying lanterns to light the way as they rode out the gates of Westminster Palace.

"That was a disaster. An utterly wasted day." Ela barely managed to save her growl of frustration until they were out of earshot.

"At least the king now knows about the missing children," said Bill. He was a little tipsy from all the good wine they'd been plied with for hours.

"If he cared enough to do anything to protect them he'd have sent soldiers out to the house immediately."

"Perhaps he did."

"I doubt it." Ela found her head foggy from all the excess. She didn't enjoy being forced to taste course after course of indigestible delicacies and would have much preferred a nice bowl of pottage at home. "De Burgh is determined to frustrate me in any way possible."

They rode along the cobbled streets. The night was quiet, with the thick, moonless darkness keeping most people inside. That and the ever-present robbers ready to waylay foolish strangers. Ela didn't feel all that safe even with a trained knight and two armed attendants. The hour was late and they were all tired and unfocused. Even her horse—one of her mother's that she didn't know well—tripped over every third cobble, it seemed, and made her feel unsteady in her awkward sidesaddle.

The road from Westminster seemed twice as long and ten times as sinister on this black evening. She heaved a small sigh of relief when they passed the familiar stone facade of St. Michael and All Angels and drew closer to her mother's street. "Tomorrow we shall visit the White Tower bright and early, before the sheriff has a chance to ride out," she said. "We can—"

A sudden hard shove knocked her from her horse and blew the words from her mouth and her mind.

CHAPTER 6

*E*la fell from her horse onto the hard cobbles. Dazed, she tried to right herself and caught the flash of a long knife from the corner of her eye. She watched with horror as Bill doubled over the blade and slumped from his horse to the ground.

She tried to cry out his name, but one hand clamped over her mouth and another tugged a dark cloth over her eyes. She struggled and tried to bite the hand, but her captor shoved a balled-up rag into her mouth that left her gagging and unable to scream. She was lifted off her feet and bundled over a hard shoulder like a sack of kindling.

Bill! Bill! She cried out in her mind, pummeling her captor's back with her fists. From the glimpse she'd seen in the last burst of lantern light, she could swear he'd been run through with the knife. Where were the attendants? Were they all killed?

Who are you? She wanted to demand of her captor, but her mouth was forced wide open, and no sound would come from her cloth-filled throat. She gagged and wriggled and struggled the whole way, trying to break his grip on her—the man was running—until she felt his arm move and heard a door swing open, then shut behind her.

The smell that assaulted her nostrils surprised her. A scent of cooked meat and under it a whiff of something like incense. Her captor strode forward, feet silent on the floor. He climbed a flight of stairs, then she heard another door open—his back didn't move to open it so someone must have done it for him.

Still struggling, unable to do more than make small choking noises, she suddenly found herself ejected from his shoulder and laid roughly down on…a soft bed.

Or that's what it felt like. Her hands—unbound—clutched at the surface and found it to be a rich, soft wool like her own winter cloak.

Where am I? She raised her hands to her face and tugged the covering from her eyes, but the room was so dark she could see nothing. Her captor had already left and closed the door. She pulled the wadded ball of cloth from her mouth and coughed until her chest ached.

She could scream now.

If she wanted to. But was that wise? Who would hear her? And would a listener be more likely to save her or kill her? She needed to figure out where she was and how to get out of here.

And then she needed to find Bill.

Her heart clenched at the thought. If Bill wasn't dead he'd have come after her with the last ounce of strength left in him. He'd always been her champion—after her husband—and vowed a thousand times to give his life for hers.

And now he had. Grief welled inside her.

She prayed that her eyes would adjust to the dark so she could see something. Now sitting, she felt for the floor with her feet. This wasn't the house of a common robber—which would smell of musty walls and tallow candles and stale bread. The scent in the air reminded her of her mother's house, with its tall beeswax candles, polished wood and dishes of spiced delicacies.

She sat in the house of someone wealthy.

She strained to see in the darkness, but no light entered from any source. She rose gingerly to her feet. Her hands weren't tied so if she could find a window maybe she could force it open and escape.

Her ears pricked, listening for any sound. She thought she heard music, but maybe it was the sound of her blood pulsing in her panicked brain.

Bill is dead. The memory assaulted her again like a blow. He'd been her constant companion since she was a girl. The prospect of life without her husband was grim enough, but without Bill Talbot the world would be a very lonely place.

You need to get out of here for the sake of your children. The urgent thought burned in her mind. *They've lost their father, and they can't lose you.* Not to mention that Hubert de Burgh would no doubt try to make them his wards so he could pillage her estate for his own gain.

She held her hands out in front of her face as she shuffled forward across the floor, wary that she could trip or bang into a jutting piece of furniture. The darkness obscured her vision as if she still had a hood over her eyes.

The floor under her thin-soled leather shoes felt like smooth stone tiles. Her hand touched a wall and found it to be smooth plaster, cool to the touch.

She could swear she heard music. Very low—almost too low to distinguish from the sound of her own breathing—but a rhythmic rise and fall like a chant. Moving her hands along the wall, she edged sideways. She reached a corner and felt her way around it to the next wall. A few feet along that she reached what felt like a wooden shutter, closed from the inside.

A window. If she could get it open she might at least get a small glow of cloud-covered moonlight to light the room or illuminate the way to the ground. She ran her fingers along the edge of the shutters, trying to wiggle them or find out how they latched. An iron bar crossed the shutters horizontally. She ran her fingertips along it until she found a lock in the middle with a large keyhole, securing the shutters from the inside. The barred shutters were intended to keep robbers out, but without the key they were just as effective at keeping her in.

The shutters hung on big hinges screwed deep into the wall, because they didn't budge when she tried to pry at them. Frustration clawed at her. If she couldn't get out through the window the only way out was through the door —into the house.

She felt her way further along the wall and soon she'd worked her way all around the small room, over the bed she'd been laid on and back to the door her assailant brought her in through. She was exploring the door with her fingertips when she heard footsteps in the passage outside.

HEART PUMPING, Ela groped her way back to the bed and sat down on it just as a key scratched in the lock. The door opened with a creak, and a shaft of light from a lantern almost blinded her.

Blinking, she tried to get a good look at the person in the doorway. The person was short but with the broad shoulders of man. A deep hood hid his face. A small boy came from behind him and carried a covered dish into the bedroom. He placed it on the bed next to her—all without looking at her. The short man stood in the doorway for a moment, then hung the lantern on a hook and closed and locked the door, leaving her and the boy alone in the room.

Ela realized when he'd gone that she hadn't uttered a word, despite all the questions hovering in her mouth. *Where am I? Who are you? Why am I here? Why did you kill Bill Talbot?* She had a feeling that if she'd let even one word escape she'd soon have been screaming.

The boy uncovered the dish to reveal three small roasted birds and an apple baked with cinnamon and honey. The boy was only about eight years old, with smooth, dark skin like polished oak.

"What's your name?" she asked.

He sat cross-legged on the floor and kept his eyes down. It occurred to her that he might be one of the captured children she was trying to help. He wore a dark green tunic trimmed with silver and blue embroidery. An expensive costume for a child servant, if that's what he was.

"Do you speak French or English?" She spoke softly, aware that her urgency had given her last question a sharp tone. He still didn't respond, and his eyes remained cast toward the floor. "Are there other children here?"

The fragrant aroma of the roasted birds turned her stomach after the endless feasting at the palace. She'd never felt less like eating. She wondered if the boy would like to eat them, then asked herself if they were poisoned.

Was he afraid of her? She climbed off the bed and crouched on the floor in front of the child. When he still didn't raise his gaze, she lifted her thumb and finger to his chin and tilted his face toward hers.

As she touched him his whole body stiffened and his eyes flew to hers with a look of terror.

She let go immediately. "I'm sorry. I didn't mean to startle you." What did he think she was going to do to him? What had already been done to him? "Do you understand me?"

He blinked. She had a feeling that he did but that he'd rather eat his tongue than admit it. "I'm here to help you," she whispered. Was she? She didn't know why she was here, but it was a fair assumption that her abduction had something to do with her quest to find Edyth. It was another fair assumption that someone was listening at the door or through a wall.

"What are they planning to do with me?" she wondered aloud. She picked up one of the little birds as if she were about to eat it but put it back on the plate. "Are you hungry?"

He shook his head.

"You do understand me."

His gaze dropped to the floor again. The lantern light revealed it to be an elaborate pattern of black and white tiles. She glanced up at the rest of the room. Colorful painted patterns and naturalistic vines covered the plaster walls. This house must be a palace of some kind to be so richly decorated.

But who did it belong to?

"Is that music?" The odd swells of sound seemed sometimes to be there and sometimes not.

The boy bit his lip. He sat on the floor, clutching his knees as if trying to curl himself into a ball.

"Are you afraid?"

He didn't look at her. He'd obviously been told not to talk to her on pain of punishment. Perhaps he'd been told to watch her and report back to his masters or to call out if she tried to escape.

She rose to her feet and walked to the shuttered window. In the light, the shutter and its iron bar looked more impenetrable than ever. Would anyone hear her from the street if she shouted for help? She couldn't tell if there was glass hidden behind the shutter, but given the ornate decor of the room there probably was. That would further deaden any sounds she might make.

Was anyone even looking for her? It was past midnight, and her mother would be asleep. With Bill dead and her attendants dead or injured as well, no one would remark upon their absence until they failed to appear for breakfast the next morning.

She turned and marched back across the small space until she reached the door. "If there's anyone out there I'm ready to meet you. Why do you have me shut up here?"

She could almost swear she heard movement in the passage outside, but no one spoke.

"I'm not going to eat in case the food is poisoned," she said coolly. She did feel oddly calm. She grew impatient for action or confrontation of some kind. Is this how men felt before battle? Of course, she was unarmed and had no way to defend herself but her wit. The people who'd taken her were clearly remorseless killers. Her predicament looked bleak.

But if they simply wanted her dead, surely they'd have killed her already?

ELA HEARD the fumble of a key being inserted into the lock and turned. Her stomach clenched as the door opened again to reveal a tall man. She couldn't tell if it was the same one who'd brought her here. If it was, he'd changed. He now wore the black robes of a friar. The hood was pushed back enough to reveal a face—except there was no face, just an odd leather mask with a protrusion like a crow's beak. The unsettling sight unnerved her, and she gasped before she managed to steady herself.

The little boy was so disturbed by the sight that he scrambled to his feet, a sob bursting from his mouth.

"Shut up, you brat," snarled the man. "Get back to the kitchen."

The boy tore past his legs and out the door.

The man spoke in English, not the courtly French she'd expect of a friar. But he didn't have the thick accent of the people who ran the market stalls or begged for alms in the streets of London.

"Where am I?" She was glad her voice came out calm and even.

"Follow me," he snapped. He turned and walked back into the hallway, holding a lantern to light the way.

Ela followed behind the man. The black robes dragged on the floor as if they were a size too large. The hallway bore a pattern of smooth black and white stone—marble from Italy, she suspected. She'd seen similar in some grand houses she'd visited. Carved wood panels decorated the hallway walls.

Her curiosity about this strange, lavish place conquered her fear, and she tried to take in every detail as they descended a narrow flight of wood stairs and the man unlocked another door and led them into a large room.

More lanterns glowed in brackets on the wall, illuminating the grand space. At the center of the opposite wall stood a large stone fireplace carved with what looked like angels. No fire burned in the grate, but a stack of wood and polished iron fire tools stood next to it.

The walls were stained dark red, and a painted pattern of yellow and blue diamonds ran along the top and bottom of the walls. Several fine wood chairs lined the walls, and a table on one wall held an open book on a stand. The book was large enough to be a great Bible, but Ela couldn't make out the text in the gloomy candlelight.

The masked and hooded man led her into the middle of the room. A large silver box on a table caught her eye. The intricate patterns in the silver had the geometric quality of work by the Spanish infidels whose God forbade them to draw men or objects from nature.

"Whose house is this?" she asked, curiosity burning her.

"You're prying into matters that don't concern you," he replied roughly. "And doing so will endanger your life and the people you care about."

"You already did that. I saw Sir William Talbot fall from his horse, stabbed by a knife."

"Then you know I mean it." He spoke low, with that same not-quite-accent. She could almost swear she'd heard his voice before, but she couldn't say where. "Go back home and mind your own business."

My business is to do what God commands me. She wanted to argue with him, but right now her priority was to escape with her life and return to her children. "I'd like to do that." She made her voice meek and quiet. Playacting was not her strong suit. Her husband, William, used to tease her about that. She'd never been skilled at pretending to like dullards or flattering pompous guests in their home. "Please let me go home to my children."

The man shifted his weight. He gave off an unpleasant smell of unwashed skin. Or maybe it was the cloak. "Your children. You want to keep them safe?"

"Of course."

"Then focus on them and don't waste your time and energy wondering about other people's brats."

I was brought here because of my search for Edyth.

"What do you mean?" Much as she wanted to escape, she suddenly felt like she was on the right path to find the girl.

"You know what I mean," he growled. "Don't play stupid."

She drew herself up. She wasn't used to being spoken to like this. But then she'd never been knocked from her horse and imprisoned before, either. Even in a palace.

In the silence, again she heard the swell of music. "Who's singing?"

"None of your business."

The sound had the cadence of a Gregorian chant. She could hear it better here than in the small bedchamber. Another object in the room caught her eye—draped over the back of a chair on the far side of the room—the pelt of an exotic animal with spots. She'd only seen such animals in drawings and couldn't guess which one it might be. A leopard perhaps?

The person who owned this place must be a collector of exotic things. Perhaps someone who traveled. "The boy who brought my dinner. Where is he from?"

She expected him to ignore her, but he didn't. "He's from the Black Coast." His voice had a bragging tone. "All the people there are black as charcoal, and it's said that they feast on human flesh."

The idea startled her but she knew he'd said it to shock her. It was probably nonsense anyway. Now that his lips were loosened, she tried again. "This palace is fit for a prince. Your master must be a great man." She could hardly believe how calm she was when this man could draw a knife from his robe and kill her at any moment. "Will you tell me his name?"

He wouldn't kill her. He didn't dare. She was a countess and kin to the king.

But, given those things, how did they dare to seize and threaten her like this?

"You must leave London tonight and not come back." His voice was slightly muffled by the odd beaked mask.

"I will. I'll leave at once." The prospect of escaping this strange place sent a jolt of energy to her fingers and toes.

"If you're ever found to be prying into the matter of

missing children again, your own children will join them and disappear without a trace."

A chill gripped her. "I would never endanger my own children." Her voice trembled slightly. "Please don't hurt them."

His posture softened, and she could almost swear he smiled under his ghoulish mask. Her genuine fear had no doubt gladdened his cruel heart.

"Don't move." He took a step toward her.

She braced, much as the boy had done when she touched him. The man pulled a length of dark cloth from inside his robe and tied it over her eyes. The cloth had a strong smell of incense, and she fought the urge to sneeze as it covered her nose and mouth as well as her eyes.

Unable to see, she felt him move behind her. He placed his hands on her shoulders and pushed her forward like she was a horse before his cart.

The door opened before her, so there must have been someone else standing there listening the whole time.

"Watch your step," he said in the oddly mocking tone he'd used earlier. "We don't want you getting hurt now, do we?"

She didn't dignify his threat with a reply but did pick up her hem so as not to trip on it. She held her other hand out in front of her to avoid bumping into walls or furniture.

He steered her along a series of passageways—different from the way she'd come in. Another door opened and the cool night air touched her skin like a kiss. She could smell distant fires and hear the barking of dogs.

"Do I find my way from here?" She raised a hand to her blindfold.

His laugh exploded out of him. "No! You'll be taken far from here. We can hardly have you coming back here with the sheriff's men now, can we?"

Ela's ears pricked. What did he know of her search for the sheriff? Who had told these people about her?

She let out a small shriek as someone—not the masked man, maybe the short one—lifted her off her feet and carried her forward a few steps, then bundled her into a wagon of some sort. She was laid down on a wood floor that reeked of refuse, like a cart used to carry animals or agricultural produce. Before she had time to right herself, the cart jolted forward and she heard the clatter of hooves on cobbles as it set out with her.

She reached up to tug the blindfold from her eyes—

"Leave that!" said a voice in French as a hand slapped at hers. Then the driver's voice, a rougher, more typically London one, scolded her. "You've no need to see where you're going."

"How will I find my way home?"

"I don't know or care."

Ela strained to pay attention to the movements of the cart —a turn to the right, a curve to the left, a halt while hooves clattered by in front of the cart—but the turns continued until the map she drew in her head devolved into a tangle of weeds.

The city's nighttime sounds—the grumble of drunks, the clip-clop of a lone horseman, the occasional shout of an angry housewife—gradually faded into a thick, dark silence as the smell of cooking fires was replaced by the rich, wet smell of damp earth.

She made another conversational gambit. "Where are we?"

"The less you know, the better off you are," was the only answer she received.

Eventually the driver up front shouted something intelligible and the stinking cart slowed to a jerky halt. The man next to her seized her in his arms like she was a sack of carrots and heaved her out of the cart.

Her shoulder hit the ground hard—before she could throw her arms out to break her fall. The coachman yelled back and berated him to have a care! He retorted with a curse that burned her ears, then the horse moved forward and the cart lurched into motion again.

She just had time to tug off her blindfold, right herself, and scramble out of the road before the horse and cart turned around and came back again toward her at a trot.

"Sleep tight, princess!" called the driver. The short man upbraided him for insolence, and their argument faded into the night as Ela found herself alone in the dark in the middle of nowhere.

CHAPTER 7

$\mathcal{A}$s the cart with its cruel occupants receded into the distance, Ela felt a powerful sense of relief. She'd escaped with her life. Next came deep unease. She was alone with no attendants and no means of transport in an utterly unknown place. Worse yet, it was night and she stood on one of the many roads leading into London where robbers and vagrants might lurk behind any tree hoping to waylay travelers.

Not that she could so much as make out a tree. A thick bank of cloud blotted out the stars and moon and made it hard to distinguish the sky from the ground.

At least she knew which direction London lay in, since the cart was now heading back there. If she could stay on the road and not be murdered by cutthroats, she'd eventually find her way back to the city and to her mother's house.

She set out walking, which wasn't easy, given the delicate, thin-soled shoes she'd chosen to wear to Westminster Palace. The embroidered hem of her gown wrapped itself around her ankles like a chain, and she had to repeatedly pull it loose. Then there was the problem of staying on the road, which was really two deep furrows made by a thousand cartwheels.

Ela hitched her skirt to her knees, grateful for the darkness, the better to stride forward. She now covered ground rapidly and soon, over the top of a small rise she saw the glow of a light in a window and smelled smoke rising from a hearth.

If it was a house, perhaps she could ask the occupant to shelter her until daylight. Or if it was an inn, she could hire a horse and attendant to take her home.

Except that she had no money.

The thought hit her like a sudden rain shower. Riding around Salisbury she always kept a purse of coins on her, for buying small items or offering alms. For her journey to the palace, however, she'd seen no such need. Bill and her attendants carried money to tip the pages or buy small notions on the way.

Her heart ached at the thought of poor Bill. She couldn't believe he was dead. It was too much to bear. She'd felt the same way when her husband died—ready to argue with providence and insist that he was still alive…somewhere. Both Bill and her husband would be horrified if they knew that she was alone and friendless out here in the dark without a coin on her person.

She did have her mother's gold-link belt, though.

How odd that they hadn't taken it from her. It must be worth a good deal of money, and she was surprised that the man in the wagon hadn't relieved her of it without telling anyone else. No doubt he was too afraid of his master to commit a theft that might draw the attention of the authorities.

And his master must have told him not to molest her. She still had all her rings as well. Perhaps she could trade one of those for passage into London.

~

ELA'S HEART beat faster as she approached the building. It sat right alongside the road, and the windows glowed with candlelight from within despite the late hour.

Ela realized she had no idea what time it was. Certainly the wee hours of the morning. Who would still be up at this time? Apprehension clawed at her as she lowered her hem back to the ground. Was she about to introduce herself into a den of thieves?

A cold drizzle dampened her skin and gown and drove her to hurry toward the lone building. As she approached she could hear the muffled sounds of horses in the stable nearby.

"Who goes there?" A voice shouted out of the darkness.

Ela, Countess of Salisbury! "A traveler seeking shelter," she managed.

"Oh, really?" The mocking tone of voice made her conscious of the French-inflected accent that distinguished herself from the common people. Perhaps she should have tried to disguise it. On the other hand, she still wore the rich attire she'd donned to visit the king so she could hardly pretend to be a dairymaid lost on the road to market.

"Is this an inn?"

"Aye."

She still couldn't see the speaker. The ground right outside the inn was slippery from the rain and the passage of many feet, and she lifted her hem slightly to keep her footing.

"You have money?" The harsh voice maintained its mocking tone.

"Um…" Ela wondered how to explain that she had valuables she could trade.

"If you're a likely lass you might not need money," the voice wheedled.

"I'm a mother of eight," retorted Ela quickly. "And not at

all likely." Part of her wanted to turn back onto the road and keep going, but the rain grew heavier and soon she'd be wet through and chilled to the bone. She might be hours away from her mother's house, especially since she didn't know the way. There was no point surviving an abduction only to catch a chill and die.

She approached the door, and the dark figure of her interlocutor emerged out of the shadows and opened it for her.

Ela stepped into the gloomy interior, which reeked of damp earth and something like parsnip and bacon pottage. She didn't see anyone eating. In the flickering light from two stinking tallow candles, she could make out eight or nine men gathered in two small groups. Why were all these men awake in the middle of the night? Dressed in rough clothing and clutching wooden cups of ale, they hardly seemed the type to be waiting for Matins service to begin.

A portly older man approached her, his hair in a tonsure similar to a monk's but shaved by nature. "How may I help you?"

"I seek passage back to London." She glanced around. "I... I fell from my horse and got lost on the road." She didn't like revealing that she was vulnerable and alone, but there was no way to explain her lack of attendants.

She could have told them what really happened, but for all she knew, her kidnappers frequented this place and she'd be digging herself back into danger.

"Come, take a seat and sip a cup of ale." He gestured to a bench on the far side of the small room.

"I'm not really hungry or thirsty," she protested. She itched to leave this place as quickly as possible. Were there no women here at all? Not even the innkeeper's wife? Maybe she lay safely abed upstairs. Ela had a sudden urge to cross herself, but she kept her hands firmly at her sides. "I'd like to hire a horse and carriage for the journey."

"We don't have a carriage." An odd smile lifted one side of his mouth. "And we can hardly discuss your needs while you're standing wet and cold in the doorway!" He placed a thick hand on her arm. Ela stiffened. "Come pull up a chair by the fire."

"Then I'd like to hire a riding horse." Ela reluctantly allowed herself to be led across the room. The floor was strewn with foul-smelling, dirty straw. She perched on the edge of a wooden chair, which lurched because one leg was shorter than the others.

"I'm afraid we don't have a sidesaddle." The man cocked his head.

"I can ride astride." She spoke quietly. He was trying to intimidate her. It was working. For all she knew the men who dumped her by the road could be among those gathered around the guttering candles.

"I presume you'll rest here until morning. We do have a bed upstairs that—"

"Oh, no." The prospect of staying here among these strange men appalled her. "I need to ride at once. There are people awaiting my arrival. They'll be looking for me." She knew that much was true.

"Our horses are well tired. They've worked a hard day and need their feed and rest." He sighed. "But I suppose I can find one if you have the right coin."

"I don't have coin but I have—" Ela glanced down at her rings. The belt was too valuable for such a purchase. One ring should be more than enough for payment. She bent her head and started to work a finely wrought gold ring off her middle finger—then she stopped with a start as her blood ran cold.

Her belt was gone.

She knew she still had it on her after her fall from the cart. She could almost swear she'd felt its reassuring weight about her waist as she'd walked the last slippery steps to the door into this God-forsaken place. Had someone snatched it off her as she walked across the room? She'd heard tell of thieves who could steal your eyeballs out of your sockets without your noticing.

She realized she'd stopped breathing. She wasn't in any position to accuse them of theft. A woman alone among strangers in the dark of night. She'd never—ever—been abroad at night without an attendant. Although her gut instinct was to rise to her feet and loudly threaten to bring the law on them—without an entourage of armed knights…

She worked her ring off. "I can pay with this ring." Her first priority was to get out of here and back to London in one piece.

She put the ring in the tavern owner's greasy palm. He raised it to his mouth and bit it, which made her flesh crawl. "It's just brass." He peered at her, and she could swear she saw a question in his gaze. He dared her to argue with him. She suspected that if she rose to the bait she'd end up stripped of all her rings and with no horse.

She looked down at her hands. She had three more rings, one with a large emerald and another with three small rubies. "Would one of these do instead?"

"This one—" He held up the one in his hand. "And the green one."

Ela's heart sank. The emerald ring was a gift from William on their tenth wedding anniversary. But William would value her life above even the most precious gemstone. She eased it over her knuckle.

The innkeeper snatched it, and she heard it click against his yellow teeth. "I'll send the lad to get a horse ready for you.

For the ruby ring as well you can have the lad ride along with you...for protection."

His voice had an odd edge to it. Would the "lad"—who might be a man of fifty for all she knew—be more likely to protect her or to harm her? Or was the offer of protection a threat that if she didn't buy it, she'd soon regret it?

Fear trickled down her spine as she weighed the two unappealing options. "Would he ride all the way to my destination?"

"Aye, and bring the horse back. Otherwise you'd have to bring it back yourself tomorrow." Ela would have had a servant do the latter, of course, but a guide all the way into the city held a lot of appeal. The outskirts sprawled in a maze of streets, and it would be easy to lose her way and end up in a dangerous quarter.

"I'd like the lad to attend me." She pulled off the third ring. Her mother had given it to her for her birthday last year. Hopefully it would buy her the right to see another birthday. She handed it over and averted her eyes as he stuck it in his mouth. She looked up in time to see him grin and shove the rings in his purse. Their true value could probably buy this whole establishment, but worth was circumstantial.

She refused all food and drink, wary of being drugged or poisoned. For all they knew she might ride back to civilization and accuse them of theft and extortion. After what seemed like an hour the innkeeper gruffly shouted that her horse was ready. Ela hurried outside, anxious to get as far away from this place as possible.

The pitch darkness of the night hadn't abated. The lad—who was indeed a lad, of about eighteen—held two horses in one hand and a crude lantern in the other.

"Take your pick." One was a wide-eyed, sturdy chestnut and the other a tall, spindly bay.

"Which one is easier to ride?"

79

"Both the same."

Both horses looked sleepy and unimpressed by their new task. Ela chose the bay because it had a kinder eye. The lad looked relieved, which wasn't encouraging. She took the reins and managed to climb on while the bay sidestepped away from the boy and the lantern.

Once she was safely astride she turned the horse in a circle to let it know she was in charge. Thank goodness it knew at least basic commands. Perhaps it had even been a fine horse at some point in its earlier life.

They set out on the road, with the lad holding the lantern aloft to light the ruts and puddles of the path. "Have you done this journey before?" she asked, after she'd had time to settle into her mount and decide it didn't want to kill her.

"Nope."

"You've ridden into London."

"Nope."

Ela did quickly cross herself. "What do you usually do?"

"I just started at the inn this week. I wash the pots and cups and feed and water the horses." He turned to her with a bright grin. "I've only been on a horse twice in my life. I'm glad you picked the tall one!"

Ela prayed that both horses would be quiet and that nothing would happen to startle them. This poor lad would be next to no use once they reached the busy streets of London—surely it would be dawn by then—and would likely have trouble finding his way home.

Still, that wasn't her problem and he seemed happy enough to go on this adventure.

THE FIRST GLOW of dawn revealed the roofs and church towers of London in the distance. Cottages and hovels of all descriptions hunkered against each other in sprawling suburbs outside the city walls, and thin whiffs of smoke rose from bakeries and cookshops. Through the thin dawn mist she could make out the tall shape of the White Tower, and the sight of the familiar landmark made her want to weep with relief.

As they drew closer, however, the great tower disappeared behind the cluster of thatched and tiled roofs that crowded around them. As she suspected it was almost impossible to guess the right way to turn in the higgledy-piggledy patchwork of streets.

The lad led the way confidently enough. He even blew out the lantern and stowed it behind his saddle as the misty dawn light illuminated their unfamiliar surroundings. Perhaps he'd lied about never making the journey before.

But as time went on she wondered if they were making real progress or just going around in uneven, looping circles. A bank of flat white cloud hid the rising sun, so she had no idea which way was north or south. Eventually he stopped his horse, turned to her and admitted that he had no idea which way to go.

"Don't worry, we'll find our way." She wanted to reassure him. "Perhaps you could ask that good woman behind the fruit stall."

A red-faced woman arranged rows of plump pears and damsons on a clean linen cloth. The lad dismounted from his horse and led it over. She heard him mumble something and the woman replied. Then he came back over to her and asked, "Where are we going?"

Ela couldn't help but laugh. She gave him her mother's address and he hurried back to the woman, dragging his broad chestnut horse along by its reins like a hound on a rope. As he gave her the address the woman shot Ela a glance of shock that turned into a look of grave disapproval.

Ela found herself looking down at her attire, which, in the stark light of morning, was shockingly dirty. She wasn't even sure how that had happened. Probably the floor of the stinking cart followed by her ejection onto the damp earth of the countryside. She lifted her chin high. It was nothing that wouldn't wash off.

The lad paid no attention to her grimy appearance but excitedly mounted his horse, muttering to himself. "Right at St. Peters, left at the old fish market, right again past the Abbey of St. Giles…."

Ela kept quiet, not wanting to chase the precious words from his head. Luckily, he had a good memory and his horse was steadier than his riding of it, and they soon found themselves on the wider, cobbled streets between the grander houses and better endowed churches in the environs that Ela knew as London.

Ela wanted to cry with relief at the sight of her mother's black-and-white gables. "Hold the horses and stay here," Ela said as she dismounted. "I'll fetch something for you."

The door opened before she could even knock, and a shout from the doorman brought her mother—screaming—into the hallway.

"Ela, my darling! May God be praised." She rushed to her and clutched her to her breast. "We haven't slept a wink all night."

"Bill is—" she didn't know how to say it. Couldn't bring the horrible words to her lips.

"Upstairs in bed—against his own wishes. No sooner were his wounds bandaged than he wanted to head out onto the streets searching for you."

"He's alive?" She could hardly believe it.

"Only just. He lost a lot of blood. The doctor said we're lucky help came at once." She glanced at the lad behind Ela. "Do come in!"

"I need coin and a morsel of food and drink for this lad, who gallantly brought me to your door although he's never been in London before."

"May God bless you, young man!" Her mother soon had him relieved of both horses and ushered into the kitchens for refreshments.

Ela's mother led her inside, exclaimed over her filthy garments and sent Hilda—whose eyes were red with weeping—to fetch a clean gown for her.

Alianore led Ela into the parlor and pressed a cup of watered wine into her hand. Ela took a sip and realized her hand was shaking.

"Where were you? Bill said you were abducted before his eyes! Who took you?" A barrage of questions flew from Alianore's mouth.

Ela blinked, struggling to believe that all these events had happened in just one night. "I have no idea."

"They stole your rings…" Alianore snatched at her hand. "And my gold belt!" She stared at Ela in horror.

"It's a long story."

CHAPTER 8

"We must tell the sheriff that you're home," exclaimed Alianore after Ela had swallowed a reviving cup of wine. "Bill raised the hue and cry before nearly dying."

"The assailants left him there in the street?"

"Yes, and both attendants are badly injured, too. Young Rufus is hovering between life and death due to loss of blood. Stabbed in the gut."

Ela crossed herself. "May God protect them. We must offer up a Mass for them at once."

"Yes, of course, but first we must get you changed."

Hilda helped Ela out of her soiled gown and into a clean one of soft blue wool. Alianore sent her away to bring a bowl of water, and when she returned Hilda still looked on the brink of tears. "Hilda, what ails you?"

"I thought you were dead, my lady. Like Drogo." A sob like a hiccup shook her chest.

Ela rose and held the girl close. "God has spared me for another day. I don't have time to die. I must look out for you and your baby as well as my children." She smoothed away the girl's tears with her thumb. She realized with chagrin that she was starting to feel tenderly toward Hilda as if she were her own wayward daughter. "I can hardly enjoy the sweet rest of Heaven with those responsibilities weighing on me."

"Hilda, do fetch your mistress a bowl of oat porridge with cream and honey," said Alianore sharply. Hilda scurried away. Alianore leaned in. "You're far too soft with the girl. You should beat the tears out of her."

"If anyone beats Hilda after what she's already been through she'd simply break. If my plan comes to fruition Hilda will be mistress of her own estate and raise her child in comfort."

"And you'll be sheriff of Salisbury," scoffed her mother as if it were the most preposterous thing in the world.

"Exactly." Ela jutted her chin for a moment. "But let's stay focused on the present task. When the sheriff is told I'm alive, be sure that he's summoned here immediately."

ELA COULDN'T EAT a bite until she'd visited Bill. She climbed the stairs to the bedroom with growing apprehension, half afraid he'd have suddenly died of his wounds. Her fears worsened when she opened the door to see him lying on the bed, pale as bone, with his eyes closed and his head sunk deep into the pillow.

"Bill!" She rushed forward and took his hand, relieved to find it warm. She squeezed it gently. "I thought you were killed."

His eyelids flickered for a moment before opening a crack. "Ela...God be praised. I'd never forgive myself if anything happened to you. Who took you?"

"I'm not sure. Someone who wanted to scare me. And

clearly someone who wouldn't mind having murder on his hands."

"You should go back to Gomeldon immediately," he rasped.

"Like a coward running from battle?" The idea repulsed her. "That's exactly what these evil-hearted men want. They want me to run home like a scared little mouse and allow them to go about their devilish business undisturbed."

Bill looked like he wanted to protest, but the effort proved too much for him and he winced in pain as a cough rattled his chest.

"Have a care!" Ela put her hand on his shoulder. "You have a wound, and if it doesn't heal cleanly it may fester. Who closed it for you?"

"The same doctor who attends the king. Your mother has friends in high places."

"And thank God for them. But now you must rest so you can protect me next time I need you. I promise you I won't do anything rash. And at least I should have the sheriff's ear now."

To his credit the sheriff arrived promptly, with a loud clattering of his entourage in the street outside. Alianore ushered him into a special back parlor she kept for private games and other covert occasions. Then she closed the door so just the three of them sat at a small table inlaid with mother-of-pearl.

Sheriff Roger le Duc was a tall man, nearly bald, his remaining dark hair shaved close, but with a thick dark beard that showed little silver. His tunic was dark brown, almost black, with silver trim—an unusual look that gave him a Continental appearance.

He bowed to Ela and murmured his relief at her safety.

"Sir William Talbot and I sought you all day yesterday," she admonished. "Even to Westminster. I had no intention of tangling with these criminals myself. I'm glad to have found you at last. I'm sure that the people who took me are involved in the secret trade in children that I'm investigating."

Le Duc blinked. "Children? What do you mean?"

Ela sighed. No one had found him and told him. "Children are being stolen from their homes and sold into some kind of slavery. My lawyer had his men look into the matter and they found a house near Westcheap—with no windows on the first floor—where at least some of these children are being kept. You must ride there at once before they can be moved."

His smooth forehead furrowed. "What does this have to do with your being abducted?"

"I came to London to search for a girl taken from her cottage in Salisbury, and it led me into the middle of this foul trade."

"And you were taken to this house on Westcheap?"

"No." Frustration rose in her. "At least I don't think so. They didn't take me far, so the house where they hid me was near here. And a very grand residence, even larger and more luxurious than this house. But the children are in danger. Please, attend to them first before we look for whomever took me prisoner."

Le Duc's mouth flattened out and turned down at the corners. "Your safety is a far greater concern to myself—and, naturally, to his majesty the king—than any other crimes that have been committed. We must find the men who took you."

"Indeed, but you must visit the house in Westcheap first." *Or I'll ride there myself*, she wanted to threaten. But she knew that would only irk him and possibly impede the investigation. She repeated the directions that Spicewell's men had given her. "Please, I beg you. I shan't breathe a word about my own ordeal until you've at least tried to rescue the children."

"I beg you also," said Alianore. "Or my daughter will take it upon herself. Her thirst for justice rivals that of her late husband."

Ela felt a burst of pride and wanted to hug her mother. But she kept her hands in her lap. She had an inkling that her mother secretly wanted her to be sheriff.

Le Duc looked highly skeptical but agreed to ride at once to the house and search it. He also promised to report back. Ela watched him leave, his entourage a flurry of gold brocade and fur trim on their fine destriers.

As they rode away her heart quietly sank. "He's not going to go there."

"Of course he is, my dear. He said he would." Alianore bustled about, fussing over the dirt his men had tracked into her front hall and parlor. "Why wouldn't he?"

"I'm not sure." Ela bit her lip. "I wish I did know. But I watched his face harden while I spoke to him. He doesn't want to rescue the children. He doesn't even want to know about them."

"But why?" Alianore only half listened as she pointed out some crumbs to a maid.

"I suspect that the trade in children is run by—or for—very powerful men. Men whose interests must be protected at all costs. Even at the cost of a tender child's innocent life." Ela frowned. "Even at the cost of my life."

"What nonsense!" Alianore stopped and stared. "You are a countess of the realm! Your children are cousins to the king."

"And yet these men dared to seize me in the street, take me prisoner, then dump me out of a wagon deep in the countryside."

Alianore's mouth fell open. She realized she hadn't told her mother—or the sheriff—that part. "You must return to Salisbury at once."

"I want to return to my quiet home and my own children more than anything, but how can I face poor Alys Wheaton and tell her that her little girl is lost forever?"

"The sheriff may find her this afternoon," said her mother brightly, plucking at a piece of fluff on her gown.

"If he does, then I'll take her back to Salisbury with me, praising God all the way."

Her mother looked up, disturbing her white veil. "And if he doesn't?"

ELA SHOULD HAVE BEEN EXHAUSTED by a night utterly without sleep, but instead she couldn't sit still. A feverish energy coursed through her, fueled by her anxiety about Bill's wounds, as well as the fate of Edyth and the other children.

She paced her bedroom, peering out the window at the rain-wet streets below, wishing she could ride after Sheriff le Duc. Hilda had spent a sleepless night fretting over her absence and was now fast asleep in the wooden chair by Ela's empty fireplace. Ela pondered whether to wake her up but decided against it. The girl was pregnant and needed her rest.

She slipped out of the room and tiptoed back into Bill's room. She vowed that if he was asleep, she'd leave him be, but his eyelids cracked open as she entered the room.

"Where did they take you?" he rasped.

Ela moved a chair up to his bedside and sat in it. "I will only tell you if you promise not to become agitated."

He regarded her through slitted eyes. "I'll try my hardest."

"That's not good enough. Your health comes before all else."

"I vow, as a knight of the realm, to keep calm no matter what you tell me. You are safe and well, and that is what matters."

Ela looked at him skeptically. "I shall take you at your word. A man snatched me and put a hood over my head, so I couldn't see where they took me, but it can't have been far from here. It's likely a house we walk past on our way to Westminster or even going to Vespers."

"A grand house, like this?"

"More so. Lavish, filled with unusual and rich objects from foreign countries." Ela frowned. Who would own such a house? "A house fit for a prince or…"

"A bishop?" Bill said the word she'd been afraid to utter.

Ela did not like to cast aspersions against God's representatives on earth. It might be different if she knew the person well—she'd had her ups and downs with Bishop Richard Poore in Salisbury—but to think evil about members of the clergy rubbed against every bone in her body.

"It is certainly the house of a wealthy person. Possibly a merchant. I'd imagine some of them are as rich as princes in these materialistic times." She shifted, uncomfortable on the hard chair. "Or a bishop."

Bill's eyes opened a little wider. "What did they do to you?"

"They shut me up in a room with a small boy to watch me. I tried to quiz him about the place and its owner, but he never said a word. They may have chosen a child who didn't speak English. He was from Africa. Possibly brought here as part of the same cruel trade in children."

She rose, too agitated to sit still, and walked across the room. "They gave me food, but I wasn't fool enough to take a bite." She glanced back at him. "You've trained me well."

A pained attempt at a smile hitched his mouth. "Praise be."

"Then a man wearing a strange mask came to fetch me. I've heard they have haunting, fanciful masks in Venice, but I haven't seen them so I don't know if it's one of those or not. It had a beak like a bird. He wore a cloak that covered his hair and body. I couldn't see him at all, though he was tall."

"Did he speak?"

"Yes." She frowned again. "And his voice sounded familiar, but I can't place it at all."

"Did he have an accent?"

"He spoke in English but he didn't have a distinctive accent." She paced across the room. "I've been racking my mind, trying to think of where I might have heard his voice before."

"Was he one of the men at Spicewell's chambers?"

The thought stilled her feet. "No. They had London accents and he didn't."

"Someone from Salisbury?"

Ela turned and walked back. "No. No one that I know well."

"Did they ever catch that strange man who seemed to be behind the murders related to the opium trade?"

"Vicus Morhees?" Ela would never forget that strange name. Not as long as he walked alive and free. She considered him at least partially responsible for the death of Hilda's lover on her own estate. Although he hadn't dealt the fatal blow—the man who did had been tried and hung for it—he had encouraged the killer to further his own nefarious ends. She realized she'd stopped walking...and breathing.

"He'd have motivation to want you to retire to Salisbury and never leave it again."

Ela blinked, trying to recall the nuances of the masked

man's voice. "He would indeed." She'd written letters to several sheriffs calling for his arrest.

Ela hurried to Bill's side and sank back into the chair. "I can't be sure. Too much has happened since I last heard his voice. And the masked man specifically warned me against looking into the children's disappearance. What would Vicus Morhees have to do with that?"

Bill's face turned pale as an attempted cough racked his body.

"Oh, you poor thing. Where did they wound you?"

"They cut me beneath my ribs but missed any vital organs."

Ela crossed herself. "May the Lord heal you with all speed. Do your best not to move at all so the flesh can knit back together."

Bill's face showed his pain no matter how he tried to hide it. She resolved to go seek some herbs to soothe him and leave him in peace for now.

ELA RETURNED with some myrrh that she'd bought at great expense, due to the distance it had to travel from the Holy Land. She'd heard it had powerful healing properties that could keep a wound from festering. You'd never be able to get your hands on myrrh in a hurry in Salisbury, so being in London had its advantages. She also bought some willow bark to make a tea for Bill to drink to ease his pain.

He was just teasing her that a nugget of opium might provide better relief when she heard the commotion of horsemen outside.

Sheriff le Duc strode back through Alianore's doorway, flanked by his deputies. Ela hurried down the stairs, peering behind them for signs of the children, but saw nothing but more men on horseback.

"Did you search the house?" she said, before even attempting a polite greeting.

Alianore rushed in front of her and filled in the required pleasantries, welcoming the sheriff back into the house. Ela's heart sank as he wasted time in introducing his deputies and accepting a cup of wine.

At last he turned to Ela. "To answer your question, my lady. We found the house. A three-story structure in the alley behind the Hog and Hound, old and in poor repair, with a stone lower story with no windows."

"You entered?" Her heart quickened.

"We knocked and no one answered." He took a sip of wine.

Ela leaned forward in her chair. "So you left?" She didn't attempt to hide her incredulity.

He looked at his deputies as if this suggestion were hilarious. "We broke down the door and went inside." He paused to accept a fig pastry from a plate carried by Hilda.

Ela managed to stop herself screeching at him to carry on.

He took a bite, chewed it, swallowed, then took another gulp of wine.

He's playing with me. She resolved not to be drawn into his snare, even though a child's life was at stake. Getting angry with le Duc wouldn't help.

He put his wine cup down. "My men entered the building and searched every room, and there wasn't a soul to be found."

"Did you see evidence that children had been there?"

"Not a whit. The place wasn't clean, but all furniture and objects had been removed."

"Were there signs of recent occupancy?"

"Yes, most certainly. There were many footprints in the floor dust and fresh scuffs on the doors as if furniture or boxes had been carried through them recently."

"They took the children and left," exclaimed Ela. "Where could they have taken them?"

Le Duc enjoyed another long swig of his wine. "We saw no evidence that children were present."

"No small footprints?" Ela was more inclined to believe Spicewell's paid henchmen than this slick sheriff.

He shrugged, which caused the silver trim on his tunic to shimmer. "Impossible to say. There was too much traffic to see individual prints."

She fought the urge to howl with frustration. "They must have been warned. They knew you were coming."

"How would they know?"

"How did they know I was looking for them?" asked Ela aloud, as much to herself as to the others. Spicewell's men knew. Could they be trusted? She knew that if she told the sheriff about them, he'd focus on chasing after them and not finding the children, and how would that help little Edyth?

"Now we must address the matter of the men who abducted you, if you don't object?" His warm smile irked her.

"Yes. I suppose we must." Ela seated herself in a chair. "I wish I could give you more solid information, but the only thing I know is that I was taken to a house not far from here. Not more than two or three streets away."

Le Duc's eyes widened in surprise, and he looked at Alianore. "Did you know you have brigands for neighbors?"

"I most certainly did not," said Alianore, crossing herself. "This is supposedly the finest part of London."

"And the White Tower." Le Duc let out a loud laugh, and

his two men joined him. "Would you be able to identify the house?"

"From the inside, absolutely. I saw a hallway with a pattern of black and white tiles and wood paneling on the floor—very fine—and a great room with frescoes on the walls and fine objects. It was not a normal household but a very grand house. A palace, even."

Alianore's eyes grew wide.

"Mama, do you know a house that fits this description?" Ela's pulse quickened.

"Well, no, not exactly." She looked like she wanted to say more but didn't. Ela wanted to prod her for more information, but the look on her mother's face warned her to stay silent. "And you must tell the sheriff about the theft of the gold belt and the rings."

CHAPTER 9

*E*la frowned. She'd begged her mother not to mention them earlier. First of all, they were stolen by entirely different people. Second, attempting to retrieve them would be a distraction the sheriff might gladly pursue instead of the more complicated matter.

"You were robbed?" asked le Duc.

"By someone unconnected to my abduction. A sneak thief, after I sought help in an inn on the London road. I never felt anyone take it so there's no one to accuse."

"And the rings?" asked Alianore.

"Those I traded to lease a horse to ride here. I gave them willingly."

Alianore clucked her tongue. "You could have bought the inn with their true value. Is that lad who arrived with you from the same inn?"

"Yes. He guided me home. I told him to head back to the inn with the horses." She'd made sure he wasn't here to take the blame for the thefts. "He bears no guilt. He wasn't even present when the theft happened or when I bartered for the horses. I was in a difficult position—a woman alone in the night—and value is dependent on circumstance, as you know."

Alianore and le Duc murmured agreement and praised God—again—for her safe deliverance. "But that belt is worth a small fortune," protested Alianore. "What's the name of the inn?"

"The boy said it's called the Eight Feathers." She'd asked him before sending him away with a silver coin for himself. "He'd have no reason to lie. I admit I don't know which road it sits on. It's not one I've taken before. But can we leave that for another time? It's the least urgent matter. At least those people didn't threaten my life or anyone else's." She turned to le Duc. "How can we determine whose house I was kept in?" Then back to her mother. "Does the black-and-white floor sound familiar?"

"Many houses have such a floor," said Alianore, fiddling with her cuff. "They bring colored marble from Italy to make the patterns."

Ela turned to the sheriff. "Can we search some of the larger houses in this part of town?"

Le Duc stared at her for a moment, then laughed. "How would your lady mother feel if we were to knock on her door wanting to explore her house to see if it looked like one where a crime had been committed?"

"I'm sure she would do her best to help you in your work," said Ela quickly, before her mother could join him in laughing.

"I don't think that the wealthy nobles and burghers of this district will appreciate their houses being rummaged by my men any more than your mother would want me rifling through her linen chest."

"True!" exclaimed Alianore. "But that could be because half of them are up to no good anyway."

Ela thought of how they'd discovered a profitable trade in

opium disguised as a trade in cheap trinkets. She could only imagine what they might find in the house of a wealthy merchant who had ships coming and going from ports across the Continent.

"I doubt I'd be sheriff for long if I got a reputation for harassing the city's wealthiest and most important residents," said le Duc. "One must always be practical, unfortunately. Unless we have a solid reason to suspect a particular house, we can't insist upon entry."

"While I was shut in there, I could swear that I heard singing somewhere in the distance." Ela struggled to remember the details.

"A woman or a man?" asked Alianore.

"A choir," said Ela frowning. "At least that's what it sounded like. High voices, so it could only be women or boys. It was a beautiful sound, now that I reflect back from a place of safety."

"The kind of choir you'd hear in a church?" asked le Duc.

"Yes, or a monastery," said Ela.

"Perhaps the house was next to a church?" suggested Alianore.

"The weather is warm, and people have their windows open," offered le Duc. "Sound can carry some distance."

"True." Ela sighed. "And there's a church on almost every street in London, it seems."

"God be praised," said Alianore.

"Indeed, but that makes it hard to know where I was. But more importantly, where can the children have been moved to?"

Le Duc frowned down at the table. "Once again we find ourselves in a situation where every building in the city looks suspicious, but we can hardly break down the doors of each one."

"So what will you do?" asked Ela.

Le Duc cleared his throat. "My men will keep watch on the house near Westcheap, and in the meantime we can send a posse to the Eight Feathers in search of your stolen belt."

ELA TENDED to Bill for most of the afternoon, with Hilda's help. He was very weak and needed complete rest, which wasn't easy for a man of action. She made him promise to stay in bed while she went to Compline with four of the sheriff's men who'd remained to keep her safe.

Alianore, sitting at her embroidery, protested loudly. "You narrowly escaped death yesterday, and now you're heading out into the streets again?"

"I won't let the actions of evil men keep me from praising God, Mother."

"God has better things to do than watch over you every minute, my dear."

"That may be, but I can hardly pace back and forth across the parlor, waiting for something to happen. At least prayer might provide wisdom about what to do next."

Her mother, fingering a pearl rosary she kept in her sleeve, looked doubtful. "Don't let yourself get abducted again."

"I'll do my best." Ela hesitated. "Now that the sheriff's gone, you did recognize the black-and-white floor, didn't you?"

Alianore looked up from her rosary. "As I said, they're not all that rare."

"Where have you seen one in London?"

Her mother shrugged, looking awkward. "Nowhere that could have been the place you were taken."

"Mother—" Ela stared at her. "Where?"

"Abbot Abelard de Rouen's house has a black and white tile floor. I saw it when I was given a tour of his art collection by my friend Ethelburga le Hinton, who's patron of his order. But you can't possibly have been taken there."

"I'm not naive enough to think all men of God are Christlike. Sometimes their greed for money—or power—makes them depart from their true calling."

"That is sadly true, but Abbot Abelard de Rouen is one of the most powerful men in London and is known for being deeply pious. He's a close associate of King Henry and his court."

"Where does he live?"

"I forget." Alianore stabbed her needle through the fabric she was embroidering. "And it can't be him. It's impossible to imagine that he has untoward activities happening under his roof."

"Unless he's unaware of them," suggested Ela.

Her mother's look made it clear that she thought this impossible.

Ela resisted the urge to growl with frustration. "I'd better leave, or I'll be late for Compline."

ELA WENT out to mount her horse. The sheriff's men, there to protect her, were already mounted. It was a short walk, but it had already been decided that being mounted was safer. Not that it had helped her last night.

The ride to the church was uneventful. Inside, Ela tried to focus on the words but found herself praying fervently. She prayed for Bill's full recovery and also for the two wounded guards. She'd heard they were out of danger, but you never knew when a wound would rot and poison the blood.

She also beseeched God for his help and mercy in her efforts to find Edyth safe and well. It was hard not to lose a little more hope with each passing hour. She dreaded the awful possibility of returning to Salisbury without the child, and having to break the news of her failure to Edyth's desperate parents. She felt bad that she hadn't written to them, but short of word that Edyth had been found alive, what tidings could she send that would comfort them?

After the service, Ela couldn't bring herself to hurry home to her mother's house. She'd been taken right here in front of St. Michael and All Angels, and the house she'd been taken to was in the same district. She told the men she wanted to exercise her horse by riding through the local streets.

With two men flanking her in front, and two behind, she set out along the road, peering curiously at the buildings around her. Twilight glowed bright enough to see the buildings clearly, and with candles and rushlights being lit inside, she could catch a glimpse through some of the windows as well. The large houses in this district had glass windows designed to show off their owners' wealth and stature.

Ela rode along, making a mental note of houses she'd walked past a hundred times but never really noticed before. One grand three-story house held her gaze. The ground floor was built of cut stone, like a castle or fortified manor, and the upper story had at least six gables, each finely decorated with an elaborate pattern of wood beams.

She wanted to stop and stare at the house, but that would cause too much commotion among the sheriff's men, so she rode past, planning to return and examine it more closely.

She strained her ears, listening for the sound of singing—and heard it. But that was hardly surprising. There were indeed churches all around them and once she paid attention she could hear bells and snatches of music in every direction she turned her head, even over the clatter of hooves and the grind of cartwheels hurrying home in the last few moments of daylight.

Several times the sight of a man in a long dark cloak made her heart trip, but each time the person turned out to be a Dominican or Franciscan brother, or a merchant in fur-trimmed finery or someone other than the tall masked man.

The sheriff's men rode along close beside her, eyes scanning in all directions, and the one flanking her to the right seemed to jump a little any time there was an unexpected noise, to the point where his horse was becoming skittish.

"What are you so worried about?" asked Ela. She realized she should turn down the next street and head back to Alianore's house before it got fully dark.

"Protecting you, my lady." The man was painfully young, with oily hair and a pimply chin. "The sheriff says he'll have our jobs if anything happens to you."

She could almost feel the older man to her left glowering at him for revealing this to her.

"I feel quite safe in your midst, and I appreciate the trouble you're taking to protect me." She'd had difficulties with the guards at Gomeldon and had to beg Sheriff de Hal for new ones from the castle garrison.

While Bill Talbot was a brave and skilled knight, and as loyal as her own heart, he was well past fifty years old now and not as fast or strong as a brigand of three and twenty. Not that she'd ever suggest that to him. It would break his heart to think that she didn't trust him to protect her.

Ela rode back to Alianore's house, frustrated to have made no progress in locating the man who stole her. In the morning she'd visit Spicewell and see if his spies could provide some further intelligence.

$\approx$

BACK IN ALIANORE'S house Ela begged fatigue and headed to her bedchamber early. She didn't want to listen to her mother scold her for foolhardy bravery or question her plans and motives while refusing to reveal Abbot de Rouen's address.

Hilda brought her water to wash and combed out her hair and scented her wrists and temples with soothing lavender oil.

"Do you feel safe with the guards outside?" asked Hilda softly. Ela had often scolded Hilda for speaking out of turn, but this question obviously came from a place of genuine fear.

"I see no reason not to trust the sheriff's men," she replied. "They're trained and seem attentive. Though I understand your anxiety."

Hilda had been abducted from her own bed at Gomeldon because she'd had the misfortune to witness her lover's murder. Luckily they'd intercepted her captor and saved her in time, but the incident had left echoes in her memory, piled on top of the horror of seeing the father of her unborn child murdered in front of her.

"I have bad dreams," Hilda admitted. She was braiding Ela's hair into two long plaits, and she stopped half-way down the second one. "They wake me in the dark, and sometimes it's all I can do to stop myself screaming." Hilda's hand, still holding her hair, started to shake.

Ela turned and took hold of Hilda's trembling fingers. "You've suffered horrors that would wake a world-weary soldier in the night."

"How can I make these cruel visions stop? The girls I sleep with were sympathetic at first, but they tire of me waking them in terror."

Ela's heart clenched. "I wish I could offer solid advice, but the best suggestion I have is that you pray as hard as you can. Pray at bedtime, pray on awakening. Pray in the middle of the night when you wake in terror."

Hilda's lip trembled. Her beautiful eyes shone with unshed tears. "I think God has forsaken me. Why would he leave me pregnant with a dead man's child?"

Ela blinked. For all the terrible things that had happened to her—including the suspicious death of her husband—nothing had shaken her faith and it was a constant comfort to her. She couldn't imagine suddenly being deprived of it. Poor Hilda must feel like the sole survivor of a shipwreck without a spar to cling to.

"God would never forsake you. Even though you can't see or hear him, he's with you all the time."

"Was he with Drogo when the knife pierced his throat?" Hilda's eyes were wide. Ela detected a hint of anger in her voice.

Her own children had never asked her such probing questions. She didn't want to brush Hilda off with platitudes when the girl was in such obvious distress. "The Lord called Drogo to his side."

"Like he called your husband?" Hilda's face looked innocent, but her question stabbed Ela right in the heart.

"Yes," she said, when she found her voice. "Much as it pains me, he chose to have my husband at his side in Heaven."

"What if Drogo isn't in Heaven?" Tears filled Hilda's eyes. "Everyone says he wasn't a good man. He was caught poaching. He took advantage of a...a..."

Of an innocent young maid.

Ela took Hilda in her arms and held her close. Hilda shook with sobs, and Ela's own emotions surged through her along with Hilda's. The cruelty of the situation was hard to fathom.

Could she safely assure Hilda that Drogo—that witty rogue who had charmed her almost as much as he'd seduced poor Hilda—had ascended to Heaven? Her own husband had prayed fervently and confessed in terror during his final days, fearing an eternity in the flames of hell. Her beloved William had died shriven and soothed of his fears, but Drogo never had the chance to make his final confession or receive absolution.

If you were to ask a bishop he might well be forced to admit that Drogo was in a very hot place.

"We must pray for his soul." Ela heard her own voice tremble slightly. She was sure her words were cold comfort to Hilda. "And in the meantime we must do everything possible to keep you and your baby safe and healthy."

Hilda seemed to calm a little, and they slowly pulled apart. Ela dried Hilda's tears with her thumb. Hilda's breathing had steadied, and her hands were no longer palsied by emotion.

Hilda looked right into her face, bright eyes clear. "What if my baby is cursed?"

"Your baby isn't cursed."

"Lizzie said she would be. She said it's the sins of the fathers."

Ela racked her brain for who Lizzie was. Probably one of her mother's gossipy kitchenmaids.

"All babies are born carrying the weight of the sins of their fathers. That's why they're baptized as soon as possible after birth. The water of the baptismal font serves to cleanse them of original sin." Ela wasn't entirely sure how a voiceless babe could carry the burden of every sin since Adam and Eve were cast from the garden of Eden, but at least the Lord had given them a means to lift the curse.

"Will my baby be baptized?"

"Of course!"

"What if the priest refuses because I'm not married?"

"He won't. They're entrusted with saving souls." And Ela made a mental note to apply a judicious application of silver to ensure that the priest wouldn't scowl at Hilda during the ceremony, either. "Are you going to finish my braid?" She said it kindly, but she wanted to pull Hilda out of her emotions and back into practical activities.

"I'm sorry, my lady." Hilda scrubbed at her eyes with her sleeve and picked up the half-undone braid. She pulled it tight again and wove the braid a few more turns. "How will I tend to you when I have a baby at my breast, my lady? And where will my baby live? I can hardly keep her under your roof. She might cry and upset everyone—" Her hands started to tremble again.

Ela took the braid from her hand. "Here, let me finish it. I can actually braid my own hair, oddly enough." She wound it quickly to the end and tied it with the small strip of ribbon Hilda had put aside.

"Why do ladies not braid their own hair?"

"How else would girls like you support yourself if we all braided our own hair?" She hoped her attempt at humor would help dispel the cloud of gloom hovering over Hilda. "Just imagine if I folded my own clothes and lit my own tapers. What would you do?"

"I'd starve in the streets, since my parents will never take me back home."

"Hilda, you're not going to starve in the streets!" She wanted to shake the girl.

"No one will want to marry me since I'm not a maid and I already come with a mouth to feed. One day you won't need me as a lady's maid anymore, and no one else will want to hire me. I talk too much, for one thing—"

"That is true," said Ela with a smile. "And I'm not sure I appreciate you looking ahead to the day I drop dead, but—"

She hesitated a moment, knowing she'd probably regret letting this cat out of the bag but somehow unable to stop herself. Nothing else seemed to give Hilda any hope for the future. "I've hired a lawyer to pursue ownership of the manor at Fernlees for your unborn child."

CHAPTER 10

*H*ilda's hand flew to her belly. She was barely showing, only a teeny bump swelling beneath her gray gown. "The manor that Drogo was hoping to get back?"

"Yes." Hilda had never seen Fernlees—although Drogo must have mentioned it to her while seducing her in the hayloft—and Ela had never given her a reason to hope for it before. She probably shouldn't even now. But with the long-term tenant and claimant missing and presumed dead, the situation looked promising. "It's a small manor and not in the best repair, but it has good grazing and if managed well it could provide an income from wool and sustain the needs of a family. There's a stocked fishpond and a mature orchard. There's also a small wood to provide timber and fuel and to run pigs."

Hilda stared at her, lips parted, hand still resting on her belly. "And you say it belongs to my baby?"

"As the heir to the rightful owner. Presuming that Drogo is indeed the rightful owner, which thus far appears to be the case."

Hilda's whole face brightened with a glow of incredulity. "So my baby and I would live there."

"Indeed you would. And"—again Ela doubted her own good sense—"the manor should provide enough income for you to have your own lady's maid as well as other servants."

"I'd be a lady of the manor." Hilda blinked, then looked down at her belly. "And my baby would be a lord!"

"Well, he wouldn't be a noble." Ela wanted to laugh. "But he'd be a landowner and you could raise him as a gentleman. When he grows up he could train as a knight, or even study the law or medicine at Oxford or Cambridge." Ela knew her mouth was running away with her, but she'd let her thoughts gallop off in these happy directions more than once while enduring a sleepless night in her bed.

Hilda stared at her in silence for a moment, then her expression clouded. "I don't believe you, my lady. How is such a thing possible?"

"Well, I'm sure I've been imprudent in giving you so much to hope for, but the fact remains that Drogo grew up at Fernlees while his father was the owner, and there's every chance the manor will return to his bloodline by law."

Hilda staggered to a chair and sat down. "Begging your pardon, my lady, but I feel a bit faint."

"As well you might. But you look more cheerful now."

"I feel as if I've banged my head and I'm seeing stars."

"But you can see that you don't need to worry about starving in the street."

"My parents might forgive me if I'm a lady of the manor dressed in silk and furs."

Ela still wanted to laugh, but she could see the poor girl was quite sincere. "It shouldn't be this way, but wealth and property do have a way of opening people's hearts. I do hope you won't waste your prosperity on extravagant clothing and fripperies. Modesty in dress and behavior becomes a fine lady as much as it becomes a lady's maid."

"I shall strive to be as much like you as I can, my lady." Hilda's eyes shone.

Now Ela did laugh. "I do hope you won't imitate my many failings but strive to put piety and duty before all else."

"What failings?" Hilda looked curious. The poor girl was woefully impertinent. But Ela couldn't help but admire her spirit to keep asking probing questions of a countess who most girls in her position would be afraid to talk to.

"I have the same failings you chastise yourself for and have had them since I was a girl. My mind is full of questions, and my voice has a way of persisting in asking them even when my sense of propriety begs me to remain quiet."

"Which is why we're here in London doing the sheriff's business when some people think you should be home in Salisbury tending to your home and children there."

"Indeed." Ela was curious. "Did you hear someone say that?"

Hilda shrugged, looking guilty. "Servants do gossip."

"They're right, of course. Most people would think I should leave the pursuit of justice to the men charged with seeking it. But when they neglect their duty I can't find it within myself to simply ignore their failings and let injustice rule the day."

"I admire you for that, my lady. I shall be just like you when I'm a lady of the manor."

"You have a lot to learn between now and then, Hilda, and I advise you to question your motives at every turn and ask yourself whether what you're doing serves you or the greater world."

Hilda's whole demeanor had changed. Perhaps she was just stunned. At least she no longer shook and wept. Ela hoped she hadn't been premature in her announcement, but

Hilda needed something to help her climb out from the pit of horrors she'd been wallowing in lately.

Still, it wouldn't do to announce the legal verdict before it was official. "Will you promise to keep this news between us until my lawyer tells me the manor is secured?"

"Yes, my lady." Hilda stared at her, clearly preoccupied with visions of herself as mistress of Fernlees. Her hand rested on her belly. "I won't tell anyone, but I shall sleep well knowing that my baby could have a brighter future than I ever dared to hope for."

"In the meantime, don't forget your duties." Ela glanced at her bed. Hilda's gaze followed hers, then she hurried across the room to turn back the covers and plump the pillows. "Thank you, Hilda. Sibel would be proud of you."

Hilda waited until Ela was in her bed, then she blew out the candle and left it on the table, before retiring from the room and closing the door. Ela settled back into her mattress with a sigh. She doubted Hilda would be able to keep such exciting news to herself.

On the other hand, no one would believe her.

ELA AWOKE TO A GREAT COMMOTION. Raised voices tugged her from sleep, followed by a woman's scream and a clattering of hooves. Still groggy, she jumped out of bed and flew to the door. She hurried along the hallway and down the stairs—people burst out of every room in the house though it was not yet dawn—and saw a group of people bent over something in the doorway.

"What's amiss?" she called.

"A child, my lady," called the housekeeper, who was still in her bedclothes. "She was wandering down the street and the guards stopped her."

Ela hurried down the stairs. A small girl, white faced and wide eyed, stood in the doorway in a plain brown shift. Ela crouched down so she could look into her eyes and took the girl's hands in hers—they were ice cold. "What's your name, little one?"

"Edyth," she whispered. "Edyth Wheaton."

"Praise be to God!" Ela hugged the girl to her chest. "I came to London to find you for your mama and papa. I know you were taken from your home in Salisbury." She wanted to reassure the girl that she wasn't just another fearsome stranger. "How did you find your way here?"

The girl stared at her. "The man brought me to the end of the street and told me to walk to this house."

"What man?"

"The bad man."

"What was his name?"

"I don't know."

Someone cleared their throat. "Begging your pardon, my lady, two of the guards have made chase."

"Good." Ela stroked the girl's tangled flaxen hair. "Come inside. You're safe here. I promise to take you back home to your parents at once."

Ela brought the girl up to her bedchamber, where they could both be away from the prying eyes of the household. She'd rushed downstairs in only her shift. She told Hilda to fetch water and asked the cook to send up food for the girl.

In her room she set the girl on her bed—she was small even for an eight-year-old—and rambled on about how happy her parents would be to see her again. Edyth rubbed her eyes sleepily and looked like she wanted to cry.

Hilda was sweet with her, washing her face and hands and gently combing her gossamer-fine hair. She even sang her a silly song that brought the ghost of a smile to the child's lips.

A cup of fresh milk and a piece of hot shortbread brought color to Edyth's cheeks.

"Stay here with her," Ela urged Hilda. "Don't let anyone in. I'll be right back."

Dressed in her gown, with the fillet and barbette pinned into place, Ela felt ready to address the guards. The two men who'd set out in pursuit of the "bad man" had not yet returned, but two more of the sheriff's men had arrived with news that the sheriff himself was on his way. The two men stationed at the door had seen the girl turn the corner—by herself. At first they hadn't thought anything of another urchin on the streets of London, but when she approached the steps, they'd guessed she was the missing girl and called for their horses—which were kept saddled and ready in the courtyard—to pursue her kidnapper.

Ela asked to be informed as soon as the sheriff arrived, or if they caught the man, then she hurried back up to Edyth and Hilda. Hilda sat on the bed next to Edyth, her arm around the girl's slim shoulders, murmuring something in her ear. Hilda jumped off the bed as Ela entered. "So sorry, my lady."

"Nothing to be sorry for, Hilda. Thank you for comforting Edyth." She approached the girl and crouched down on the floor in front of where Edyth sat on the bed. "The sheriff is on his way and it's important that you tell him everything you know about the men who took you and where they kept you, so he can catch them."

The girl's eyes grew huge. "I can't."

"Did they threaten you? They can't hurt you now. You're safe."

"Not me." She looked up at Ela. "He said he'd hurt the others."

"Other children?"

The color had already fled from the girl's cheeks again.

"I'm not to tell you anything at all or he'll…or he'll kill them." The last words were spoken in a shocked whisper and sounded horribly wrong in the mouth of a tender child. At the taste of them in her mouth the girl started to cry.

∼

THE SHERIFF ARRIVED NOT long after dawn with a phalanx of four men. He jumped down from his horse, dressed in a black cloak trimmed with silver fox fur. He bowed low to Ela. "God save you, my lady."

Ela blinked at the odd form of address. "God has indeed saved me, my lord sheriff. And we have been blessed with the return of little Edyth Wheaton."

"So I hear. And I have further good news." He reached inside his cloak, where he had a tooled black leather purse attached to his belt. He removed his glove and slid his fingers into the purse. They emerged with the rings she'd traded at the Eight Feathers…and the gold belt.

"God is great indeed, my lord sheriff." She held out her hands, and he deposited the treasures into them. "I certainly had not hoped to see these again. How did you—?"

Sheriff Roger le Duc bowed slightly. A sly smile snuck across his face. "Let's just say that the proprietors of the Eight Feathers did not wish to disturb the king's peace. When they learned that they had entertained a great countess unawares, and had taken advantage of her position as a lone woman in a strange place, they saw fit to mend the errors in their conduct."

So he'd shaken them down somehow. Impressive, if a bit alarming. She'd traded the rings in good faith, after all. Still, this was a gift horse and she felt no need to pry its mouth open and examine its teeth. "I'm truly grateful for the work of yourself and your men."

"It's our pleasure to serve the Countess of Salisbury." Another slight bow. "Now that you have the girl back and your jewels returned, I wish you a safe and speedy return to Salisbury."

"I've spoken to Edyth and she says there were other children being held captive along with her. The men who took her threatened to kill her if she said anything. I've not managed to get a word out of her about them."

"The poor moppet must be so frightened and exhausted. Better for her to return to her mother's loving arms than to trouble herself with reliving her ordeal." His expression spoke of sympathy, but his body language felt like a door quietly closing.

"But surely you want to catch the men responsible for stealing her. There's clearly a child slavery ring operating under your nose right here in London."

"And we shall find them and rout them forthwith. With much gratitude for all the help and information you've given us." His expression was pleasant.

Too pleasant.

He didn't mean what he said. He wanted her to leave—happy—and never mention the matter again. "Surely you want to speak to the girl before she returns to Salisbury?"

"What would be the point, if she refuses to say anything?"

The rings and chain cut into her palm, and she realized she was clutching them tight. "It pains me to think that there are other children suffering—right now—and that the men who took Edyth could strike again tomorrow and continue their evil trade."

"Unfortunately, there is no end to the evil that men do, my lady." The sheriff tossed his cloak back over his shoulders, revealing his silver-trimmed tunic. "We can but do our best to keep the tide of evil from engulfing us."

Ela frowned. This was an alarmingly defeatist attitude for

a man entrusted with keeping the peace and protecting the innocent. "I should stay in London until we discover who abducted me."

"You'd be far safer in Salisbury while we do the work of hunting the criminals."

"That is no doubt true, but my retinue is injured and I find myself without an adequate guard to travel. Bill Talbot is too gravely ill for the rigors of the journey, and I am loath to leave him."

"I'm sure he's well-tended here at your mother's house. And I shall provide you with a guard to ensure your safe journey home. Four of my finest men shall accompany you all the way to your door."

Ela blinked. "That would be kind." His desire to see her delivered immediately from London disturbed her, but she was itching to take Edyth home and this did provide the means. Bill would indeed be well cared for here, and she could return to her own children, at least for a time. "Are you sure you can spare them?"

"For you, my lady, it is a pleasure. Your bravery and fortitude in the face of evil is a tonic to us all."

A dangerous pride flared in Ela's chest. But something nagged at her. "Why did the girl suddenly appear on our doorstep?"

"No doubt the criminals sensed our hounds closing in and chose to let the little bird escape their snare."

"If they did this in the hope that you and I would abandon our efforts to find and catch them, I do hope they won't be satisfied."

"Indeed not, my lady. My men will not rest until the perpetrators are in custody." His self-satisfied expression irked her. She couldn't help but wonder if he hadn't come to some kind of mutually satisfactory arrangement with the child smugglers. But accusing him of such would achieve nothing.

"I'm glad to hear that. I look forward to seeing them tried for their crimes. I will gladly bring young Edyth back to London to testify against them."

"I'm sure it won't be necessary to frighten the child by having her meet her captors again. There will be other witnesses."

Ela could feel his impatience to be rid of her. Naturally it made her want to stay. But was that really the most sensible course? She knew it wasn't.

"I thank you for your work in retrieving my jewels. I truly had no hope of their recovery so it's a most pleasant surprise."

Le Duc bowed and pleasure shone in his eyes. "Delighted to be of service, my lady."

"Will you join us to break your fast?" She knew her mother would be scandalized if she didn't offer.

"I thank you for the kind offer, my lady, but duty calls. There were three murders committed last night that my men are already looking into." This was his sly way of explaining how the child-abduction ring would slide to the bottom of his list of things to investigate.

"God speed in finding the killers." She didn't want him to think he could entirely dismiss her from his thoughts. "Until we meet again."

"God willing, my lady." He took his leave with another bow and a volley of orders to his men. Four men on fine coursers remained to escort Ela, and Ela sent Hilda to inform Cook to provide them with sustenance for the journey.

IT DIDN'T TAKE LONG to pack for the return journey. Hilda

was in high spirits. She hurried about the household, sending messages to the cook and the stables and folding and packing Ela's belongings.

Alianore seemed relieved that Ela was headed home. She promised to remain in London to oversee the care of Bill and the other two injured men.

By midday they were on the road. Little Edyth sat in silence, easily startled by any noise or movement. Hilda sat next to her, at first quietly, just soothing her with occasional reassurances that she was on her way home. As the journey wore on, Hilda told Edyth stories and sang her songs. Ela felt a wonderful sense of happiness at the sight of the two young girls, both brought so close to death and destruction, now on the path to enjoying the rest of their lives in peace and safety.

Ela did not enjoy the restless night spent in rooms above a noisy inn—a necessity due to the length of the journey and the need to rest the horses—and they set out at dawn the next day. She didn't want to delay Edyth's return to her parents by one single moment.

As they grew closer to Salisbury, Edyth started to come out of her shell and smile and laugh more like a normal eight-year-old. She told them about her pet rabbit called Annie, who was white with black spots and liked to eat dandelions that Edyth picked on the roadside for her. Edyth also had a favorite rooster, George, who liked to dance in circles around her, strutting and fluffing his feathers. Hilda told her that soon George would be dancing with happiness to see her home again.

Instead of returning to Gomeldon and sending Edyth on, Ela headed straight to New Salisbury from the London road, so she could deliver Edyth to her family. Edyth and Hilda eagerly leaned out the window as they turned the corner onto the Fugglestone Road, where the small cottage would come into view above the hedgerows.

Except that it wasn't there.

The thatched roof didn't rise above the hedgerows where it should have. As they drew closer, Ela's breath stuck at the bottom of her lungs. The entire cottage and its fencing and outbuildings had all been burned to the ground.

CHAPTER 11

"Saints preserve us," murmured Ela, crossing herself as they drew up in front of the destroyed cottage.

"Mama!" Edyth's mournful wail pierced the air. "Mama!"

Hilda grabbed the girl and hugged her close, but Edyth fought and kicked. "Mama! Papa!"

Ela climbed down from the carriage, stunned and breathless at the horrible sight. The blackened remains of the house's wood frame no longer smoldered—all was damp with recent rain—but the acrid smell of scorched timber rose to sting her nostrils.

Nausea gripped her gut. There were no chickens or Edyth's pet rabbit. Everything they'd cajoled and soothed Edyth with on her journey home was gone.

And where were her mother and father? Had they perished in the fire? Ela's brain rang with questions. Was the fire deliberately set by cruel neighbors? Or was it an accident? Thatch could catch alight from lightning, especially at this dry time of year. Were Alys and John Wheaton home at the time, and if so, had they managed to escape?

It seemed too much to hope for.

Many footprints had ground the ashes and debris into mud. Coroner Giles Haughton must have been here in the aftermath. She'd ask him what happened.

Ela prayed fervently, eyes closed for a moment, that Edyth's parents had been spared. For the girl to survive her ordeal at the hands of evil strangers only to return to find her family gone seemed cruel beyond belief.

She turned back to the carriage. "To the castle, at once."

Her weary driver and horses and the sheriff's men were all no doubt desperate to rest after the long journey from London, but they didn't complain.

Edyth screamed and cried and pummeled poor Hilda, who tried to bundle her back into the carriage. Ela had no idea what to say to the girl. What assurance could she give that wouldn't turn out to be a lie? She'd promised her all day that she'd soon be safe home in her mother's arms, and now this.

DUSK DARKENED the landscape as they arrived at the castle, and they'd been on the road since dawn. Ela's entire body ached from sitting stiffly, braced against the roughness of the road. But energy surged through her, fueled by fear and dread and painful shards of hope.

Edyth had stopped screaming and now sat mute and pale, her face streaked with tears. Hilda's shoulders shook with sobs that she tried her best to suppress. She'd been through enough, and Ela had watched her put her heart into cheering and soothing Edyth only to see her devastated and bereft.

Castle servants helped Ela down from the carriage and greeted her so warmly that she felt bad telling them they'd come on urgent business. She hurried into the great hall, where the household was sitting down to their evening meal.

Sheriff de Hal rose from his seat, visibly annoyed to be disturbed at his dinner. He didn't move toward Ela but waited for her to approach. With a bare minimum of pleasantries, she announced that she'd brought Edyth back from London but found her house destroyed by fire.

"Ah, yes. It happened almost a week ago. The blaze raged fierce and all-consuming."

Ela glanced back to where Edyth stood silent, holding Hilda's hand.

"The girl's parents—" She spoke softly. "Did they perish?"

"They did not. They were at this castle at the time of the fire, causing a public disturbance."

Ela's knees almost buckled with relief. "Where are they now?"

"Far from here I hope. They've been driven from Wiltshire, and I hope never to see them again." His hard face had a sneer built into almost every expression.

"Why? What have they done?"

"Inflamed the people of Salisbury to near madness," he muttered. "They abandoned the religious life to live in sin. I've heard far too much about them, and I'll be glad to never lay eyes on them again." He glanced at the large platter of roasted pig with nut and apple stuffing that steamed aromatically on the table in front of him. "Your party is welcome to join us for dinner."

Ela had never heard a less welcoming invitation. She felt fairly sure that if he could have banished them all from Wiltshire, he'd have done it. "I thank you, but no, we must return to Gomeldon." Ela burned to know more and to speak with Giles Haughton, but since he didn't appear to be at the castle, that would have to wait until tomorrow.

She contemplated apologizing for the interruption but decided against it. "God go with you, my lord sheriff." The words tasted bitter in her mouth. Simon de Hal cared nothing for justice and only for the perks of the job. She prayed for the day when he'd pack his chests and leave this castle. She'd be glad to smack his horse on the rump on the way out.

Ela turned to her weary little party. "Your mother and father are alive, Edyth!" She tried to raise some enthusiasm as the girl looked ready to faint from sorrow and exhaustion. "Tonight we must return to Gomeldon, but tomorrow we shall set out to find them."

~

"Mama, we were so worried about you!" Ela's children swarmed the door of her manor house at Gomeldon as soon as the carriage pulled up.

"Why? I wrote to you every morning."

"But your first letter only just arrived," protested Richard. "And you didn't say when you'd be coming home."

"We've brought Edyth back with us, safe and sound," said Ela with all the mock cheer she could muster. "And tomorrow we'll find her parents. Tonight, please welcome her and include her in your games. Stephen, please ask Cook to prepare us a meal at once."

They ate and Petronella and Ellie tried to excite Edyth by introducing her to the dogs and letting her hold Ellie's favorite wool-stuffed dolly, but the girl would barely touch her food and drink and wouldn't talk at all.

Finally, Ela asked Hilda if she'd mind taking Edyth to bed with her. Hilda, clearly exhausted, gladly agreed and took the girl up to her room.

A kitchen maid called Mary was pressed into service to help Ela undress and ready herself for bed. Unlike Hilda, the girl was quiet to the point of sullenness—probably nervous—

and fumbled so with removing her barbette and fillet that Ela worried she'd stick her in the head with a pin.

When the girl finally finished, Ela fell gratefully on her knees at her prie-dieu and thanked God for the strength to say a full rosary before she climbed between her cool sheets.

IN THE MORNING Ela felt so sore and stiff from sitting cramped in the carriage for two whole days that she sorely wished she could summon Giles Haughton to the comfort of her parlor. But she wasn't sheriff and no one was dead, so she'd have to ride to him herself and pay a social call.

Edyth's eyes shone red with weeping, and Hilda looked like she hadn't slept a wink either. Not good in her condition. Ela prayed they'd find the girl's parents quickly and that they'd have somewhere safe to live. Preferably somewhere friendlier than Salisbury had been to them.

Then she scolded herself for being as unfeeling as Sheriff de Hal. Did she expect unpopular people to remove themselves from the county so as not to inconvenience her? It was hardly their fault that their neighbors had taken against them.

Then again maybe it was their fault. Why would anyone leave the peace and joy of the religious life for the tumult of the secular world? She'd heard of bishops and priests having children with local women and even raising their children with a degree of respectability. It wasn't even rare. Men were sadly vulnerable to the pleasures of the flesh. But she'd never personally known of a nun daring to leave the cloister.

No doubt Alys had been tempted down the same thorny path as Hilda—coaxed and cajoled into trading her innocence and purity for a man's brief, sweaty pleasure. Not that Ela hadn't enjoyed intimacy with her husband. Their embraces and caresses had sometimes stirred almost feverish desire. But she couldn't imagine abandoning propriety and decorum—throwing away her whole life—for a few moments of passing passion.

Ela found herself grumpy and disconsolate on her morning rounds, which wasn't like her at all. She chastised herself for ingratitude. *The Lord has delivered Edyth into your hands.* Better still, the girl did not seem to have been raped or otherwise physically mistreated, though admittedly Ela hadn't dared to quiz her about that. No doubt such abuse would reduce her value on the black market in babes that these foul villains operated, which might be the only reason she'd been spared thus far.

Ela tasked Hilda with distracting Edyth while she rode back to the castle mound to find Giles Haughton and find out what he knew about the fire and the Wheatons' whereabouts.

The sheriff's men had set off back to London after a night's rest, so Ela took two of her own guards with her. The drizzly and disconsolate morning matched her mood. She arrived in Salisbury damp and anxious and her horse, Freya —who'd apparently sat in the stable unridden while she was away—proved every bit as nervy and jumpy as Ela herself.

Ela had a guard dismount his horse and knock on the coroner's door, in case he was abroad at the castle—or the Bull and Bear—but his wife answered and called to him in a flurry of excitement.

Ela greeted Mistress Haughton and let the servant take her damp cloak to hang by the kitchen fire. She accepted a cup of wine and made small talk about the weather and how busy London was. Haughton's wife was a well-preserved woman a few years older than herself who clearly enjoyed company. She could hear the coroner moving about upstairs, probably getting dressed.

When he finally came down, his wife seemed in no rush to leave them and kept making conversation about trivial matters. Eventually Ela cleared her throat. "I brought Edyth Wheaton back to Salisbury last night and found her family burned out and driven away."

"The girl is safe?" He looked astonished.

"No thanks to the relevant authorities. Do excuse my bluntness, Mistress Haughton. It seems her captors released her in order to see me leave London as quickly as possible."

"We received news that you and Bill Talbot were set upon and that he was badly wounded. God be praised that you are unharmed."

"Indeed the praise lies with Him and not with the sheriff of London, who seemed little interested in the trade in children happening right beneath his nose. I think Sheriff le Duc was as happy to see me leave as the perpetrators, who are no doubt still going about their repulsive business." She could see she'd scandalized them with her frankness, but she was in no mood to prevaricate.

And there was now more urgent business. "Where are Edyth's parents? I promised her all day yesterday that she'd spend the night in their arms. To find their whole house destroyed was a blow that almost felled the poor girl."

"I suggested they seek alms in the priory at Wilton. Once it was determined that no one had died, the sheriff told me to waste no more time on the matter."

"What happened to their livestock?" Ela couldn't help thinking of Edyth's pet rabbit and rooster which she'd talked so fondly of.

"Probably stolen by the townsfolk in the commotion. There wasn't so much as a stray hen when I arrived."

Ela sighed. This lawlessness apparently proceeded unpunished under the sheriff's gaze. "Who put out the fire?"

"The rain, I'd imagine. I gather that none of the townspeople would lift a finger to help the Wheatons. I can hardly picture them carrying buckets from the stream for them."

"Do these people not understand the principles of Christian charity?" Ela resolved to speak to the bishop about the need for a sermon on the subject. "It's their duty to help the needy, whether they approve of them or not."

Giles Haughton lifted his hands in despair. His wife had bustled away out of sight. "Unfortunately, I have no idea who started the fire. The husband and wife were at the castle pleading for help in finding their daughter when it happened."

"Were there witnesses?"

"No doubt," he sighed. "The persons who started the fire. But they'd hardly admit to it."

"And de Hal seems happy that the Wheatons are driven from their home and no longer a tiresome bother to him."

"Indeed." Haughton glanced over his shoulder as if to reassure himself that his wife was out of earshot. Then he spoke low. "I've heard some disturbing rumors about Sheriff de Hal." He hesitated.

"What?" Ela leaned in, ears burning with curiosity. Haughton spoke so low she could barely hear him.

"There were apparently complaints lodged against him while he was sheriff at York. He became very unpopular with the local businessmen and eventually he was removed from the office."

"Removed from that office and installed here at Salisbury." After she'd made her wish to be sheriff plain as day to the king himself and everyone else within earshot. Ire burned in her gut. "Well, this is interesting news that bears some reflection and research. But in the meantime, I must find Edyth's parents. I shall send two men to the monastery in search of them."

"I'm afraid I don't know if they would have even been received there or turned out on the road again."

"Surely the monks have at least a shred of Christian charity in their hearts?" It was a rhetorical question, and Giles Haughton simply lifted his hands in reply.

"I'd imagine you'd be well within your rights to deposit Edyth at the castle and leave it up to the sheriff's men to find her parents," he suggested.

"From what I'm hearing I might as well deposit her in the king's forest and leave her to be raised by wolves."

"I won't argue one way or the other, but anyone can see that you've more than done your Christian duty by the girl."

"I'm not just a Christian, I'm a mother. If this were my child, stolen and separated from me, I'd hope that whoever found her would take on the responsibility of returning her to my arms."

"I heard a rumor that another child has disappeared." Haughton spoke with visible reluctance.

"What? When?"

"More than two weeks ago, it seems. Her disappearance wasn't reported at first."

"Before Edyth vanished?" Ela couldn't believe her ears. "And I was in London within reach of these evil—" Ela suddenly found herself so angry she could barely speak. "They abducted me and threatened me and left Bill Talbot and two of my men for dead. And they continue their evil business unchecked. Sometimes I feel like the devil himself walks the earth among us."

Mistress Haughton, who'd rejoined them, crossed herself and Ela and Giles Haughton followed suit.

"Who is this missing girl?"

"One of the Brice children." Haughton looked a little sheepish. "Do you remember them?"

"I'll never forget the case. And now the children have

neither mother nor father. I heard they went to live with an aunt."

"They live with their mother's sister. She and her husband have a farm quite far outside the town. The girl went into town with a basket of eggs to sell but didn't return home by dusk and hasn't been seen since."

"How long was she gone before they reported it?"

"At least a week. One of her siblings came to the castle to report her missing."

"Jesus wept." Ela sighed. "I was at the castle last night and the sheriff never breathed a word of this. She was probably snatched by the same child thieves."

Why wouldn't the sheriff—or anyone else there—have mentioned another missing girl?

Ela itched to leave. "I must ask Edyth about her. She wouldn't talk about her ordeal or her captors because she said they'd kill the other children there if she said anything. Hopefully distance will give her the courage to reveal what she knows."

She turned for the door, then stopped. "Do you have any suspicion about who started the fire that destroyed the Wheatons' cottage?"

Haughton looked at her for a moment, then glanced at his wife, then back at Ela. "No one saw it start."

Ela stared at him. That was quite a nonanswer. She suspected he wanted her to mull it over. She said her good-byes and hurried outside to mount her horse.

ELA WOULD HAVE PREFERRED to pursue the Wheatons herself —at a brisk trot—to put the weight of the earls of Salisbury behind any request for their safety, but she knew it would only make people talk. They had plenty to talk about already.

She repaired to Gomeldon and from there sent two men to the monastery with instructions to find the Wheatons and report to them that their daughter was alive and well. She also gave them a small purse of coins—which she counted in front of them—to offer to the monastery as a donation for their generosity in caring for the distressed family.

She wished Bill Talbot were here to entrust with this sensitive mission. Or even her son Will, who made up in honesty what he lacked in tact. But they were both elsewhere and she'd have to make do with hired men.

Edyth remained quiet and listless, despite the best efforts of the children and Hilda to engage her in their games or even their lessons. Eventually Ela told them to leave her be and tried to reassure the girl that she'd sent out men to find her parents.

She could hardly bring the parents back here and house them at her home, so she prayed that the monastery would shelter them until a new home could be found for them.

No one saw the fire start. The Wheatons were at the castle when it broke out, begging for help from the sheriff. Could the sheriff's men have started the fire to banish them from the town and be rid of the responsibility? Sheriff de Hal had little motivation to help them. The townspeople already shunned the family and there was no money in the search for a missing child.

Then there was the mystery of who'd stolen the girl. From her own experience of being abducted and threatened, Ela could tell she'd jerked the robes of an important man. Someone who might even have Sheriff de Hal on his payroll.

"What's wrong, Mama?" Her daughter Petronella approached with a frown.

"I'm becoming suspicious of everyone," Ela admitted. Mostly because she couldn't come up with another convincing answer fast enough. Why had Haughton not wanted to talk frankly in front of his wife? Was she likely to whisper gossip in the town square?

"Are the men who stole Edyth going to come to our house?"

"Good Lord, no." *At least I hope not.* "But we'll all be safest when they are locked up tight in the dungeon or hanged for their crimes. That's why I won't let the matter rest until we've found them."

"Is it dangerous for you, Mama?"

Ela had made sure that her children knew nothing of her abduction, simply that Bill Talbot and the guards had been hurt. "Less dangerous than letting evil roam the land."

"Isn't the sheriff supposed to catch criminals?"

"Indeed he is, my love."

"But he's not doing his job, is he?" Petronella was perceptive.

Ela sighed. "He's new to the position. We must give him time to rise to his responsibilities." She certainly didn't need her children knowing her complaints about de Hal.

But she did need to find out the details of what had happened in Yorkshire. With that in mind she wrote at once to her lawyer, Spicewell. He could conjure documents from the four winds and she knew that he could lay his hands on an official complaint within days. She also told him there was another girl missing and that she was very far from letting the matter rest.

And that afternoon she mounted her horse again and set out to visit the Brice children and their aunt and uncle. She made sure her men were armed and ready, since she knew she might be anything but welcome.

CHAPTER 12

$\mathcal{T}$he farm Ela sought was remote. She had to ask directions three times before they found it at the end of a long, narrow, leaf-littered track that was muddy even in autumn and must be all but impassable in winter and spring.

Elizabeth Brice's sister Martha was married to a man called Thomas Brown. Their rustic cottage had a strange, uneven greenish roof that looked to be a mix of thatch and turf with a layer of moss growing on it.

There were children all around—scores of them, it seemed—ranging in age from crawling babe to half-bearded young man and budding girl. They all gathered in a group, staring, as the party from Gomeldon approached.

"Hello, my name is Ela. May I speak with your mother or father?" She didn't want to frighten them with her full name. They might well know it as the name of the acting sheriff who'd presided over the arrest and trial of their mother for the murder of their father.

"My mammy's dead," said one little girl. "And my daddy."

Ela's heart ached at the sound of her brave voice. "Who's

looking after you?" She knew the answer but didn't need them to know that.

"Our auntie."

"Our parents are at the market to buy a cow," said a boy of about fifteen. "When they come back we'll have cheese and butter to eat."

Ela looked around. She didn't see any other livestock, not even a mangy chicken to produce the eggs the missing girl had taken to market when she disappeared. The entire vista was one of extreme poverty. "What do you normally live on?"

"We have a good crop of parsnips and carrots growing," said one boy of about eleven, brightly. "And last week they bought a sack of flour to make bread."

"How many of you are there?" They kept moving so she couldn't manage to count them.

No one answered.

"Too many mouths to feed," piped up the first little girl. "That's what our auntie said."

Ela's chest hurt. Poor mite. She must have overheard them complaining about the added burden—an intolerable one from the look of it—of Martha's sister's children. No wonder they hadn't run to the castle at the first sign of one less mouth to feed. At first they might be relieved that she'd be supping at someone else's table for a night or two.

Ela chastised herself for not looking in on the family sooner. She'd meant to see if they needed alms, but had been wary of a hostile reception after the trial and had somehow kept busy with other things.

"I heard that one of your sisters is missing. I'd like to help find her. What's her name?"

"Elsie," said a girl of about thirteen.

"How old is she?"

"Older than me and younger than Tom," piped up a boy of about ten.

"So she's about eleven?" They all looked back in confusion. Did they not know their numbers? How would they count their eggs for market? Or their sheep to make sure none were missing? "What color are Elsie's hair and eyes?"

"She has brown hair and brown eyes," burst out two or three of them at once. "Her hair's really long," said a smaller girl. "She always wears it in a plait down her back. Will she be coming back soon?"

"God willing. What color was she wearing when she left?"

"Brownish." None could provide more useful detail. They were all dressed in various natural hues in garments made from homespun wool.

A girl with brown hair and brown eyes, dressed in brown. She might as well be looking for a leaf in the forest. Half the girls in England wore their hair in a long braid.

"Does she have any distinguishing features? A birthmark or a chipped tooth or anything that makes her stand out in a crowd?"

They all just stared at her.

BACK AT GOMELDON ELA busied herself with inspecting the gardens and sties and bee skeps. The gardens were coming along well considering how little time they'd had for preparation and planting in the spring. They still enjoyed fresh greens and baby carrots, and it looked certain they'd have a good crop of root vegetables to store for the winter.

Gomeldon's orchard had been neglected in recent years while the manor was rented to a tenant, but the trees had since been pruned and manured and the fruit selectively plucked so they'd coaxed a harvest of apples, pears, plums and quince to be had before hard frost. The apricots and walnuts also looked promising, the grapevines much less so.

But England was a difficult place to grow a good crop of grapes.

Her greyhound, Grayson, followed Ela as she made her rounds and spoke with the gardener and the boys who tended the pigs and chickens. It was a brisk autumn day, the sky a clear, bright blue with the occasional wisp of feathery cloud. She wanted to stay out here in the peace and abundance of the garden, surrounded by buzzing bees and the cheerful tapestry of changing leaves. She couldn't bring herself to go back inside, where she'd glimpse Edyth's mournful face with still no fresh news to report of her parents.

At last the two men returned from their ride to the priory at Walton. Ela hurried around the house to meet them as they rode up the drive.

"Did you find the Wheatons?" she asked, before they'd had time to dismount.

"Yes, they'd stayed a night at the priory, then been told to leave at dawn the next day. Not wanting to stray far from Salisbury—in hopes of finding their daughter—they started walking back this way. The sheriff's men stopped them on the road about two miles outside of Salisbury and turned them around again, and that's where we found them."

"They're on the road?"

"Aye. I gave them the coin for their sustenance. I hope that wasn't wrong."

"It was right...but none of this is right. We must take Edyth to them at once to ease their minds, but she can hardly tramp the roads with them." Ela racked her mind. She couldn't take in every waif and stray in Wiltshire. She'd already gone too far down that road. Still, there was no time to waste and she could come to a solution as they traveled. "Please have my carriage brought around. You can escort me to them."

Ela hurried inside to tell Edyth that her parents had been found and they must wash the tears from her cheeks so she'd be ready to see them. Edyth looked so happy and excited that there was no way she could tell the girl they had no place to stay.

In the past she might have offered the shelter of her barn, but since it was the recent scene of a brutal murder she imagined they might prefer to sleep under the stars.

Hilda came along as well because her presence so soothed and cheered Edyth. If the Wheatons were already most of the way back to Salisbury the journey should be short, so she'd better think fast about what to do with the little family.

The idea that Simon de Hal's men might have torched their house lit a flame of rage in her heart. She'd probably never know for sure, but she was fairly certain that's what Giles Haughton had hinted at.

The sunny afternoon clouded over as they topped a rise and headed down through a broad vista of sheep meadows. The leaves on a great oak had turned a rich burgundy color that shone like a jewel in the landscape.

"They're up ahead," called one of the men.

Ela poked her head out the window and saw a man and a woman sitting by the roadside in the shade of another massive oak tree. They pulled up next to them. The man and woman rose nervously to their feet as Ela alighted from the carriage, coaxing Edyth to come with her.

The sight of her parents stunned Edyth to silence. Her mother rushed forward and hugged the girl to her breast. Her father praised God for her safe return and said he didn't want to let her out of his sight again as long as he lived.

Ela had to blink back a tear at the sight of the touching reunion.

But now what?

It shouldn't be her responsibility to put a roof over their

heads tonight. It wasn't her responsibility. Just as it wasn't her responsibility to bring Edyth back to them.

She knew in her heart that it was her duty as a Christian, though.

"Thank you so much for your kindness," said Edyth's father. "I don't know how we can ever repay you." He bowed. "I have the advantage in knowing that you are Ela, Countess of Salisbury. My name is John Wheaton, at your service." He spoke in French, and Ela could tell he was an educated man.

"God must receive all praise and gratitude due for Edyth's return," protested Ela. But an idea occurred to her that would offer them shelter without embarrassing them further after all the humiliation they'd suffered. "And I do have a favor I could ask of you."

John Wheaton looked excited by the prospect of serving her to repay his debt. "Tell me and it shall be done."

"I've had the misfortune of having a murder committed in my hay barn, and I'd appreciate the services of a man and woman of prayer to…" How to put it? "To cleanse the space of any evil that might linger there as a result of that terrible crime."

John Wheaton blinked. "I'm not a priest. I can't cast out demons."

"The space is not haunted or possessed by spirits, as far as I know. In fact, I'm not sure anyone has entered it since the week that the deed occurred. But I feel sure that a night of prayer would lift the spirit of the place and make it safe to hold feed or animals again. And prayers would be most welcome for the soul of the murder victim, who was a brave knight who once saved my husband's life." She didn't mention that he was also the father of Hilda's baby.

"Both my wife and I have a spiritual education and long years' experience of prayer." He looked anxiously at Alys. "I feel confident in speaking for both of us that we'd be glad to pray inside your barn and combat any dark forces that might have taken up residence there."

"Wonderful. Please climb in my carriage." They didn't have so much as a bundle of rags with them. Just the clothes on their backs, which luckily for them were young and strong. They helped Edyth into the carriage and climbed in behind her. Soon they were turned around and rolling back along the road to Gomeldon.

Ela didn't believe in spirits or ghosts. She'd seen no evidence of them in her lifetime. But surely prayers could bring no harm and would keep this small family safe while she figured out what to do with them.

She hated that they'd been deprived of all their possessions and banished from Salisbury. She swiftly resolved that —with her as their champion—they'd be reinstated in the village and secured from the hatred and fear of the villagers.

But how?

BACK AT GOMELDON ELA ushered Edyth's family into the house and had the cook prepare them a simple meal. After it was done she took John Wheaton to the barn and explained what had happened there.

The blood from the murder had been cleaned up, but no one had been in there since for any reason. The hay had not yet been harvested, and there were other barns and sheds in use on the manor for the animals.

"If I had holy water I could cleanse it properly," he said.

"How is holy water made?" Ela thought it odd that she'd never wondered this before.

"It's blessed by a priest."

There was a moment of awkward silence before Ela

spoke. "We have a pond filled with fresh, clear water. I presume that as a former novice, you know the words..."

John looked doubtful. "Not only am I no longer a novice, there are many who think I'm less than a man since I left the order."

"Why did you leave the order?" It was an impertinent question, but curiosity seared her. Most men would conduct an affair in secret and hold fast to their title and position. Did they get caught?

"I fell in love with Alys. I wanted to live with her as man and wife. I often think it would have been better for both of us if our paths had never crossed." He sounded deadly serious.

"The Lord has his own plan for us," said Ela. "And we're not often blessed with knowledge of it."

"That is true, but I've brought her and our child into poverty and danger. I truly thought the Lord had burned our house and taken Edyth away to punish me for my sins."

"Your sin is loving Alys?"

"I could have loved her from afar like a knight in a song. A chaste love wouldn't have wrecked her vows and upended her life." Distress carved at his young face.

Ela's heart ached for him. "Did you join the order of your own free will?"

"My father paid for me to join because my older brother was to inherit our lands."

"So you had no choice?" Holy orders were considered a suitable career for landless younger sons, and they were often pushed into the religious life.

"I tried to make the best of the path laid out for me, but I strayed from it."

"You were tempted by her beauty?"

"And her kindness. I was foolish—reckless—and she became pregnant."

"You do realize that happens literally all the time?" She didn't have enough fingers to count the instances that she'd heard of. "There are bishops and abbots and priors all over England who've fathered children that are being raised right under their nose in their own parish."

"I've heard of such. But I couldn't continue to live a lie."

"Ah, you're a man of principle. That's always dangerous." She smiled. John's honesty and candor—of words and spirit —touched her. "I don't think you've done anything wrong but be a man instead of a holy statue. I don't believe the Lord means to punish you either. I believe he brought us together for a reason."

He looked at her curiously, but he didn't dare ask what the reason was.

"Never mind about holy water. I shall leave it up to you to cleanse and prepare the space as you see fit, if you're willing to have your family sleep here tonight."

"I shall do my best. But how else can I repay your kindness?"

Ela hesitated for a moment. "Pray for the soul of my dear husband, William, who died an unexpected, painful and premature death in March of this year." *And for my soul*, she wanted to add. She still burned with fury about her husband's untimely death. Her anger—and her desire to one day see his murder avenged—was most unchristian.

But she didn't need to burden John Wheaton with her sorrows. He had enough of his own.

THE NEXT MORNING Ela had a spring in her step as she went about her daily rounds. She could finally breathe a sigh of relief that Edyth was back safe in the arms of her parents. Yes, Elsie Brice was missing, but having found one child she knew there was at least a chance she could find the second.

But now there was the problem of restoring the Wheatons to their home and livelihood, and teaching the citizens of Salisbury—and its sheriff—a lesson in the process.

She'd made some scented oil in one of the bottles she bought from Sibel's husband. She'd bring that with her today. She could tell that Bishop Poore used oil as a pomade in his luxuriant silver locks, and she imagined he'd enjoy one that smelled of lavender.

She dressed in a finely embroidered gown and wore the rings recently restored to her by the sheriff of London. Hilda pinned on a veil so fine and delicate that it might have been spun by orb weavers. Today Ela wanted to look like the Countess of Salisbury.

She rode to Bishop Poore's house, where a cowled brother explained that Bishop Poore was "in prayer." Ela suspected that he was simply sleeping late—as he was rumored to do quite often. "It's a pressing matter. I'll wait," she said with a polite smile.

The monk ushered her into the bishop's lavish parlor, where she noticed a handsome new set of iron fire tongs with an embossed design in gold on the handles. After some time spent admiring a beautiful tapestry with a woodland scene that might be biblical but probably wasn't, she heard footsteps on the stairs.

A grumbling voice called for wine and spice cake, and she rose from her chair as Bishop Richard Poore swept into the room.

"My lady countess, what a very great pleasure."

He pressed her hands, and she decided to surprise him by kissing his ring. Which was one of the most magnificent jewels she'd ever seen. While he was still blinking with shock, she shoveled on a heap of flattery.

"Bishop Poore, you're known throughout the land as a true good Samaritan. You're a man who cares about children —creating a school for them—and who feels deeply the suffering of the poor. The almshouses you're building here in Salisbury are a model for other cities to follow."

She paused to take breath and assess the effect of her blandishments.

He looked worried. Good. "Perhaps you've heard of a terrible injustice committed right here in Salisbury in this past month?" She looked at him curiously.

He seemed to be consulting a long list of injustices and trying to consider which one she meant.

"Not only was Edyth Wheaton spirited from her home by child thieves, but her parents were burned out of their house while they visited the castle to seek help."

"Very sad. Very sad. I'll keep them in my prayers." He twisted his huge ring.

"I'm afraid prayers won't keep the rain off their heads, my lord bishop. They're in need of sturdier roofing. I hoped that perhaps they could take up residence in the newest of your almshouses. Perhaps the one that faces the cathedral close?"

She knew the property she referred to wasn't an almshouse, but was in fact to be a grand new mansion for some burgher or other—no doubt in lieu of a generous donation to "the church."

"I'm afraid the new buildings are all filled, indeed over-subscribed and—"

"Then perhaps the church can see fit to provide men to help rebuild their small cottage at the crossroads. They own the land, inherited from Alys parents, and such a modest building surely wouldn't take more than a few days to build."

A gray look descended over Bishop Poore's face. "I really feel this is outside the purview of my—"

"Do you resist because you know that they're both

formerly cloistered? It's surely God's will that they left their holy orders to dwell among us. I feel sure that the Lord would wish to see his sheep well sheltered from the upcoming winter."

Bishop Poore's hair smelled of some rich Eastern resin. Perhaps her offering of lavender oil would be used to scent the rushes on the refectory floor.

The bishop's mouth opened. Then closed.

"Do you feel it's just that some cruel individual can take a torch to their house without fear of censure or rebuke, simply because they're disliked?"

"They did choose to flout the laws of God and the conventions of society."

Ela wondered how often Bishop Poore flouted the laws of God. He certainly paid no attention to the Rule of St. Benedict, which would require him to forsake worldly goods and consider himself "inferior to all." Although she wasn't aware of him having sired any children, she had heard rumors that he was himself the illegitimate son of a bishop. "Have we not all sinned in the sight of God? These are good, hardworking people. Although John Wheaton has been working lately as a farm laborer, he's an educated man. Perhaps you could find him a position serving the church?"

"I'm afraid that I have no need of another—"

"Bishop Poore, let me speak plainly."

CHAPTER 13

*E*la paused for effect and watched a look of alarm rise in Bishop Poore's pale eyes. "As Countess of Salisbury I find it my duty to see God's will done in this small part of his creation."

"I believe Sheriff de Hal has been charged with—"

"Sheriff de Hal has not seen fit to interest himself in the matter of the Wheatons. He showed little concern when their daughter disappeared and now does not care that they've been cruelly abused by the people of Salisbury. His lack of interest does not mean this matter can be swept away with the rushes. The good people of Salisbury—and I use the word *good* reservedly—need to be taught a lesson about Christian charity. I intend to see that the Wheaton's house is rebuilt in its former location."

"I don't believe Sheriff de Hal will be happy about that." The Bishop's lips closed in a tight rosebud, and he wound his plump fingers in front of his robe.

Two servants entered at that moment, one carrying two cups of wine and another a fine platter bearing a spice cake rich with cherries and currants and dates.

Ela took the cup offered her but politely refused the sickly sweet cake. Her stomach wouldn't tolerate such overindulgence this early in the day.

After the servants had left, she sipped her wine, then put the cup down on the table. "Simon de Hal may be sheriff of Salisbury at this moment, but he will not be sheriff of Salisbury forever. The king, whom I visited while in London, is in favor of my taking on the role once my period of mourning is over."

His mouth formed a tiny round O.

"So I do not intend to sit quietly at my manor embroidering while the town of New Salisbury becomes a place where a family can be robbed of their children or driven from their home."

"Quite." She could sense his brain working fast beneath his scented hair. "But I fail to see how I fit into this…scheme."

"Good triumphing over evil is hardly a scheme, Bishop Poore." Ela drew herself up to her full height. "It's your role as the Bishop of Salisbury—and God's highest representative here—to ensure that His will be done. Do you think that God wants innocent children to be stolen from their homes?"

"Well, no…"

"Do you think God wants the people of Salisbury to decide who gets to live here in a trial by fire?"

He hesitated and for a horrible moment she thought he was actually asking himself this question. "No. But there are other places to live than Salisbury. Neither of them grew up in this area."

"Where you born in Salisbury, Bishop Poore?"

"Well, no—"

"Yet you find yourself here and I know you take a keen interest in the spiritual and physical health of our residents. You've no doubt saved countless lives with your weekly exhortations that children not be left unattended near fire or water."

"I have prevented a few tragedies, I trust." He glanced at the cake.

"One tragedy prevented enriches countless lives, and I am inspired by your example." She cleared her throat and went in for the kill. "John and Alys Wheaton may have left their cloistered existence, but they have not abandoned the Lord their God and I feel sure that he has not abandoned them. Together we must prove it to them and to all Salisbury."

Bishop Poore seemed to sag. "Would you please sit down?" he said quietly.

She realized he was waiting for her to sit so he could sit and enjoy his cake. She obliged by sweeping her skirts under her and perching on the edge of one of his extravagantly carved chairs.

His chair creaked under his weight as he sat down hard. He reached for the slice of cake that the servant had placed on a napkin for him and took a large bite. Ela waited while he chewed it.

"If you can find employment for John Wheaton so he can support his family, I will provide materials and labor for the restoration of his home. He's an intelligent man, and I have no doubt that he'll prove an asset to the parish."

"His presence might encourage the monks to desert their calling."

"If their calling is so weak as to be easily broken perhaps that is for the best." She gave him a stern look. "I intend to seek the peace of the cloister myself one day when the time is right. The time is not yet right for me, and apparently not for John and Alys Wheaton either. That does not mean we aren't still devout children of God."

Bishop Poore looked like he wanted to cross himself, but

his hands were full of cake. "Perhaps I could find a secular role for him. The leper hospital might suit."

"The leper hospital is not a suitable place of employment for a man with a wife and child. John Wheaton reads and writes and knows French, English and Latin."

Bishop Poore nodded and took another bite of cake. He looked defeated.

"I shall send him to meet with you this afternoon."

He looked like he wanted to protest but then thought better of it. "Send him to the monastery counting houses. I'll meet with him there."

Ela smiled. "Excellent. The Lord has already blessed Salisbury with our magnificent new cathedral—for which I give you credit—and I hope to see our town thrive as a shining example of God's will being done on earth."

"Quite, quite."

JOHN WHEATON'S meeting with Bishop Poore led to him being offered a job traveling between the various manors belonging to the cathedral and its monastery. Throughout the year there were fleeces and cheeses and cut firewood and candles and even spun and woven wool to be gathered from the manors for sale at the market in Salisbury.

Poore preferred not to have his monks riding about the countryside, which clearly bristled with temptations. John accepted the job and Alys wept with joy.

Ela then set men to cutting down three great trees in the woods of Gomeldon, explaining that they were in the way of a new lane being cut between two meadows. The Gomeldon woods proved a rich source of willow and hazel stems and other sticks for the wattle. A thick stand of reeds clogged the fishpond on one of her other nearby manors, and Ela ordered them cut and stacked for thatch.

Cartloads of manure and straw were gathered for the daub, some of them surreptitiously gathered from the castle floors and stables by her old friends on the castle staff. Ela expanded the Gomeldon fishpond which produced several cartloads of clay and sand to add to the daub mixture.

Within days, the wood was cut, dressed into stout beams, and lifted into place on the foundation stones of the burned cottage. Ela—with the help of a rousing sermon by Bishop Poore—managed to shame the townspeople of Salisbury into turning up to help. They wove the wattle and trampled and smeared the daub and laid the thatch in exchange for the bishop's blessings for the safety of their eternal soul.

Three of the Wheatons' chickens, a rooster, and two rabbits were even returned. Edyth was thrilled to find them pecking and hopping around the bright new house on the morning the family arrived to take possession of their newly dried home. Ela took this as a sign that the people of Salisbury realized the error of their ways and looked to right the wrongs they'd done, for they could have easily eaten the animals and no one would have been the wiser.

WHILE THIS WENT ON, Ela didn't forget about Elsie Brice. Part of her wanted to return to London immediately and exhort the sheriff to retrieve the second girl.

But that wouldn't keep other children out of danger.

Ela also didn't want to excite Bill Talbot into rising from his sickbed prematurely. He needed time for his wounds to heal properly, and he'd never sit quietly indoors while Ela rode around London seeking help for her cause. It would do no good to either of them if his wounds reopened. She needed to restrain herself at the sidelines of this particular battle and gather her strength for the next fight she could win.

Ela had plenty to do in overseeing the education of her younger children and the smooth running of Gomeldon and the other manors in her possession. It was a busy time of year, with the harvest underway and preparation for winter storage of the crops.

The Wheatons had lifted the spirit of the barn by their cheerful presence and—while Hilda wished to never enter it again—the servants no longer stared and whispered or crossed themselves when they walked near it. Its loft soon filled with fresh summer hay that would keep their horses and cattle fat over the winter.

No one raised a fuss about the missing Brice girl. Her aunt and uncle probably had their hands full with the harvest as well as all the other children. While her siblings must miss her and pine for her, no one in authority raised a finger to help her.

But Ela prayed daily for the girl's safe return. She wrote again to Spicewell and told him to keep a watchful eye on the whole operation. If a little pressure caused them to release Elsie, like they did Edyth, so much the better.

After about two weeks, burning with impatience to search for Elsie and to hunt down the men who'd abducted both Edyth and herself, she resolved to return to London.

ELA BROUGHT HILDA WITH HER, and an entourage of men-at-arms. She didn't want to take any chances on being attacked again.

Her mother had retired to the countryside, leaving Bill

Talbot with the run of the house and a full staff of servants, who were also caring for the other injured men.

Ela found the wounded men in good spirits and recovering, though she suspected it would be some time before they could be counted on to protect her again. Bill greeted Ela at the door when she arrived, and the housekeeper told Ela ruefully that no amount of pleading could make him rest in bed while the sun was high.

After the initial greetings she told Bill there was another missing child.

"But she's been gone almost a month?" Bill looked appalled. "Why didn't you send word? I could have been looking for her this whole time."

"That's what I was afraid of. I can see you're healing well but that's in part because you weren't trotting about London on your horse or—worse yet—getting into fights with a band of criminals."

Bill looked offended. "I've been most careful. At this point I've probably sustained more injury from the housekeeper's scolding than from the dagger that pierced me."

"He views taking the stairs one at a time as resting quietly," muttered the housekeeper, who was a brisk middle-aged woman with pointed features. "I will say he has an appetite, though."

"They're trying to fatten me like a hog for market." He patted his belly. "I need some exercise or I'll start to look like Hilda." Hilda's condition was now clearly visible. "I'm fine for activity, truly. My wound was just a small puncture."

Ela lifted a skeptical eyebrow. He'd bled so copiously that they'd feared for his life. But he did look hale and hearty now. His color had returned, and he actually did have the beginnings of a belly. She didn't say that, though, as she knew Bill could be quite vain about his appearance.

"Well," she said cautiously, "I've sent a message to

Spicewell informing him that I'm back in London and wish to pursue the matter of the missing children urgently, and I await any intelligence his men can provide me. Perhaps we can both go visit him tomorrow."

SPICEWELL DID INDEED INVITE her to meet him, but in his grand chambers near the law courts rather than his business quarters down by the docks. He welcomed them in and congratulated Bill on his speedy recovery, then immediately launched into a dissertation on how Hilda's child would soon be proved the rightful owner of Fernlees.

Ela grew impatient. "That's encouraging, but what news do your men have of the child slavers?"

Spicewell cleared his throat, pushed his chair back and rose to his feet. Then he paced across the room, with his hands oddly tented together. At last he spun around. "I'm afraid they've turned up no further information."

His expression was pleasant enough, but Ela sensed an iron portcullis closing behind his warm gaze. Suspicions unfurled inside her. "They didn't learn anything or they're afraid to look into the matter?"

"Did you not find the girl you came to search for?"

"She found me. Her captors set her free, and I attribute her release to the pressure that we applied to them during my last visit. They returned her in the hope that I'd leave London and never trouble them again."

"No doubt they did," he said, looking down the length of his nose at her. "And for your own safety that would perhaps be the wisest move."

Shock ran through Ela like a splash of cold water. "You're surely not warning me away from the matter?"

"As your friend and a dear friend of your mother's, I feel

it's my duty to warn you that you've poked a dangerous beehive."

"Whose beehive?" He did know something.

But he held his hands up as if in despair. "It's not my privilege to know that, but both of the men who gave you the information last time are dead. Their bodies were found at low tide in the River Thames near Richmond."

Ela gasped and felt the blood drain from her body. Dalziel and Bray were both dead? She took a moment to gather her thoughts. "Surely you want to avenge their deaths?"

"I'm an old man, my lady," said Spicewell. He moved behind his big desk and rested his hands on it. "I've had a long and successful career in the law that I consider myself officially retired from. I take on cases that interest me and for friends that I wish to help. This matter is sadly outside my purview."

Ela stared at him. *He was afraid.* Further, he was unwilling to help her probe deeper into the matter. "Someone powerful must be behind this." Spicewell's expressionless face angered her. "You must have some idea of who it is."

"If I knew any more than you do I would tell you. Whoever it was boldly abducted a countess while gravely wounding her guards. Not a person to be trifled with."

"I also am not a person to be trifled with," she said quickly. She felt Bill stiffen. He clearly did not enjoy her displays of bravado. Perhaps he worried that he'd be called on to draw his sword to defend her again.

Ela let out a sigh. "The guards are recovering well, thanks be to God."

"That is good news. But I still advise you to steer well clear of this dangerous matter."

"And let an eleven-year-old girl—an orphan whose mother was recently hanged for killing her father—be doomed to a fate worse than death?"

Spicewell drew in a long breath as if calling on reserves of patience deep inside himself. "Be careful, my lady. I know you seek the office of sheriff of Wiltshire. Is it not better to gather your resources toward winning that prize?" He walked over to a carved oak chest and unlocked it with a key that hung on the belt at his waist. "I have some information about Sheriff de Hal's conduct in Yorkshire."

Ela's interest piqued. "What is it?"

"It's a written complaint by the burgesses of Scarborough." He unfolded a piece of crisp parchment and read aloud a vivid account of de Hal and his men terrorizing the farmers, fisherman and merchants of Scarborough, a market town on the north Yorkshire coast. They accused him of demanding their goods at half price—or outright stealing them—and promising to burn their homes or imprison them if they refused.

The burgesses insisted that he'd destroyed all business in the town because people were afraid to come to the market there and have their goods seized or their lives threatened by the sheriff's men. The complaint was lengthy and detailed and very damning.

Ela hadn't formed a good opinion of Sheriff de Hal. He was greedy and seemed uninterested in pursuing cases that didn't promise to fill his coffers in some way. But this was different. He stood accused of outright villainy such as you'd expect from a band of pirates or highwaymen. As Spicewell read on, she could hardly believe her ears. "How was de Hal made sheriff of Salisbury if he so grossly misused the office in Yorkshire?"

Spicewell shrugged. "I asked the same question myself. He's clearly an aggressive man, ruthless and fearless in his misdeeds."

She blinked, trying to make sense of it. "In bringing him

to Wiltshire, it almost makes you think that someone deliberately wanted to sow trouble in Salisbury."

Hubert de Burgh. The man who killed her husband.

"Once again, my lady, you're asking me to speculate about matters that do not concern me."

"When were these complaints made?"

"In the eighth year of his majesty's reign."

"Just two years ago?" Ela rose from her chair and paced across the room, fury burning in her veins. "This is outrageous. Simon de Hal runs riot in Yorkshire, earning the official complaint of the good people there, then is summarily installed in my ancestral castle to bring his reign of terror to Wiltshire?"

"Has he done such things in Salisbury?"

"Not yet." She frowned. "At least not that I know of. I moved my household to Gomeldon because it's near the castle and I wanted to keep a close watch on him."

"That may be the reason he's behaving himself," said Spicewell with a lifted brow.

"I've certainly tried to be a thorn in his conscience." Ela walked back to her chair and sat. "And I shall be sure to breathe down his neck at every opportunity."

"Be careful," warned Spicewell. "You can tell from this complaint that he's ruthless and unafraid of violence."

"Against a countess who's kin to the king himself? I don't think he's that much of a fool." The idea of Simon de Hal being a renowned reprobate was starting to warm her heart. It would be all the easier to convince King Henry that she'd be a better sheriff for Wiltshire. Yes, she'd still have to pay for the privilege—as de Hal might well have done himself—but even de Burgh could hardly make the case that de Hal was more suited to be sheriff. "Though I do appreciate being forewarned."

"Under the circumstances," said Spicewell slowly. "You

may wish to spend more time in Salisbury and less in London."

Ela cocked her head. "Did someone suggest that you tell me to stay away from London?"

"My dear lady, neither I nor anyone else would presume to tell the Countess of Salisbury where she should or should not conduct her business. I simply warn you to have a care for your own safety and that of the members of your household."

"I appreciate the warning. May I keep that copy of the burgesses' complaints?"

"Indeed you may." He handed it over. Ela folded it up and stowed it in the small purse at her belt.

She resolved to return to the one matter that didn't seem to disturb Spicewell. "If Hilda's child is born healthy and alive, God willing, he or she will be owner of Fernlees. What is Hilda's status with regards to ownership?"

"She should claim her status as guardian of the rightful heir and take up residence there forthwith."

"If, God forbid, the child dies, either during pregnancy or some years into the future. Then what happens?"

"Then the vultures would circle and likely one of them would pluck the manor from her."

"Meaning de Hal or the king or some far-distant male relative of Drogo Blount's?"

"Exactly. It is essential that the child be alive and healthy and installed at Fernlees as quickly and firmly as possible."

"Understood."

Ela didn't like that Hilda's toehold in her new role as lady of the manor was so tenuous and circumstantial. She resolved to help the girl acquire the skills to support herself in the style she was about to become accustomed to, should her new status be snatched away at some time in the future.

Truth be told, the people of Scarborough were an inspiration to her. She admired them for joining arms and standing tall in the face of tyranny, and she wished she could meet with them and congratulate them on ridding Yorkshire of Simon de Hal.

But right now she had more urgent matters to attend to.

CHAPTER 14

*O*utside Spicewell's chambers they remounted their horses. "Should we ride to Westcheap and view the building to see if it's still empty?" Ela was itching to act but wanted Bill's moderating wisdom.

Bill rode up close to her. "We should keep our thoughts and our movements visible and knowable to as few people as possible." He spoke so softly she could barely hear him. With his eyes he gestured at the four guards that rode with them, two in front and two behind.

Ela fought the urge to roll her eyes. What could you accomplish in this life if you could not even trust the men hired to defend you? But perhaps they should wait to discuss the matter in private. "Heard and understood."

BACK AT THE house Ela ushered Bill into her mother's private study, where Alianore wrote her correspondence and kept her important documents locked up, and closed the door. Then locked it from the inside.

"They've murdered both of our informants," she hissed, still in disbelief. "They threaten and frighten and browbeat their way into continuing their foul trade unmolested."

"Like Simon de Hal did in Yorkshire."

"Indeed. But what kind of England would we live in where such behavior is allowed to run unchecked? Surely the forces of law and order are an equal match for such brazen iniquity?"

Bill watched her in silence for a moment. "The profit motive can trump all other considerations for some men."

"Those who have no thought for their immortal souls," she spat.

"Some would argue that's most men," said Bill with a wry smile. "We're hardly trained in the arts of war so that we can better follow the teachings of Christ."

"You are an excellent example of a man who's both knightly and Godly." She frowned. "And you're far from being the only one. Though the quest for riches and the lust for pleasure do tempt many men from the path of right-eousness."

Her own husband, for example. But William had certainly never enslaved children or burned a family from their home. His sins were those of a lusty man well able to enjoy the bounty that this world offered and who answered the call of his king promptly in times of war.

And he'd repented in the end.

Ela inhaled deeply. "I'm keenly aware that my greatest responsibility lies with my family and seeing my children raised to adulthood and settled into their lives—"

"Three down and five to go," quipped Bill.

Ela smiled. "Indeed. But I would dishonor my ancestors if I allowed crimes to go unpunished under my very nose."

Bill held her gaze. "And I have a calling to serve and protect you."

"Indeed you do." She smiled. "And I'm so grateful God has spared you to continue his work." She sat at the small table where her mother wrote her correspondence. Her mother's seal and sealing wax sat ready in a small wooden box. She indicated for Bill to sit in the chair opposite her. "We must find the children."

"And we must discover who abducted you. I shall have to keep one eye open at night until we know that."

"Your concern is appreciated, though I doubt they'll expose themselves to study by doing such a brazen thing again."

"Your bravery does you credit." His tone suggested this wasn't entirely a compliment.

"You think me foolhardy?"

"I think you more courageous than half the king's knights. You're made of the same unrelenting stuff as Empress Matilda."

"I hate being compared to her." Ela glared at him. She'd heard this backhanded compliment before. "She's my husband's ancestor, not mine. She was cheated of her rightful throne and couldn't gain the support to take it back. I have no wish to walk in her shoes."

"People speak of her difficult and tyrannical nature, but perhaps that's a mischaracterization. History is written by the victors, after all."

"I had no idea you carried such a torch for Matilda." She paused. "Or are you trying to warn me that people are already speaking of me in the same terms?"

Bill swallowed. "What other people think is none of my business."

"Let them talk. I refuse to concern myself with the whispering of gossips. I also refuse to let crime flourish under my gaze. And I will find that house with the black and white tile floors. Shall we walk out and take the air this afternoon?"

Bill looked wary. "You mean walk around looking for that house?"

Ela's ears pricked as a chime sounded in the distance. "I think I heard the bell for Vespers. We should attend and ask for the Lord's intercession in our work."

WITH AN ENTOURAGE of armed men in tow, Ela walked past the small church on her mother's street and kept going toward the larger one, St. Michael and All Angels, two streets away. She'd never been inside, but she'd certainly noticed it. The dressed-stone structure rose nearly three stories tall and boasted stained-glass windows and intricately carved oak doors.

It was the kind of church likely to have a sizable and accomplished choir.

Bill maintained a placid expression while she led them to the doors and past the black-robed brothers flanking it. Instead of heading to the front of the church, she took up a seat near the back of the nave, where she'd have a better view. Two attendants stayed outside, and two came in and stood near where she sat.

Aside from the brothers, the altar boys, the priest and sundry other ecclesiastical persons, there were only three other congregants inside the body of the church at that hour. Two older women prayed the rosary on their knees at the front of the church. A middle-aged man in a moss-green cap stood behind them and might have been there as the attendant of one or both of the women.

She snuck a glance around the interior of the church. Gold embroidery ornamented the rich red fabric of the altar cloth. The candlesticks on the altar looked to be of solid silver. The side chapels contained life-sized painted wooden effigies of various saints.

Ela realized with a jolt that the floor was a pattern of black and white tiles. Her blood pounded louder in her ears as a procession of twelve choirboys entered singing a sweet incantation and took up their places to the right of the altar.

Ela resisted the urge to glance at Bill. She kept her gaze ahead, toward the altar, while trying to absorb as much information as she could through her peripheral vision. If this church was somehow associated with the person who'd abducted her, they'd be watching her.

The windows around the altar, though small, shone with brightly colored stained glass and must have cost a small fortune. Pillars of carved stone flanked the nave and side chapels. If there were any tombs or memorial plaques, she didn't see them. The church gave the impression of being newly constructed—at great expense—rather than being ancient.

The priest was a tall man with a long, mournful-looking face like a saint from an old manuscript and an air of authority.

The service proceeded as normal, the psalms sung with great beauty by the choir. No one else came in. After the service, Ela ventured into a side chapel with a carved effigy of a saint. She couldn't tell which saint it was. Or maybe it wasn't a saint. Maybe it was actually a likeness of the rich patron who'd paid for this beautiful place.

She lit a candle for her husband and dropped a coin in the box, then knelt and prayed for her husband's soul, for the health and safety of her children and her household—including Hilda and Bill—and for the wit and cunning to find Elsie Brice and take down the ring of child thieves.

It was a lot to ask for and she suspected the Lord might find her greedy. But at least she didn't ask for his interces-

161

sion to make her sheriff of Salisbury. She intended to accomplish that on her own, and the document Spicewell had given her would surely help.

OUTSIDE ON THE STREET, Ela tried not to look around curiously but suggested to Bill that she felt lightheaded and wanted to get some air before returning home. The sun still hovered above the rooftops, casting a rosy glow over the city. Bill murmured some nonsense about what a fine evening it was, and they set out walking slowly along the street.

Great houses sat on either side of the church and across the street. The house next door had a chiseled stone foundation that rose almost to shoulder height, topped with a pattern of black wood and white lime. She had a better view of the house across the street, which had a fine clay tile roof instead of thatch, and at least eight chimneys.

"How can we find out who owns these houses?" she whispered to Bill.

"The king's tax collectors must know who pays taxes on them."

"I hardly think they'll open their books to me."

"Perhaps the sheriff could ask them for that information."

Ela hesitated. She'd felt leery of Sheriff le Duc ever since he'd all but shoved her out of London. Was he in the pay of someone powerful who'd told him to get rid of her? The damning document listing de Hal's crimes vividly illustrated that sheriffs were liable to fall prey to the same greed, opportunism and fear as other mortal men.

"I've not yet found the chance to even mention that the opium trade still likely continues at Pinchbeck's old shop. I hesitate to involve him in yet another matter. Perhaps my mother will know." They walked down the street and turned around the corner. These fine houses lay apart from each other, with walled gardens in between. Gates that pierced their brick and stone walls through which she caught glimpses of the gardens, with their espaliered pear trees, stone fountains and sundials.

They rounded another corner, and Ela noticed that one wall continued around the corner without another house in sight and no gate to provide a view inside. This house sat on a large plot, one large enough to fit two dozen houses in a more cramped quarter of the city.

As they walked she saw a man emerge—seemingly from the wall itself—about fifty feet ahead of her. He didn't glance her way and turned to walk in the same direction they were heading. He wore a long black cloak—not a monk's robe but a cloak.

Ela felt the tiny hairs on her arms stand on end.

"Let's walk faster," she whispered. If only she didn't have to bring an entourage of armed men with her everywhere. It made subtlety challenging.

But there was something about that man. Something that quickened her steps and made her heart beat faster. As they passed the part of the wall he'd emerged from she turned and saw a solid wood door right in the wall. Above the wall rose the gables of a tall house with diamond-paned windows.

Are we being watched? She felt eyes everywhere, but it was likely her imagination. The man walked fast, his cloak flying out behind him. His thick, black hair was slightly curly, and she couldn't shake the feeling that she knew him.

Up ahead he turned and crossed the road just as a pony cart came by. He paused and cursed at the cart, which blocked his way for a moment. He turned just enough for her to see his face.

"It's Vicus Morhees," she rasped. She grabbed Bill's arm. "I'm sure of it." The man had haunted her nights since he escaped untried while suspected of being an instigator in two murders.

She knew they couldn't continue to chase him in this manner. Sooner or later he'd turn to see a noble lady with four well-dressed guards striding briskly toward him. He might even recognize her.

But she needed to know where he was headed.

She tapped the guard to her left on the arm and whispered, "Follow that man as if your life depends on it. I want to know where he goes and what he does." Then she turned to the man on her right. "Follow your fellow guard. As soon as he arrives at that man's destination, report back to me. God speed."

As soon as they left, she spun around and she and Bill circled back with the other two guards. "My mind is spinning," she admitted. "Vicus Morhees? What could he have to do with this?" She kept her voice barely above a whisper as they were still in the vicinity of the mysterious house with its large garden. She didn't want to be overheard by someone hanging washing or plucking herbs—or spying on them.

Bill frowned and kept walking straight ahead without looking at her. "I don't like this at all." His face was pale. "And it's getting dark."

"Are you all right? Do your wounds ache?"

"My wounds are fine, but I was sure we'd seen the back of that reprobate. Was he in the church with us?"

"I don't think so. I'm not sure how that house and its wall connect to the church."

"I think they back up to each other."

"So, if I was in that house I'd be able to hear the singing of the church choir." Her mind whirled. "Does the same wall enclose them both?" It was hard to see where the wall began and ended, especially with the sun sinking below the rooftops.

"It's possible."

Whose house could it be? Not Vicus Morhees's own house. He was a devious criminal who'd manage to take temporary control of both a manor and a business by trickery just a few months earlier, but he wouldn't have risen to these dizzy heights that quickly.

He must be working for the person who lived there.

BACK SAFELY INSIDE her mother's house, Ela paced around the parlor, thinking aloud while Bill listened. The candles on the table guttered every time she walked past them, but she was too anxious to sit still. Hilda—who she didn't like to leave alone for too long as she was prone to brooding—sat in the corner, mending a pair of stockings.

"Morhees plied the opium trade between Exmouth and London. He fell under suspicion for two murders connected to the trade, and both times he had an iron-clad alibi in Exmouth at the time of the killings. He proved highly strategic and skilled at getting others to do his dirty work, while keeping his robes high and dry in the meantime."

"Could he be the one who recognized you and alerted the child slavers that you're investigating them?"

"He could. I had words with him one day at Fernlees when I went there looking for Osbert Pinchbeck." She frowned. "But what do the child slavers have to do with the opium trade?"

Bill sipped his cup of spiced wine. "These underworld organizations—that trade in stolen goods or goods disguised to avoid taxes—are just as likely to be involved in the traffic in humans. To them the children would be yet another product. They have ships coming and going to various ports already and are quick to realize where there's fresh profit to be made."

"But that's so…messy."

"Not really. You have sheep on one manor and crops on another and milk cows on a third."

"I have all three and pigs as well on several of my manors. The cows graze the rich pasture, sheep graze the poorer land, the oats and wheat and rye and barley grow on the good arable land and pigs root in the woods."

"See? It's the same principle at work. Diversification for maximum profit."

"I suppose he could have laid eyes on Edyth Wheaton when he was in Salisbury trying to establish himself there. He saw an opportunity—a pretty young girl with poor, friendless parents—" She stopped pacing and stared at Bill. "But he can't have visited Salisbury recently enough to kidnap the girl. He's a wanted man, and the sheriff's men have orders to arrest him on sight."

"Unless they've been paid off."

Ela stared at him. "That does sound like something de Hal is capable of. And he could have sent a subordinate with instructions to kidnap the girl. Morhees wouldn't have done it himself anyway. That's not his style."

"Indeed. And he might have seen another opportunity in the orphaned Brice children."

"But the Brice children are tucked away deep in the countryside. How would he have learned about them?"

"The murder case was cause for gossip. He could have heard people murmuring about the orphaned children in the market."

"That is true." Ela's mind whirred. So this one man might be behind two murders, another man's disappearance and the kidnapping of two children? "If this is true Vicus

Morhees is one of the craftiest and most dangerous men in England."

"He might have ordered your kidnapping." Bill's face was taut with concern. "In which case he knows you're watching him and he's certainly watching you."

"Then why would he emerge from that garden and walk right in front of us?" Ela had seen that as a stroke of luck.

"To lead us somewhere?"

"I suppose he is cunning enough for that." She played with the base of a candlestick. "You think he was trying to lead us into a trap?"

"I suppose we'll find out when the guards return."

Ela sighed. "I hope these men-at-arms are as skilled as they say. Such hardened criminals are not to be trifled with."

"Are you thinking we should alert the sheriff and share your suspicions?" said Bill hopefully.

"No, but clearly you're thinking that. I'm afraid I have almost as little faith in Roger le Duc as I have in Simon de Hal."

"He did find the girl."

"He didn't. She appeared in the street."

"Surely it amounts to much the same thing?"

"Not at all." Ela inhaled deeply. She hated that she'd developed such deep mistrust of so many of her fellow men in recent months. "Le Duc putting pressure on the kidnappers—without being seen to do so—almost amounts to him being part of the widespread web of this criminal enterprise, in my opinion."

Bill regarded her in doubtful silence, then rubbed his chin with his hand. "You think the sheriff of London is in their pay?"

"I can't prove it," she replied. "But I don't dare assume he isn't."

"You could go straight to the king," Bill suggested.

"And right into the hands of de Burgh." Ela lifted a brow. "Who would like nothing better than to see me disgraced or disappeared or dead. He might even see this as a wonderful opportunity."

Bill's pained expression tugged at her heart. "I feel like we're locked and bolted behind our castle walls, friendless and under siege from all quarters."

"Except we don't even have the castle walls anymore, thanks to de Burgh. At least I assume de Burgh was behind the king's decision." She walked across the room again. "I feel strangely calm. Is that normal when one is under siege?"

"Your husband was always calm in a crisis." Bill's expression brightened. "He could find humor in the most desperate of situations."

"And he survived enough of them." Ela felt a surge of reassurance, as if William had suddenly appeared in their midst, armed and ready to fight. The thought warmed her, then sadness followed with the realization that it was a momentary illusion. "Though ultimately he didn't live to a great age."

Not many powerful men do. The unspoken words hung in the air between them. If they didn't die in battle they might perish in a tournament or fall victim to a plot, as her husband had.

She'd had painful moments late at night when she wondered how long her sons would be granted to live. No doubt every noblewoman thought the same in the privacy of her chamber. Young noblemen were raised to put honor before all, even their own life.

As they should. And she should lead by example. "Let's leave the king out of it for now. He's young, and although he's been king for years, he's only just now old enough to find his way in the role. I count him as an ally, but I know better than to call on him for every favor I need."

Her ally Spicewell had begged off this battle too. And she had to remember that Bill was injured. Her armies were depleted, and the enemies gathered at her gate.

Suddenly a loud bang on the front door made her jump and Hilda shriek.

CHAPTER 15

*E*la froze. She heard footsteps in the hallway as a servant ran to answer the door.

Bill jumped to his feet. "My sword!" He looked around. A page had taken it away for cleaning.

"Shhh," said Ela. She wanted to listen.

Hilda rose to her feet and screamed at the top of her lungs.

"Hilda, calm yourself." Ela rushed to her.

"Someone's trying to get in." Hilda stared at the door, eyes wide with terror.

"Don't move," said Bill. He dove for the back door, which led to the kitchen passage. "I'll be back with my sword."

Ela wanted to beg him to stay still and not injure himself, but she knew it would do no good. "Hilda, stop screaming. I need to hear what's going on."

She heard a commotion in the hallway with a scuffling of feet and the sound of something heavy being hurled down and hitting both the wall and the wood floor.

A momentary lull followed, and there was a measured knock on the door. "My lady, the guards have returned."

Ela's heart pounded. "Hilda, sit right there in that chair and don't move. Everything will be fine." She didn't want to invite whatever was going on outside into the parlor. Poor Hilda was still battling demons from the murder she'd witnessed. "I'm coming." Ela hurried to the door, turned the handle and peeked out into the hallway.

The porter's lantern illuminated a shocking scene. One of the guards she'd sent after Morhees stood just inside the front door, his blue tunic splashed with blood and his sword unsheathed. He stared down at the floor where his foot sat propped on the slumped body of a man in a black cloak, who was bleeding profusely onto the floor.

Ela felt a small scream rise in her throat, and she mercifully swallowed it. "What happened?" The body on the floor didn't move. "Is he dead?"

"Close to it at any rate," said the lad with a rustic accent and a good deal of swagger. "Came at my cohort with a dagger and I ran him through."

Ela blinked. Was it Vicus Morhees?

The sound of screaming alerted her to Hilda's presence in the parlor doorway.

"Hilda, could you please draw me a bath?" She wanted the girl anywhere but here. Hilda stared at her for a moment as if she—Ela—were demented, then turned and ran toward the kitchen.

"Please show me his face." The guard bent down, grabbed the cloaked shoulder and heaved him over like a sack of turnips.

Ela held her breath as the porter lowered the lantern for her to get a better look. The face was blood-streaked and caked with grime, as if he'd been dragged along the ground, but it was unmistakably Vicus Morhees.

"Where did this happen?"

"Down by the river," said the lad, his voice quaking. The

171

courage and fire of battle were giving way to the realization that he'd just survived a fight—and killed a man.

"Where's your companion?"

"Still there. He's injured. I secured this one"—he glanced down at Morhees—"to my saddle and rode back with him."

Ela examined Morhees for signs of life. Unsurprisingly, there were none. He'd been dragged half a mile or more, apparently by his foot, which still had part of a rope tied around it. If Morhees was dead, he could never lead them to the stolen children.

"Good work," she managed, though she wasn't at all sure that it was. "We must bring back your companion and tend his wounds. God willing, he's still alive."

"I hope I did the right thing securing the attacker."

"I'm sure you did." The young man's bravery had now ebbed, and he looked fearful. "Your valor will be rewarded. This man was a true villain and deserved to be dragged through the streets of London."

She took a moment to thank God that it was Morhees and not some random, black-cloaked stranger.

"We must call the coroner, but more urgently we need to rescue your brave companion."

"I'll go with him." Bill, shining sword unsheathed, appeared in the hallway. "I've called for fresh horses."

"You'll do nothing of the sort," she retorted. Then she realized she'd been rude. "I'm sorry, Bill, but you're too valuable to me to have you test your wounds riding around in the night."

Ela ordered two men to accompany the blood-stained guard to where the incident had happened. She sent another to the White Tower to raise the hue and cry. The sheriff would now be involved whether he wanted to or not.

THE SHERIFF'S men arrived in a commotion of pounding hoofbeats and clanging weapons. Vicus Morhees still lay slumped against the wall inside the front door. No one had ever been deader. At least that meant he was no longer bleeding onto the floor.

Ela greeted the men and looked around for the sheriff.

"Sheriff le Duc is dining away from home, my lady." Their leader had windswept dark hair and flashing eyes. "Word of the incident will be sent to him. My name is Raymond le Forester and I am at your service in his stead, my lady." He suddenly noticed Vicus Morhees's body on the floor behind her, surrounded by rags intended to stop his bodily fluids leaking into the walls and floor. "This is the victim, I take it."

"Victim?" Ela glanced down at the awkwardly sprawled limbs. "No, this man was the attacker. He set upon my guard —" She hesitated a moment before admitting the next part. "Who I'd ordered to follow him."

"Why was your guard following him?"

"I'm sure you're aware of the child who was abducted and then released last month. I'm back in London seeking another child who was taken from Salisbury around the same time. This man—his name is Vicus Morhees—was implicated in two murders that occurred in Salisbury in the spring. He managed to escape conviction because he convinced others to do his dirty work, but it occurred to us that he might have seen an opportunity to abduct the children while he was in Salisbury. Both families are poor and have no influence, and the latest girl is recently orphaned and—"

Raymond le Forester held up his hand. "Begging your pardon, my lady, but this story grows too complex. You say his name is Vitus Moray?"

"Vicus Morhees, I know it's a strange name. It may not be

his real name. He seems a slippery character with his finger in many pies."

"Please describe the incident that led to his death."

Ela realized she had no idea what had happened. "My guard will have to describe it for you."

"And where is he?"

"He set out to retrieve his injured companion." Ela blinked. They should be back by now. A messenger had ridden to the White Tower, waited for these men to mount, then returned with them in the time he'd been gone. "That's a good question. They followed him from the walled garden behind St. Michael and All Angels. He said the incident happened by the docks."

"But why did you ask them to follow him? Did he have the child with him?"

"No, but I was surprised to see him emerge from the place. It seemed an odd coincidence that someone who'd caused me so much trouble in Salisbury should suddenly appear under my nose here in London."

"He caused *you* trouble?" His voice rang with disbelief.

"I have cause to believe that he ordered the murder of my friend Drogo Blount, which took place in the barn on my own manor." Her voice rang louder—with indignation.

"I see."

"And, as I'm sure you also know, I was abducted and held prisoner in a house near here. When I heard the choir at St. Michael's, it reminded me of the sound I heard while captive and I began to wonder if the grand residence behind St. Michaels—which Morhees emerged from—might be the place I was held."

"Ah." His big hand rested on the handle of his sword. "Naturally I need to question your guard for his version of events. I'll send my men out to find them. Which direction did they go?"

Ela tried to give him directions but admitted she had no idea which route they took. They'd been gone far too long. Had someone killed the second guard and lay in wait for the first to return in order to finish him off as well?

And where were the other two men she'd sent?

The metallic stench of blood turned her stomach. She wanted the body of this foul villain removed as soon as possible. "Has the coroner been sent for? We can hardly come and go over this dead body in my doorway."

Le Forester's face betrayed a hint of exasperation. "How did he come to be inside your house?"

"My man dragged him inside. He's young and lacks experience." She was starting to wonder at the young guard's judgment. Dragging a man through the streets of London was hardly a normal practice and would confound the coroner's task in examining the body and exonerating him of wrongdoing. And bringing him inside the house... She hoped he was truly provoked into the killing and didn't do it in a fit of nerves that might be hard to explain in court.

"How are you sure this man is Ficus...What did you say his name was?"

"Vicus Morhees. It's certainly him. I had words with him myself in Salisbury. You can see he has a distinct style of dress, black with silver trim, and rings on several of his fingers." She refrained from observing that Sheriff le Duc had a similar sartorial style. Which was odd, now that she thought about it.

"Who else might positively identify the dead man?"

Ela racked her brain. Who, other than her—and a host of people who were now dead—could confirm his identity? "Sheriff de Hal in Salisbury had words with him, I believe." She might as well have mentioned the man in the moon. She knew de Hal wouldn't ride from Salisbury for something so unprofitable as identifying a corpse. "And I presume that since he emerged from the garden gate behind St. Michael and All Angels, that someone there could identify him as well. Do you know who owns that house?"

An odd expression passed over his face. "I'm sure inquiries can be made. But I still don't understand why you sent your own men to pursue this individual? This sounds like a matter for the sheriff."

Because I don't trust the sheriff. Ela cleared her throat. "Sir William Talbot and I attended Vespers at St. Michael and All Angels, and decided to take the air by walking a long way home. It was an utter surprise to see Morhees emerge from the gate behind it. I was simply curious to see where he would go. And, unfortunately, I don't really know what happened after that."

Le Forester's face had a dark expression. "It would have been better if you had sent for the sheriff."

Who would have ignored me, since no crime had yet been committed. "Indeed. Would you like a cup of wine?"

"No, thank you, my lady. I shall leave two men here to wait for the coroner while we look for your guards. Make sure the body is untouched until then."

MORHEES' blood had dried into the floor by the time the coroner arrived. Theobald Crux was a corpulent man with a thatch of whitish hair. He fussed around the body for a few moments, his young assistant scratching notes on a much reused piece of parchment.

Ela told him everything she knew about Morhees and the incident, which wasn't much. She mentioned that he was implicated as an accomplice of sorts for two murders in Salisbury, but that he had an alibi in Exmouth for both.

"I see. And I daresay you were surprised to see Master Morhees in London."

"Indeed I was. And in connection with a building where I believe I was recently held prisoner against my will."

Now his eyes widened. She explained her abduction and her investigation into the disappearances of the two children.

His expression shifted gradually from surprise to disapproval. "It sounds like you're involving yourself unnecessarily in dangerous affairs, my lady. Surely this is work for the sheriff's men."

"The sheriff's men are busy with a long list of crimes that expands every day. Where are they? My two guards should have returned a long time ago."

"Indeed. I need to question the one who killed Morhees. Until I do, I have no evidence that this wasn't an unprovoked attack on Master Morhees."

Ela wondered if—as the guard's employer—she might find herself liable for his actions if he was convicted of an unlawful killing. Morhees's family might even sue her for damages. While she didn't have any tears to shed over the death of Vicus Morhees, she hoped the young man had a good explanation for it.

THE GUARDS DID NOT RETURN.

The sheriff rode up late at night with his men. He dismounted and was invited into the house, where Ela met him in the parlor. She could smell drink on his breath. Bill Talbot joined them.

"My men have found no trace of your guards."

"What?" Ela had assumed by this point that they had been taken to the Tower for questioning. "You didn't find them down by the docks?"

"We didn't find anyone down by the docks that wasn't engaged in their usual business."

"There must have been bloodstains leading the way to the place where the fight occurred."

"Because your man dragged his victim back here by horseback."

"Well, yes." Her guard appeared in a less favorable light each time he was mentioned.

"Did he have orders to do so?"

"Indeed not! He had orders only to follow him and see where he went."

"For what purpose?"

"I suspect him of being involved in the abduction of young children, including little Elsie Brice of Salisbury. I hoped he might unwittingly lead us to where the children are being held."

"So you were conducting a sort of…investigation?" His eyes narrowed.

Ela stiffened. "In a way. I thought he might be involved in my abduction last time I was in London. To my knowledge you still have no suspects. On reflection, Morhees might be the masked man who warned me away from looking into the child abductions. I felt at the time that he seemed familiar, but I couldn't place him."

"Are you sure you didn't order your guard to kill him?" The sheriff asked the question in a matter-of-fact way—with a half smile, even—that made it easy for her to say yes.

"Most certainly not. I would never seek to pervert the course of justice to my own aims."

"Except by conducting your own investigations into missing persons."

"That's hardly the same thing as commanding an execution," she said darkly. "I think you should interview the inhabitants of the house behind St. Michael and All Angels and ask them what Vicus Morhees was doing there."

The sheriff's brows lowered. "That house is the residence of Abbot Abelard de Rouen. I hardly think he'd have any business with low criminals."

"Then other members of his household did. I saw Morhees emerge from the garden with my own eyes." She glanced at Bill. "And so did Sir William."

Sheriff le Duc looked at Bill. "And you recognized him?"

Bill looked distressed. "Well, I'd never seen him before but—"

"You took your mistress's word about his identity, naturally."

"Indeed I did," said Bill. "Countess Ela has a keen eye and an excellent memory." Ela wished she could enjoy his vigorous defense of her finer qualities. Instead she felt oddly patronized.

"You must question the members of Abbot de Rouen's household," she said, barely keeping her anger contained. Why did she feel like she was under investigation instead of Morhees?

Le Duc hesitated and looked behind her to the tapestried wall. "I shall call upon them tomorrow when it's light."

Frustration surged inside her. "You don't consider this an urgent matter?"

"Not for Master Morhees. He's dead."

"What about my two young guards? Where can they be?"

He cleared his throat and looked around the room. "Probably out drinking. You know how young men can be after their first taste of blood."

Ela found herself lost for words. "They're in my employ. They'd hardly take off drinking without asking permission. Besides, one of them was injured in the exchange and the other returned to retrieve him."

"I'm sure they'll turn up." Le Duc swept into a sudden bow. "I have urgent business to attend to. I'll call on you tomorrow. In the meantime, please refrain from interfering in matters that are better left to the men entrusted with those duties."

~

EARLY THE NEXT MORNING, the household was stirring when one of the sheriff's men arrived with news that the two guards had been found dead.

"Washed up in the shallows at low tide," explained the sheriff's man gruffly. "Bound and gagged, they were."

Ela felt a wave of nausea. "Has the coroner attended them?"

"Yes. The bodies are at the Tower, and he's there right now."

Ela saw no point in rushing to the Tower and further irritating the sheriff. Her presence would hardly bring them back to life. She'd have to inform their families of their death, and that weighed heavily on her heart. Both of them were young men from the countryside near Salisbury who'd trained in the king's garrison. Although they had indeed died in a battle of sorts, their families would hardly feel them to be covered with glory by these events.

"Has the sheriff visited Abbot de Rouen's house yet?"

"I don't know, my lady." The young man's wide face was impassive as a stone block.

"Do you have any suspects in the killing of my guards? Naturally, I take this matter very seriously and intend to pursue their murderers to the fullest extent of the law."

"I don't know, my lady."

"Well, who does know?" Ela pulled a shawl around her

against the morning chill. "Surely there's an investigation underway?"

"Yes, my lady."

"Must I ride to the sheriff to ask him myself?"

"He sent me here to inform you of the deaths, my lady."

"I thank you for that," she said with as little irritation as she could manage. "I shall seek out the sheriff myself."

"I, er, I believe he's—"

"Busy with more important matters?"

"Well, not more important but…" He turned and glanced over his shoulder at two fellows behind him. They shifted awkwardly in their saddles.

"Fine." Ela crossed her arms. "Never mind. Tell the sheriff I shall take matters into my own hands."

If that didn't get his attention, nothing would.

CHAPTER 16

"What is he going to do? Kill me?" Ela marched around the parlor.

"These people are ruthless," said Bill. He absolutely hated her idea of calling on Abbot de Rouen. "There's no telling what they'll do."

"But Abelard de Rouen is a man of God."

"He might not even be in residence right now. He might have manors all over the south of England. There could be someone usurping his house for a criminal enterprise."

"An abbot's residence is certainly a good place to hide. All the more reason we need to dig deeper."

"But the sheriff…" Bill tailed off.

"The sheriff is not going to go knock on Abbot de Rouen's door any more than he would go ask the king if he was involved in child smuggling. A religious house is the perfect cover for iniquity because it's considered to be above reproach." The more she thought about it, the more she grew convinced that Abbot de Rouen's grand residence was her black-and-white-floored prison. "I shall knock on the door and introduce myself as their neighbor. They'll have to invite me in or risk affront."

Bill tried—unsuccessfully—to hide his exasperation. "If these men are as bloodthirsty as they seem I hardly think they'll care about seeming impolite."

"You'd be surprised." Ela adjusted her barbette, which was tight enough to give her a headache. "Having something to hide makes people awfully circumspect. And I'll leave my guards outside to wait for me. They can hardly make me disappear if my entire household knows where I am and eagerly awaits my return."

"I'll come in with you," he said with a tilt of his chin.

"Good." She smiled. She could tell he was hoping she'd protest but in truth she did want him there. He was a moderating influence on her that she suspected she'd need if she came face-to-face with the man behind the child abductions. "And while we're there be sure to pay attention to every detail of the household and its occupants."

HILDA DRESSED Ela in finery fit for a royal visit. A long robe of blue so deep it was almost purple, trimmed with braided silver and gold thread and tiny silver leaves. She wore her rescued rings and would have worn her mother's heavy gold belt again if her mother hadn't spirited it safely back to her country retreat.

Her veil shone like new snow, and her fillet was starched so stiff it might have been chiseled from white marble.

"You look so beautiful," said Hilda, admiring their work.

"I'm not trying to look beautiful," said Ela. "I'm trying to look important."

"You look rich, too. If a woman is beautiful and rich, then she's powerful," said Hilda, still looking pleased.

Ela found this idea disconcerting. Poor Hilda's beauty had brought her nothing but suffering so far. But if she'd been an earl's daughter she'd likely have made an advantageous marriage already. "I hadn't thought of it that way." Still, she didn't want Hilda's head being turned by visions of herself as a glamorous lady of the manor. "Beauty and riches can be gone in an instant. Piety and a sense of duty give a woman her strength."

"Oh, I agree." Hilda rested her hand on her growing belly. "I've been praying every morning and night for the health of my baby. And I've been eating as well as I can so he'll be big and strong."

"I'm glad to hear that." Thankfully Hilda's nausea had lessened, though she was still a picky eater. "Though don't forget you might well have a daughter."

"Will I still inherit Fernlees if I have a daughter?"

"I believe so. Spicewell didn't make a distinction as to the sex of the baby."

"I shan't let myself get puffed up thinking about the possibilities," said Hilda with an expression that managed to be both gay and deadly serious at the same time. "My duty is to serve you. And if your current appearance is anything to go by, I'm doing an excellent job."

Hilda's smile cheered her. "I appreciate your efforts on my behalf, Hilda." Oh, dear Lord, she did hope this girl's prospects developed as they intended. With her natural ebullience and loquacity, Hilda didn't have the humility and self-effacing nature required of a good servant. "Now I shall go see if they have the intended effect on my neighbor."

ELA DID NOT BRING Hilda to the abbot's house. If Hilda knew her mistress might be walking into a den of kidnappers, she would have prostrated herself on the floor in a fit of weeping. While it might have been useful to send Hilda below stairs at the abbot's house for refreshments—and to ask probing questions—her present condition was too delicate for any further shocks.

Ela took Bill and four guards with her. She sorely regretted the loss of the two men who'd been killed yesterday and she warned them to be on their guard at all times. She chose two to come inside. She also told Bill that he was not to exert himself physically in any way, no matter what happened.

She knew her warning would prove futile if the need arose to defend her, but she was fairly confident that it wouldn't. Everyone in the household knew exactly where she was headed and had instructions to immediately inform both the sheriff and the king if they failed to emerge within a reasonable amount of time.

Since the house was so close, Ela and Bill walked. Two of the guards came on horseback, in case a pursuit of any kind should be required. They would remain outside, paying close attention to anyone who entered and exited the abbot's house and grounds.

Ela found herself strangely calm as they approached the door. Dark oak, carved with a pattern of chevrons and studded with heavy iron nails, it looked as defensive in nature as the cut stone of the house and its high garden wall. A small brass bell hung next to the door and she watched while a guard rang it. She waited, holding her breath, as the chime resounded off the stone walls.

Just when she began to wonder if anyone would ever come, the door opened slowly, revealing a floor made from big slabs of the same gray cut stone as the walls.

Ela's heart sank slightly. "Good morning, brother," she said to the monk who answered, a short man with beady dark eyes. His remaining hair bristled out sideways beneath his tonsure like a dark halo. "I am Ela, Countess of Salisbury, and I wish to make the acquaintance of my esteemed neighbor." She forced a smile to her lips.

The monk stared at her. Surely it wasn't so unusual for neighbors to introduce themselves in London? Perhaps it was odd for a countess to make the rounds, but this was a grand house and no doubt they'd be even more shocked if the fishmonger's wife paid a social call.

"I find myself at a disadvantage, brother." She managed after an awkward silence. "You know my name, but I don't know yours." She didn't want to make the mistake of assuming this was a mere novice when in fact it might be Abbot de Rouen himself dressed to display piety and humility.

"Brother Sebastian at your service, my lady," he muttered. "The abbot is not here."

"May I wait for him?"

"It will be a long wait. He's in Rome."

Interesting. "Then who is in residence here in his absence?"

"No one of consequence." His beady eyes narrowed. "We all eagerly await his return."

"You are here." She tried to curb her irritation. She needed to be invited in so she could look at the floors, but that wouldn't happen if she pushed too hard or asked about Vicus Morhees. "I'm sure the abbot would be pleased to have you make the acquaintance of his neighbors in his absence." She smiled mildly.

"I'm afraid we have to prepare for Nones." He fidgeted with the wooden crucifix at his waist. "You must excuse me."

Panic flared in her chest. If he closed that door—and if the sheriff refused to investigate here—she'd never find out if this was the place she'd been held. "I'd like to make a donation to your beautiful church. Sir William Talbot and I attended services at St. Michael and All Angels yesterday, and we intend to visit regularly."

Brother Sebastian hesitated. He clearly wanted to close the door firmly in her face, but no doubt he knew someone as richly dressed as she could make a substantial contribution to their coffers. If word came out that he'd refused it he might be in trouble.

She took a step forward, placing a foot over the threshold. "Perhaps we could discuss how I might support the abbot's good works?" Her syrupy smile did nothing to lessen the grimly reluctant expression on his face.

He hesitated. "You really must speak to the abbot."

"But I shan't be in London for long," she said with mock regret. "Just another day or so and then I'll have missed my chance. Who is the priest conducting services in the abbot's absence?"

The prospect of her disappearing in the near future seemed to soften him. "That would be Father Dominic. Perhaps he could discuss the arrangements. I'll see if he's available."

Ela stepped in through the door before he could exclude her. Bill followed close behind her. Brother Sebastian muttered something in rapid English to a servant who then scurried away down a dark passage.

Ela studied the floors. More bare gray stone. The interior of the house did not match the grandeur of the exterior. With rough plastered walls and low timbered doorways, it seemed much older than the elaborate church building behind it. Or this could be the oldest wing of a very large residence.

They turned a corner and Brother Sebastian opened a door. The doorway was so low that she had to stoop so as not to catch her fillet on the door frame. Once she went through the door, however, she found herself in a wide, bright room with high ceilings, of quite different construction than the low stone passages they'd just walked through.

And with a floor of patterned black and white stone.

A surge of excitement warred with an equal twinge of terror. *This is the house.* A different room, though. This one had a row of diamond-paned windows and fine wood paneling but no exotic objects or extravagant tapestries. A large silver cross, with gems at each corner, was the only decor in the room apart from a heavy, plain wooden table and three sturdy chairs.

"Wait here, my lady," said Brother Sebastian.

As soon as he left the room, Ela turned to Bill and whispered, "Don't eat or drink anything."

His eyes widened. "This is the place?"

"We're probably being watched," she whispered. They could save discussion for later. She strained her ears and didn't hear any singing. But her suspicions were confirmed when the door opened and the young boy with dark skin entered carrying a jug of wine. Behind him came a taller, fair boy carrying two cups.

When the first boy saw her, his shock almost made him drop the jug. But he got hold of himself and placed the jug on the table. Without glancing at her again, he hurried out of the room.

So whoever sent this same boy to serve her had no idea she'd seen him during her sojourn here. This household did seem large enough that the west wing might not know what the east wing was doing.

The fair one, a boy of about ten, poured the cups of wine and hurried away, leaving the door open. Ela and Bill left the cups sitting on the table.

After a short while, the tall priest who'd led the Vespers service the previous evening entered. "What an unexpected pleasure, my lady." He spoke in courtly French and bowed low. Ela felt oddly reassured by this fawning greeting. She was more accustomed to toadying than to Brother Sebastian's prickly reception. "I am father Dominic de Poitieu, the present shepherd of our blessed church in the absence of our beloved abbot, who is visiting our father, the pope, in Rome. We humbly welcome you." His delight seemed quite genuine.

Which, upon reflection, was unsettling.

"Some wine?" He gestured to the cups.

"Thank you. We simply wished to make the acquaintance of the guardians of this church so we might offer our support for your good works and for the maintenance of the blessed church." A wild idea unfurled in her brain. "Could you give us a tour of the church that we might enjoy its features—its tombs and statuary—and learn of its needs? It is of most beautiful construction and quite new, I suppose."

"It was completed in the second year of our king's reign, so it is quite new by ecclesiastical standards. Fortunately for that reason it's in excellent repair, but it has few tombs to speak of."

"There was an interesting statue in a side chapel I visited to light a candle for the immortal soul of my late husband. I couldn't tell which saint it was."

"Perhaps St. Ebrulf. A small church in his name stood here before they built this one."

"How fascinating. I've never heard of St. Ebrulf. Does the church contain his relics?"

"Some relics are in the catacomb beneath the building. They're too delicate to be on display."

Catacomb? An underground crypt where one might perhaps hide something...like stolen children.

"I'd be most honored if you'd show me the relics of St. Ebrulf. I could offer a donation of five pounds for the upkeep of the church."

His eyes widened. Five pounds was a tidy sum of money under any circumstance, and she knew it would be hard for him to say no with such an incentive dangling under his nose.

She rearranged the purse at her belt, making sure to clink the coins together.

Father Dominic seemed to wrestle with the situation for a moment. Which only deepened her suspicions that he had something to hide. "We don't typically offer such visits. The saint's bones are very delicate, after all."

"But I daresay few visitors offer five pounds for the privilege. As I said, I'm your neighbor and I'll soon be gone back to the countryside. I'd consider myself graced by God—and St. Michael and all his angels—if you were to take us into the saint's presence." Ela smiled enthusiastically.

"I suppose..." Father Dominic shifted awkwardly from foot to foot. "I could show you the relics. If you were to deposit the offerings in our coffers first."

Did he really think they'd try to cheat him? She pulled gold coins minted in Constantinople from her purse and gave them to Father Dominic, who tucked them somewhere into the folds of his robe.

"Your guards will have to wait outside."

Ela hesitated. Fear pricked her spine. But could he really kill her while four of her guards waited outside? "All right."

The guards were led back to the front door. Ela felt oddly naked without them. But Father Dominic was a priest. A man of God. Hopefully that meant something.

Father Dominic picked up a candle in a wooden stand and walked to the door. Ela shot a glance at Bill. She knew this house was the place she'd been held, since the African boy was here. And Father Dominic must not know that she'd been brought here, or he'd never take the chance of leading her through the house.

Which meant Father Dominic wasn't part of the conspiracy.

He led them down a hallway with a crisp pattern of black and white stone, then into another. Up a flight of wood stairs and along a narrow wooden passage—almost like a covered bridge—that led to an adjacent building. Then down a steep, spiral flight of stone steps into a dark passage that smelled of damp.

What if he's leading us down into the catacombs with a plan to seal us in there until our bones are as fleshless and brittle as St. Ebrulf's?

These people had shown no hesitation in attacking two of her guards and killing two others. Had she made a terrible mistake coming here? *It's too late to turn back.* "Have you lived here long, Father Dominic?"

"Only since St. Swithin's Day."

Just over three months. Was that a long time, or a short one?

"Which order is this church associated with?"

"The Blackfriars. Come this way."

They stepped through a round arch supported by two stone pillars and into a damp-smelling space too dark for her to see her own hand. Father Dominic used the candle he carried to light candles in two sconces on the wall. The smell of the tallow candles turned her stomach, but they illuminated the cut stones of the ancient walls. "Is this the catacomb?"

"It is. It's much older than the church. There are graves down here from the time of St. Swithin himself. They were left undisturbed when the new church was built." He led them over to a long, narrow wooden box. The lid was painted with a cross and two doves, but the paint had flaked and peeled in the damp atmosphere. "This box contains relics of the saint's body."

Ela thought for a horrible moment that he might open it up and expose the moldered body of St. Ebrulf. She braced herself for the sight of a shriveled, blackened skeleton, or even a corpse half eaten by rats.

But he rested his hand on the lid. "The lid is nailed shut to protect the relics. You may pray here if you like."

Ela heaved a silent sigh of relief, closed her eyes and lifted her hands in prayer. *Dear St. Ebrulf, please guide us in our search for these precious children and deliver them from the hands of these vile men who deprive them of their families and their futures.* She hoped Ebrulf was a real saint and not one made up by Father Dominic for convenience.

She doubted this box contained his entire body. Relics of a true saint ended up spread far and wide. They probably kept no more than a knuckle bone or a lock of hair down in this damp cellar. If even that.

She ended her prayer since she was clearly not in the right frame of mind to commune with a saint. The foul and oppressive atmosphere reminded her of the castle dungeon, but thank goodness no living people were chained to the walls.

"Is there access to the church from here?" She had a violent desire to leave this lightless vault.

"Come this way." He led them across the room. There were a few more ancient-looking tombs and some boxes and barrels piled in the corners and along the walls. "This staircase leads up into the sacristy."

Ela climbed the second spiral stone stair gratefully. Light from the windows above gave her courage to ask the question that had burned in her mind the whole time. "What business does Vicus Morhees have here in this place?"

CHAPTER 17

*E*la could swear she saw a hitch in Father Dominic's step. "Who?"

"Vicus Morhees. A tall man with curly dark hair. Wears a black cloak."

"Never heard of him." He reached the top of the stairs and stepped into the sacristy.

Ela and Bill hurried behind him. Two windows high in the walls lit the small chamber where the priest prepared for services. A large Bible on a wooden stand lay open to one of the gospels, and an embroidered vestment hung nearby. "We saw Vicus Morhees leave the garden of this house yesterday evening. My guards followed him toward the river." *And killed him.*

Did Father Dominic know that already? Or did he know nothing of the whole sordid business proceeding under his nose?

"This illustrated gospel was donated to the church by Bishop de Burgh himself," said the priest brightly, as if her question simply didn't interest him. "As you can see, the illuminations are quite extraordinary."

The illustrations were indeed vivid and detailed and the work of a master. Did it matter that Bishop Geoffrey de Burgh was her sworn enemy's brother? "What a blessing for the church to possess such a beautiful book." She would have loved to spend some time admiring it. But that was not why she'd come here or why she'd parted with five pounds. "I've seen Vicus Morhees here before, too." *When he warned me to leave London or die.*

"I've never heard of such a person." Father Dominic's face now had a taut quality, a blue vein rising in the pale skin of his forehead.

"I wonder if he uses another name?" Ela persisted. "The man in the black cloak?"

"Many men wear black cloaks. Our Dominican brothers, for example. I have one myself." He headed toward a tall door that must lead into the church. She knew they wouldn't be able to talk about such matters in the sacred space.

Ela could feel Bill tensing. She was sure his hand already rested on the hilt of his sword. But she wasn't about to leave here without probing deeper into the matter of the children. "Where did that brown-skinned boy come from?"

"I don't know. As I've said, I haven't been here long."

"He looks African."

"He may well be."

"Is he a servant here in the house?"

"He is." He turned a key in the door. "The abbot takes a special interest in unfortunate children—orphans and those who've been abandoned by their parents." Then he stepped through into the church.

Ela turned and stared at Bill. Could Abbot Abelard de Rouen himself be the keystone of this child slavery ring? The thought chilled her. She wanted to dismiss it. She knew men of God were prey to the same temptations as ordinary men, but she'd never heard of one involved with an underground criminal network.

There had to be some other explanation.

Father Dominic walked into the church, turned toward the altar and genuflected. Ela followed suit, crossing herself and asking forgiveness from the Blessed Virgin for any impious thoughts she brought to this holy place.

Father Dominic gave them a quick tour of the four side chapels and waited while Ela lit a candle for her husband and one for her late father. He then walked them to the door, blessed them dismissively and all but shoved them out into the bright afternoon sunlight.

AFTER THE DOOR closed behind them Ela took a bracing gulp of smoky London air. She felt oddly deflated, which didn't make sense, since they'd achieved their main objective in entering the abbot's house.

"This is definitely the place where they held me," she whispered, as they walked along the wall back to where their guards were still—hopefully—waiting. Two of the men had wisely stationed themselves at the corner of the wall, watching the church entrance, and they strode toward Ela and Bill. Ela signaled for them to fetch their fellows and return to her mother's house.

"The same dark-skinned boy sat with me in the room where I was held prisoner. He was finely dressed, like a little prince, that time." Just now he'd worn a plain wool tunic, more typical clothing for a young servant.

"Why would they let you see him?" Bill looked astonished.

"I suspect the people there today didn't know that I'd been there before. I don't think Father Dominic would have led me through the house if he thought I'd recognize it."

"And did you?"

"Not the exact rooms, but the floors were similar tile and it had the same grand construction. But the boy was unmistakable. The masked man, who I'm now sure was Morhees, bragged about him being from Africa."

"Very odd." Bill scratched his chin. "It occurs to me that perhaps they wanted you to know it was the same place."

"But why?"

"To frighten you."

"Do I look frightened?" She lifted a brow. She'd certainly felt a twinge or two as they'd walked through the bowels of the house, across the raised passage, and down into the dark catacomb, but now she felt like she'd got away with something. "If they wanted to frighten me I think they'd have tried a little harder. Last time they dumped me alone in the countryside in the middle of the night. That was a much better effort."

Bill laughed. Then winced.

"Don't laugh. It tugs at your wounds."

ELA WAS SITTING down to an early supper when the porter announced the sheriff. "Send him in."

She didn't rise when he entered but gestured to an empty chair at the table with her and Bill Talbot. "Sheriff le Duc, what a pleasant surprise. Please join us for a dish of eels in a sweet wine sauce." She wanted him to think that she didn't need his help.

He hesitated. She'd been sure he'd say no, anxious to be gone as fast as possible, but to her surprise he accepted. Hilda took his cloak and sword and brought him a bowl of water to wash his hands.

To Ela's surprise, le Duc shared engaging and interesting

details of two cases he'd dealt with that day. He didn't seem at all intimidated by her high rank and made surprisingly frank conversation. He had good manners and, relaxed and loquacious, looked quite handsome.

"More wine, sheriff?" She poured it herself, keen to loosen his lips. "I can hardly believe how you have time to sleep with all the crime that takes place in London."

"It's a question of priorities," he admitted. "If there's a killer to be caught, we must catch him first. That's where we focus our efforts."

She could restrain herself no longer. "Have you caught the men that killed my two guards?"

"Indeed we have." He took a swig of wine. "They're imprisoned at the Tower."

Ela gaped for a moment. "Who are they?"

"Two low criminals who've crossed our path before. They'd been tried and punished for stealing, and one of them lost three fingers for it. Apparently the punishment did not serve as an adequate deterrent. Now they'll hang for certain." He beamed with satisfaction.

"D'you think they were killers for hire?"

"Undoubtedly. One of the wretches admitted that he'd been offered two pounds to make sure the guards were dead."

Ela's eel curdled in her stomach. She could see where this was going. "Who hired them?"

"They didn't know." *Of course they didn't.* One of le Duc's eyebrows rose slightly higher than the other. "They said that Morhees came up to them and offered them coin to kill the men who returned with him."

Ela blinked. "He told them he planned to return with my guards? How could he possibly know that they'd follow him?" This made no sense. "And why did they let my guard kill Morhees?"

197

"The hired men didn't arrive in time. They both worked as door guards for a nearby warehouse and were in the vicinity but had just spotted Morhees returning when he was killed."

This was all far too convenient to be believable. Still, her interest was pricked. "Which warehouse?"

"How do I know? They all look the same." He took a big bite of eel and roasted carrots. "What matters is that we caught the killers and they'll hang for their crimes."

Ela felt ill. If these men were the ones who'd killed her guards—and she wasn't even half sure that they were—they were scapegoats doing the dirty work of the man who'd ordered the murders—and who was stealing and selling innocent children.

The true killer was the one who'd paid them.

And since that was Vicus Morhees—now conveniently dead, too—that left no trail to follow.

Except that she'd already discovered where the trail led… if she could convince the sheriff to follow it.

"Vicus Morhees emerged from the house of Abbot Abelard de Rouen before my men started to follow him. Today Bill and I went to pay a call on the abbot."

Le Duc looked alarmed. "He's away in Rome," he said quickly. "For an audience with His Eminence the Pope."

"I'm aware of that. We convinced Father Dominic to give us a tour of the church, and as he led us through the house I could see it was the same building where I was held prisoner." She hesitated a minute to let that sink in. "I recognized a small servant boy who served us wine."

"You must be mistaken."

"I most certainly am not. The young boy had the dark skin of an African. How many young boys fitting that description are in London right now?"

"Quite a few, I'd imagine, given the sea trade."

"I'm absolutely certain it was the same boy. And the same black and white stone tile on the floor. And I'm increasingly certain that the masked man who threatened me, and who ordered me dumped out in the countryside, was none other than Vicus Morhees."

"Who, God be praised, is now dead." A smile spread across le Duc's mouth. It didn't reach his eyes.

"They took me prisoner so I'd be frightened away from investigating the ring of child thefts. I can now see that Morhees was part of that ring. It must be connected somehow to the opium trade that brought him into Salisbury. But he's just one soldier in a dark army of evil men." An idea occurred to her. "He may have been sacrificed on purpose to throw us off the scent."

"He can't have known he was about to die when he ordered someone to kill your men."

"No indeed. But my guard who killed him said that Morhees assaulted his companion with a dagger, so my guard ran him through." Ela tilted her head, trying to make sense of it. "If Morhees had been told to initiate the conflict, then perhaps the other two killers were instructed—he thought—to rush forward and help him. Perhaps they'd really been ordered to hang back until Morhees was dead and then kill the guards."

Le Duc looked amused and perplexed at the same time.

Ela bristled. "I'm glad you find this entertaining. Two of my loyal men are dead for simply following my instructions and defending themselves under attack. It's all too neat and tidy that their killers are just men for hire employed by a man who's now dead. I want to know who is the mastermind behind this evil enterprise."

"Unfortunately the hired killers don't know any better than we do. Whoever ordered the deaths managed to stay well behind the battle lines."

"It can't be Abbot de Rouen, since he's overseas."

Le Duc burst out in laughter. "I hardly think an abbot in God's church would involve himself in such nefarious matters."

"Indeed not." Ela was relieved about this. "But events related to it are taking place under his roof in his absence."

"You suspect this Father Dominic?"

"Oddly enough, no. If he knew I'd been kept there I don't think he'd have led me through the house. It's too distinctive. And he certainly wouldn't have shown me the African boy who sat in my room with me." A thought occurred to her. "He did claim that he had no idea who Vicus Morhees was, though. I can't believe that's true. Morhees was obviously familiar with the house and had been there on more than one occasion. So either Father Dominic was lying about that, or Morhees was using a different name."

"Let me guess, you'd like me to search the house."

Ela hesitated. "I'm not sure that would produce results. The house is large and sprawling enough that someone could escape through the church or out a side door." Flushing the inhabitants out like grouse didn't seem sensible. Any guilty parties would just come out protesting their innocence and they'd be none the wiser. "It occurs to me that a more subtle method of investigation might be more effective."

Le Duc accepted another cup of wine. "What did you have in mind?"

"Could we insert someone into the household—as a servant, perhaps—so they could wait and watch until the criminals reveal themselves?"

"Difficult to do." Le Duc swigged his wine. "The staff will be mostly monastic brothers."

"Or young children. In addition to the African boy we were served by a blond boy of about ten."

He looked exasperated. "You expect me to send a young child in as a spy?"

"Well, no. Of course not." Ela needed time to think. "What do you suggest?"

Le Duc sighed heavily. "I can station some men to watch the house."

"But what will that tell us? They'll be wary now. And we have no proof that they were bringing the children there. I suspect the children—if they're even still in London—are down by the docks."

"But, as you just suggested, if Morhees went there as a decoy, he may not have been going to anywhere in particular at all. My men have kept an eye on the building you originally told us about, near Westcheap. There's been no activity there." He took another bite of eel. "This sauce is delicious."

Ela's eel now sat like lead in her stomach. "Elsie Brice is in terrible danger. She's an orphan. Her mother was hanged after the last assizes for killing her father."

"How are you so sure she's in London? Or that these same people took her?"

Ela swallowed. "I'm certain she was taken by the same people who took Edyth Wheaton from Salisbury. This girl was taken before Edyth."

"Why did you not mention her when you were here last?"

"I didn't know about Elsie, then. She wasn't reported missing until some days, or perhaps even weeks, after she disappeared."

He frowned. "Why not?"

"She's an orphan who went to live with her aunt and uncle. They already have many children and no money." She hesitated to say it. "They may not have been too downcast about one mouth being absent from the table."

"Might they have sold her?" He said it through a mouthful of candied carrots.

"What? No! Who would do that?"

"You'd be surprised. Was it the uncle and aunt who reported her missing?"

Ela racked her brain for what Giles Haughton had told her. "I think the coroner said it was one of her siblings. I never spoke to the parents. They were away at market buying a cow when I arrived."

"If they were so poor, where did they find the money to buy a cow?" Sheriff le Duc lifted a brow.

Ela blinked. If it wasn't for sitting at her husband's side in his role as sheriff all these years, she'd never have believed ordinary people capable of a tenth of the shocking things they did. And the children said they'd recently bought a sack of flour. So the family had money, where before they'd had none.

Perhaps, for some people, selling a child—one of too many—was no different from someone else selling a sheep or pig they'd hand-reared from birth. An involuntary shudder rose through her. No. She couldn't imagine that. It seemed far more likely that the girl was stolen.

"Can you have men watch the entire compound, including the church and the abbot's residence and any other structures within the walls? Then we can at least get an idea of who's coming and going. They can't hide in there forever. And perhaps your men could disguise themselves—as a beggar or a knife grinder or similar—to evade notice."

Le Duc nodded. "I can do that."

"And you'll send word of what you see?" Ela had no intention of leaving it entirely up to le Duc, but she didn't want him to know that.

"Of course."

"This band of child thieves is not only responsible for ruining the lives of innocent children, but they have the blood of several men on their hands. They clearly think nothing of slaying anyone who stands in their way. And using the house of a man of God as a cover for their crimes makes their behavior that much more heinous."

"I couldn't agree more, my lady. I look forward to seeing them all twisting at the end of a rope."

That prospect didn't interfere with Roger le Duc's digestion in the slightest. He stayed for a plate of rich date sweetmeats and several more cups of wine. He talked much of the peace and prosperity of the city under King Henry III. Ela got the impression that le Duc counted anyone and everyone of importance in the city of London as a friend and that he probably had a finger in every pie worth tasting between St. Giles and the White Tower.

FOR THE NEXT FEW DAYS, Ela and Bill attended nearly every Mass at St. Michael and All Angels. Father Dominic's expression was amusing—and interesting—to watch as he witnessed their repeat appearances in his congregation at Prime, Tierce, Sext, Nones, Vespers and Compline.

Ela took the opportunity to study the monks in attendance, carrying the great candles, preparing the host and waving smoking censers up and down the nave. She watched the choir boys and observed the other patrons, who were all wealthy-looking residents—widows mostly—of this leafy and prosperous district.

On their way to and from the church, she and Bill walked slowly around the entire perimeter of the church and its close, making a mental note of the buildings. In addition to the abbot's grand house there were two smaller houses with their own entrances within the walls. Monks came and went on errands to the market—Ela sent various of her mother's watchful servants hurrying after them at a distance—and returned with loaves of bread and baskets of vegetables. Their eggs and any meat they ate must come from within the walls. Or perhaps they ate Lenten fare all year long.

There did not appear to be any women in the entire compound. At least none that she saw come and go. The abbot's cook must be a man and his housekeepers, too. But that was hardly unusual in a monastic community.

The choirboys never left the walls around the compound.

Ela grew impatient with watching the routine comings and goings of the monastic occupants. The sheriff's men reported findings that exactly matched with her own, and it became clear they were losing interest in the pursuit.

Until one very early morning on the way to Prime—in the dark hour before dawn—she saw something that made her blood seize in her veins.

CHAPTER 18

 la walked along the dark street, taking her usual route, circling around the houses that ringed St. Michael and All Angels, when she saw a dark-robed monk emerge from a building *across the street* from the abbot's house.

It wasn't directly across the street, but about thirty feet down and set back from the road behind a gate. He slipped out through the gate and closed it behind him. He didn't see her and her sole attendant in the predawn darkness, and hurried away in the same direction they were walking.

Ela hadn't paid must attention to the buildings on the other side of the street before. She could barely make them out in the darkness, but from her recollection they were fairly ordinary houses—newish, largish—that she'd assumed were the residences of successful merchants.

"Follow that man at a distance," she whispered to her attendant. He looked startled but obeyed. She, naturally was going with him. Partly because it wasn't safe for her to walk the streets alone in the dark and partly because she burned with curiosity to know this monk's identity and destination.

His cowl covered his head and obscured his face completely. His short, squat stature, however, strongly suggested that this was brother Sebastian, who'd greeted her at the door of the abbot's house. Thus it was even odder that he'd emerged from an apparently unconnected building on the other side of the road.

Ela pulled her hood over her head to cover her bright white fillet and veil. She wanted to disappear into the darkness and follow him like an invisible presence.

Her attendant was armed—of course—and she whispered to him to make sure his sword didn't clank and betray them. The monk hurried onward, dark robe swishing about his ankles, a sense of urgency to his steps.

Ela glanced behind them to see if anyone had watched them depart their course and saw no one. Not even a sleeping beggar who might be one of Sheriff le Duc's guards.

Her heart beat faster as the monk took a turn toward the river.

"Put up your hood," she whispered to her young guard. His smooth pale skin and shock of blonde hair shone like a beacon in the thin light from the moon which still hovered above the rooftops. "We need to follow him closer." She knew that the streets became more cramped and winding as they approached the busy neighborhood of the docks, and she didn't want to lose their quarry down a sudden alley.

Where was Brother Sebastian hurrying to before dawn? Shouldn't he be in the church preparing for Prime services along with the other monks?

If Sebastian was involved in the child-stealing ring he shouldn't have let her into the house. The temptation of a large donation must have been too much to resist. But why? If it was a donation to the church it would hardly line his personal coffers.

The monk took a hard right just in front of them. Ela

quickened her steps. She grew breathless, unaccustomed to this much activity so early in the morning. Her young attendant strode like a colt itching to break into a gallop but working hard to contain himself.

They turned the corner to see the monk still walking briskly, the hem of his robe lifted with one hand as he made his way over the uneven, rutted stones of these ancient roads.

Another turn led them onto Thames Street, where other Londoners stirred, unlocking their warehouses and shops and readying their horses and donkeys to make early deliveries.

"Stay with him," Ela commanded. She didn't want to lose Brother Sebastian, if indeed it was him. She let her long-legged guard lope ahead and follow the monk down one more alley toward the water.

I hope they don't kill him. The horrible thought charged her as the bold young man disappeared from view. These criminals were beyond ruthless. Maybe this was a trap of the kind that had lured her guards into killing Vicus Morhees? She reached into her robes and tugged her knife free of its sheath as she took the final turn.

The sun was still buried behind the great Tower to the east, but the dark water of the Thames shimmered in the moonlight at the end of the alley. Tall, windowless warehouses rose on either side.

And she didn't see Brother Sebastian or her young guard.

Ela stopped, her breath coming in unsteady gasps. She glanced behind her, to where a big cart came creaking down Thames Street at the top of the alley, its driver hurling a string of foul invective at someone in his path.

The water glittered menacingly to her right.

Once again, she was all alone in the dark, in an unfamiliar district. But she was damned if they were going to kill another of her men. Aware she might be watched, she walked forward, keeping her knife concealed in the folds of her cloak.

The church bells tolled for Prime, pealing out over all quarters of the city. How did a city with so many houses of God harbor so much wickedness? Maybe that alone explained all the churches. People trying to buy, beg and borrow salvation for their misdeeds.

Ela spotted a door in the stone wall to her left. A great double door, tall and wide enough to admit a horse and cart, but with a smaller door cut into it. She pushed it and it opened.

She lifted her skirts and stepped silently over the threshold and into the pitch-dark interior.

"My lady." The tiny whisper almost made her jump out of her skin.

It was her guard, tucked into the wall next to the door. She whispered back, "Thank Heaven you're safe. Where's he gone?"

"Up the ladder."

Ela peered into the darkness but couldn't make out her hand in front of her face, let alone a ladder. Theo was young and had better eyesight.

But now they knew where to come with the sheriff's men.

She strained her ears to make out any sounds—the voices of children, cries for help or similar, but she couldn't hear anything beyond the pealing of the bells and shouts from nearby Thames Street. "Let's leave. We've learned enough."

She fumbled her way out through the door, knife handle slippery in her sweating palm. The rising sun now cast a thin yellow light over the warehouses and transformed the Thames into a sinister runnel of urine.

They hurried back up the alley toward Thames Street, and she finally drew a full breath as they blended back into the crowd there. "I don't think anyone saw us," she whispered. "You were brave to follow him into the building."

"I couldn't risk losing him." He held his chin high. "Should we wait until he comes out?"

"No. We must get word to the sheriff to search this warehouse. Any day those children could be put on a ship. If they aren't gone already." Their slow progress in finding the children ate at her. "We should hurry back home and send a messenger on horseback." She frowned. "Then again, perhaps the sheriff will find it too easy to ignore an ordinary messenger. Let's walk to the Tower."

The walk along Thames Street took forever as they wound their way through the morning traffic of peddlers, pie sellers, merchants loading their wares onto carts and beggars reaching up their gnarled hands and begging for alms.

BY THE TIME they reached the Tower, the risen sun had vanished behind a bank of menacing gray clouds. Ela, already irritated by the tiresome walk, had to shake out her expensive veil and become haughty with the sentries just to pass through the main gates.

She soon learned that Sheriff le Duc didn't live in quarters at the Tower but in his own fine house and he'd have to be summoned. Someone rode to get him and she paced back and forth in the courtyard, enervated by the situation unraveling in front of her.

A monk—supposed to be a man of God—served this foul enterprise. What had he to do with Vicus Morhees? And with the killings? Could a monk even be tried by the jurors of the hundred or would there be a special ecclesiastical court called? Would the pope himself be called upon to adjudicate?

Or would the church try to cover up the whole sordid affair by denying it or somehow excusing the kidnappings as acts of charity toward poor children?

A persistent drizzle began, and Ela and Theo took refuge in a chamber of the guardhouse. Each flurry of activity—a changing of the guard or a fuss over a sentry who'd fallen asleep—provoked her to fresh fits of impatience.

At last the sheriff arrived on a grand black charger. Several men rushed up to him with their own fresh pieces of news. She hung back, not wanting to be interrupted by them, until she could stand it no longer.

"Sheriff le Duc, my guard and I followed a man from the abbot's residence to a warehouse at the docks. I feel sure there are children hidden there. We must go at once."

Le Duc had the temerity to look amused. "You've been there this morning?"

"Yes, we were walking to Prime when we saw him leave and followed him."

"Are you sure he wasn't a decoy to distract you from some other more iniquitous activities happening in the place you abandoned?" He jumped down from his horse.

He was joking—infuriatingly—but his words did give her pause. As sheriff of London he must see crimes the like of which she could barely imagine. Perhaps he examined all motives for cross-purposes.

"Will you grant a search warrant to open the warehouse?" She wouldn't let him distract her.

"Where is it?" He pulled off his gloves and shook rain from his cloak.

"I don't know the name of the alley where the building entrance lies, but it was hard by the river, off Thames Street. I could lead you there."

He stared at her, observed that she wasn't going to let him have a moment's peace until they went, then barked orders to his men. Then he turned back to her. "I shall come myself and be your search warrant," he said with a characteristic smile. He handed his damp gloves to a servant. "You came on foot?"

"We did." A mistake, in retrospect. They could hardly all stroll back there like a gaggle of dairymaids.

"Fetch a palfrey for the countess!" he commanded. "And a horse for her man-at-arms. We leave at once."

Mounted and encouraged, Ela led them back to the warehouse. The crowds of people, animals, carts and children parted to make way for the clattering hooves of the sheriff's men so the return journey passed swiftly.

Ela's heart swelled with hope and fear as they rode up the alley toward the river, and she pointed to the door. Maybe Brother Sebastian still lay within and would be arrested for kidnapping.

Outside the building she reined in her horse and glanced at Sheriff le Duc. The look on his face startled her. He sat on his horse outside the warehouse, frowning. Then he ordered for one of his men to knock. A man dismounted and pounded on the door, calling that the sheriff wished to enter.

Ela was appalled. "Won't that alert them to flee?"

"How else are we supposed to gain entry?"

"Force the lock?"

"It's barred and bolted. These warehouses are secured like fortresses. Sometimes their cargo is more valuable than a king's ransom."

"That is certainly true of the life on an innocent child," muttered Ela. The knocking and calling—then waiting—made her wonder if he wanted to alert the occupants to abscond with the children. "Someone should guard the river entrance so they don't escape that way."

Le Duc ordered two men to ride to where the alley ended in a quay that jutted out into the murky gray river. Two men unloaded crates filled with live birds from a bobbing skiff onto a wagon amid a commotion of clucking and squawking.

Ela turned to Theo. "Did the monk unlock the door?"

"Yes. He had a key on him."

They stood, still mounted, around the door. "How are we going to get in?" Ela felt like one of the caged chickens, clamoring to no avail. "You said we'd have a warrant."

"Perhaps we could return with a siege engine?" mused le Duc.

Ela was not in any mood for the sheriff's dry sense of humor. "Do you know who owns this warehouse?"

He pursed his lips in an odd way, then rubbed his beard. "I believe it belongs to an important man."

"Who?" Her heart beat faster.

"I'm not at liberty to say."

Ela's mind furled through a list of barons and bishops, trying to imagine who it might be. "What does he import?"

Le Duc shrugged. "I really don't know."

His obtuseness infuriated her. "Did your men find another door? There must be one at the water. And perhaps on the other side of the building. They might be escaping right now." Frustration burned in her chest.

Le Duc commanded his men to check the other side of the building. Where no doubt the door—if there was one— would be locked and barred.

"If I didn't know you to be an honest and upstanding servant of the king I'd almost suspect that you were in the pay of these people," hissed Ela. Shock at her own words slapped her in the face almost as soon as she'd said them. She hesitated to look at le Duc for his reaction.

But he let out a guffaw as if it was the funniest thing he'd heard all week. "I'd hardly be sheriff of London if I could be bribed by merchants."

"Indeed not," she said curtly. "But if a murder is being

committed behind a locked door do you simply stand outside calling for entry, or do you break your way in?"

"I don't think a murder is being committed."

Ela wished she could lean from her horse and strangle him. "Five men are dead! Admittedly they were all foot soldiers of a sort and none of them is titled or monied or important to anyone except his family and friends, but is it not your duty as a servant of the crown to seek justice for their deaths?" She'd included Vicus Morhees to pad the number, which wasn't entirely honest. But did le Duc not want to know who'd paid to kill him, too?

If they found the answer to who'd ordered Vicus Morhees' death, they'd be one step closer to the center of this evil enterprise.

"Every violent death is a crime against God and nature," murmured le Duc. "But we have no reason to believe those deaths are associated with this warehouse."

"Did you not discover where Morhees was killed?"

"We don't know, because your man dragged him to your doorstep instead of leaving him in situ."

"But he must have left a trail of blood in his wake and possibly a pool of blood at the site where he was killed."

Le Duc laid his reins on his horse's neck and held up his hands apologetically. "My men had to search for your guards, who'd already been seized by whoever killed them. As you can see, this is a bustling district. Blood on the ground might easily be taken for spilled wine or piss or the blood of a fresh-killed chicken."

Ela glanced at the ground in the alley, a mix of well-trampled earth and worn, uneven cobbles. Any bloodstains there would have disappeared with the first drizzle.

"Sheriff le Duc," she assumed her most imperious voice. "I must see inside that warehouse." Was he going to deny a countess of the realm?

"I'm afraid we'd have better luck breaking into the royal vaults."

She glimpsed a small window, tightly covered on the inside with a stained cloth, high up in the wall. "Can we not bring a ladder and enter through that window?"

Le Duc peered upward. "We'd need a very tall ladder."

"I can hardly imagine such a thing is hard to find in a district filled with warehouses."

He made an odd expression with his mouth. "I will give you my word, Ela, Countess of Salisbury, that I will investigate this warehouse before the end of the day."

She frowned. "But first, what? You must seek permission of the owner? Is he a personal friend?" Her questions were rude and pointed and the kind of thing that might cause offence enough for him to challenge her to an illegal duel—if she were a man.

Le Duc cleared his throat. "He is a friend. Well, more of an acquaintance."

"And you don't dare break his door down without permission?"

"It's not a question of daring, my lady." He lifted his hands again. "It's a question of respecting the man's good reputation."

Ela's strange horse shifted under her, clearly disturbed by the discomfort she must be transmitting to it. "But surely even a powerful and influential man must be subject to the laws of the kingdom?"

There was an uncomfortable silence that gave Ela time to reflect that Hubert de Burgh—the man who'd killed her husband in cold blood—could not be brought to justice, or even accused, because he was too powerful. Any attempt to accuse him would bring repercussions that could destroy her entire family.

She cleared her throat. "I see how it is. I shall return to my home and break my fast. I can see I made an error in seeking earthly justice instead of attending Prime as I'd intended."

"Justice shall be served in God's time," said le Duc, looking relieved.

"I prefer not to wait until the Day of Judgment in such matters, but if I must, I will. My attendant and I will ride your horses home and have them returned to the tower."

Ela had no intention of waiting for the Day of Judgment. She did, however, intend to seek the intervention of a higher authority—the king.

CHAPTER 19

"**My** God, where have you been?" Bill Talbot's scandalized reprimand reminded her of her mother. "When you didn't return from Mass, I sent out the guards to search for you and they returned empty handed and ignorant of your whereabouts. I sent them to alert the sheriff."

"I'm sure he'll be delighted to see them," she said drily. "Since I left him moments ago. I'm sorry to disappear with no warning, but I was safe in Theo's hands."

She dismounted the strange horse, feeling stiff and uneasy after so much activity early in the morning on an empty stomach. "No thanks to Sheriff le Duc."

Inside, and her fast broken with fresh pastries, fruit and soft cheese, she told Bill of the morning's events and her plan to approach the king.

Bill was not pleased. "You're going behind the sheriff's back?"

"I feel like all I do these days is go behind the back of one sheriff or another. Would that I didn't have to." She sighed. "But our young king is a God-fearing man. I feel sure that he'll want to help shut down this ring of child stealers."

"Even if the man at the head of the organization is a powerful one?"

"No one is more powerful than the king." Ela hoped to convince herself as much as him. "I'm sure he won't sit idly by while such iniquity unfolds less than a mile from Westminster."

Bill looked doubtful. "He didn't offer to rush out in search of the children last time."

"Last time we'd simply gone there in search of the sheriff. I wasn't prepared. This time will be different."

ELA AND BILL rumbled toward Westminster Palace in her carriage. Like her, Bill wore his most glittering finery. He tried not to wince from the pain of his injuries as the wheels hit a rut. "Do you really think the king is going to gain you entry to the warehouse?"

"You don't usually question my plans like this." She wasn't sure she liked it. She was used to him obeying her every whim without complaint. "Is your pain making you pessimistic?"

"Perhaps." He frowned, looking ahead, as they approached the sentries. "I don't want to see you disappointed." The carriage rolled through the gates into a palace courtyard.

"I'm not a child who'll cry if she's told no."

"I certainly didn't mean to imply that, my lady. It's just that—"

She didn't know what it was, because at that moment the sentry recognized her and whispered her name to a porter and a fanfare of trumpets blasted across the courtyard.

They were ushered into the palace, where, as usual, a gaggle of courtiers and hangers-on hovered in every corner. "Countess Ela of Salisbury!"

She maintained a serious expression. She hadn't come here to make small talk with anyone. She asked for an urgent audience with the king.

The page who took her request kept a calm face but she sensed he was astonished by her audacity. He returned a short while later. "The king is attended by several barons in the green chamber. You may join them."

Ela blinked. This was not at all what she'd hoped for. But it would have to do.

She followed the page into a great chamber usually reserved for private feasts. Seated at a long oak table were a group of men, including William de Warenne, Gilbert de Clare and young Simon de Montfort, relaxed and with their wine half drunk as if they'd been there for a while. And, of course, the dreaded Hubert de Burgh. He probably followed Henry into the garderobe. They all rose as she entered.

"Countess Ela," said King Henry. "What a pleasure." She approached him and held out her hands, and he kissed them. "I'm sure you know the assembled gentlemen?"

"Indeed I do." She bowed her head in a greeting. What were they doing gathered here in private? Perhaps planning an overseas conquest. She'd heard the young king was obsessed with regaining the territories lost by his father. They offered murmurs of sympathy for the loss of her husband and congratulations on the marriages of her children. Then there was an awkward moment when they all—no doubt—silently wondered why she'd come.

"I'm here for three reasons, which I will elucidate in order." She hadn't anticipated such an audience, but it would serve her purposes.

Witnesses.

"First, I brought Sheriff le Duc with me this morning to investigate a warehouse in search of the missing children we seek. He refused to search it, saying it belonged to an important gentleman of the city. I find this inexcusable and now worry that children's lives are being traded for coin and that the sheriff is putting some of those coins in his own purse."

It was an outrageous accusation and was met with stunned silence. She moved on quickly before any protests could start.

"Second, I have brought with me a complaint…" She held out her hand for Bill to give her the parchment. He pulled it from his scrip and gave it to her. "Against Sheriff de Hal of Salisbury, brought by the burgesses of Scarborough in Yorkshire, where he was lately sheriff."

She read out a few of the more pointed accusations and watched with pleasure as the eyes of the barons widened and the king leaned forward in his chair. De Burgh shifted, brows lowered, and glared at her. "As you can hear from this complaint," she continued. "He wreaked havoc in Yorkshire, using violence, fire and imprisonment to extort and threaten, to the point of extinguishing trade in the region as people were afraid to leave their homes to come to market."

She paused and looked around. "I cannot understand for even one moment why a man with such a reprehensible record should be made high sheriff of Wiltshire and installed in the castle of my ancestors." Her voice rang out and echoed off the paneled and painted walls. "How did such a thing happen?"

"Indeed how?" asked Henry. "These accusations are shocking indeed." He turned to stare at de Burgh.

Who cleared his throat. "He was an experienced sheriff, with a cadre of well-honed men. He seemed ideal for the role of—"

"Had you not seen this complaint?" Henry interrupted his

justiciar. "It implies he should be brought before the sheriff, not installed as one."

"He made a very persuasive argument," said de Burgh.

"One involving a large number of gold coins, perhaps?" said Ela.

This was war. She knew it. She'd raised her sword against de Burgh. Would he now try to slay her?

She lifted her chin. "I find it unacceptable that a man with a record for extortion and exploitation, let alone violence, should continue to rule as sheriff in the land of my fathers. I have expressed my own desire to continue in my husband's role as sheriff. I believe I've demonstrated my ability to fulfill the role, and I seek immediate installation as sheriff of Wiltshire. As to the third reason for my visit I am pleased to offer the sum of five hundred pounds to the crown in exchange for the restoration of this office and the castle of Salisbury to my family."

Now she paused, heart pounding, to let her words sink in.

No one moved. The barons stared. De Burgh fumed. Henry peered at her in amazement. Eventually they all turned to look at the king. Who looked at Ela.

"Five hundred pounds, you say?"

Ela hesitated. It was an enormous sum. An outrageous sum. She'd chosen that number because she knew few mortal men could refuse it. It would be a strain on the estate for years to come, but she was a good manager and could rebuild the coffers. And if it worked—

She drew in a breath to steady her nerves. "To be delivered within the week, if you are in agreement with my terms."

"That you be declared high sheriff of Wiltshire and castellan of Salisbury."

"Exactly." She held his gaze. She resisted the urge to glance at de Burgh, which took a lot of willpower, as she could feel waves of fury rolling toward her from his direction.

If she could get the king to agree—now, in front of these influential witnesses—the deed was done. She would be sheriff of Salisbury and could move back into the beloved ancestral castle her soul and body ached for like a missing limb.

"Has Simon de Hal done any of those things since his installation as sheriff of Wiltshire?" cut in de Burgh.

"Not that I'm aware of," said Ela coolly. "I presume he was warned to be on his best behavior."

"No doubt he's realized the error of his ways," said de Burgh. "No man is born with experience for the roles he shall assume in life and must learn in situ."

"Happily most men are born without the desire to bully, threaten and rob their subjects," said Ela. She'd waded up to her neck in this. Either she'd walk out of this room with her castle and the role of sheriff, or she'd probably never possess either of them again.

"And you think Sheriff Roger le Duc of London is similarly iniquitous?"

"I find Sheriff le Duc a delightful man, and I have no reason to believe he isn't an excellent sheriff. But he did balk at investigating a building where I have good reason to believe that children are being held by a criminal gang that has killed two of my men, two associates of my lawyer's office, and who have wounded two of my most able guards and my valuable and trusted man-at-arms, Sir William Talbot." She gestured at Bill. Who didn't move a muscle. He knew how high the stakes were at this moment.

"You were attacked, Sir William?" asked the king of Bill.

"And injured. But far worse, they took my countess hostage and threatened her before abandoning her alone at night outside the city."

The king blinked in astonishment. "How have I not heard of this?" He asked the question of de Burgh.

Who shifted awkwardly. "The countess was warned of the danger to herself and urged to leave the city for the safety of her manor." He tented his fingers. "And the child she sought was returned that morning, completely unharmed."

"Exactly as if some coin was placed on the right palms, or the appropriate warnings issued between the sheriff's office and the villains themselves," said Ela drily.

"Impossible," protested de Burgh. "I can vouch for the honesty of Roger le Duc."

"You vouched for the honesty of Simon de Hal," murmured the king, surveying de Burgh through narrowed eyes. "He was your suggestion, if I recall correctly."

"Indeed. I believed him to be a capable and efficient dispenser of justice."

"You'd not seen this complaint that Countess Ela has a written copy of?"

"I had not," said de Burgh. But without much conviction. Ela was almost sure de Hal had slipped him a sizable bribe.

The king stared at de Burgh for a moment. Then he looked at Ela. "I accept your offer. For a fine of five hundred pounds, payable within the month, you shall regain shrievalty of Salisbury castle and you shall be sheriff of Wiltshire for the term of one year, as is customary. After which time, the question of your continuing as sheriff will be addressed again."

Ela didn't much like the conditional terms of the agreement, but if she paid the money she'd be back in the castle. Once there she knew she could impress the king, and the people of Wiltshire and of all England, with her ability to dispense swift and fair justice as sheriff.

She stood and held out her hand. She knew that if the king shook a man's hand, the agreement was sealed as if it were written in ink on vellum and stamped with a wax seal. As a man of honor—and a young, idealistic one at that—she knew Henry would stand by his word. "I accept."

Henry looked surprised for a moment, then rose from his chair and shook her hand. A wave of relief rose through Ela. If de Burgh wanted to keep her from being sheriff of Salisbury—as part of an extended revenge against her and her family—he'd have to kill her. And she did not intend to give him the opportunity.

"I appreciate the trust you've placed in me." She met his gaze. "I look forward to serving your grace as sheriff of Wiltshire."

"Your reputation for piety and good works has spread far beyond Wiltshire," said the young king. "And I appreciate your drawing my attention to the reputation of the current sheriff of Wiltshire. If I'd known of these accusations he would not have been appointed to the role in your stead."

Ela bowed her head in acknowledgment. This was tantamount to an apology and more than she'd hoped for, or even wanted.

Now, in the wake of her great triumph, she had to return to the pressing question of how to find the missing girl. It had been a good excuse for gaining an urgent audience with the king, but it wasn't just an excuse. Elsie Brice—and the other children—were in urgent danger, and murderers walked the streets with their heads held high.

"I hesitate to ask more of your grace, but there remains the question of the warehouse and the missing children."

Henry's face was expressionless. "That is a matter you'll have to address with Sheriff le Duc."

"Unless you wish to present yourself as sheriff of London," quipped de Burgh, with a nasty expression.

Ela ignored de Burgh and looked straight at the king. "But

I took him to the warehouse myself and he wouldn't force entry."

"No doubt he has his reasons." The king leaned back in his chair, as if he was done with the matter. "You'll have to take those up with him."

She was dismissed. The king apparently did not deign to meddle in such small local matters. He preferred to mull over his intended reconquest of the Angevin lands.

"I shall do that, your grace." She bowed her head. "And I look forward to serving you as sheriff."

There were some polite mutterings as she and Bill excused themselves. Once out in the hallway, Bill congratulated her with much excitement.

"Indeed I am pleased," she said quietly. "But that is in the future. We have work to do that cannot wait. We must take the warehouse ourselves."

CHAPTER 20

"*W*hat do you know of Roger Le Duc, the sheriff of London?" Ela asked Spicewell. She'd begged an urgent appointment, and he'd welcomed her into his chambers near the law courts. With its ornate furniture and colorful tapestries it was a far cry from his business quarters down by the river.

"Le Duc has a good reputation. He's held the office of sheriff for multiple terms, which wouldn't happen if the guilds and the burghers weren't happy with him in the role."

"Is it possible that he bought their favor?"

"Of course."

Of course. She'd done just that herself this morning at Westminster.

"Then they might be happy with the money he provided rather than his performance as sheriff."

"Money alone would not induce the people of London to tolerate a sheriff who allowed theft and fraud and violence to go unchecked."

True. And the king would not have granted her the post of

sheriff if he thought her inadequate to the role. The thought cheered her.

"So, as far as you're aware, he's honest and concerned with the pursuit of justice?"

Spicewell narrowed his eyes. "I suspect you're hoping I'll disagree with you."

Ela told him how they took le Duc to the warehouse they'd followed Brother Sebastian to and how he'd refused to gain entry.

"What street was it?"

"I've discovered that they call it Water Street. It's little more than an alley. The warehouse is a large, unmarked building of three stories. The first story is of stone. It's an imposing building for a warehouse."

Spicewell let out a sharp laugh. "That warehouse belongs to the king himself."

"What?" Ela almost fell out of her chair. "Why does the king own a warehouse?"

"Why else? To hold his imports of wine and spices and silks and—"

"Does the king know children are being held in his warehouse?"

"How do you know children are being held there?"

"It's a strong suspicion."

"And you expected the good sheriff of London to break down the door of the king's warehouse?"

"He never told me it belonged to the king. He was most evasive."

Spicewell sighed. "He'd hardly be likely to implicate his majesty in a crime now, would he? The king might not know it belongs to him, either. He's not concerned with such matters. His stewards and treasurers would be responsible for the space. It might well be rented out."

"Might it be rented to a religious order?"

"Entirely possible."

"The man we followed there is called Brother Sebastian. He lives in the order of Blackfriars connected to St. Michael and All Angels. I visited the house behind the church, and I'm certain it's the place where I was held. We saw Vicus Morhees come out of the courtyard there before he was killed."

"Vicus Morhees is dead?"

Ela realized that a lot had happened since she last saw Spicewell. She explained it as best she could.

"So you think that the trade in children is connected to the opium trade?"

"It's possible that Vicus Morhees is the only connection. He's almost certainly the connection to Salisbury. While he was in Wiltshire attempting to seize hold of Fernlees Manor, he saw an opportunity to profit from two young lives. Morhees was a very devious man who, I suspect, would do anything for gain. After we disrupted his profitable opium trade with our criminal investigation, he may have tried to strike up with new business partners."

Spicewell nodded. "He seems to have met his match here in London. It sounds like his masters sacrificed him to your men like a spring lamb."

"Perhaps because his efforts to warn me off and banish me from London were to no avail."

"He clearly didn't know who he was dealing with," said Spicewell.

"Are you referring to me or the child thieves?"

He chuckled. "Both."

"Well, he's dead and gone and reckoning with his maker. But unfortunately Elsie Brice is still missing and I fear she's only another one in a long chain of unfortunate souls. I can't rest until we locate the girl and uncover the foul villains behind this cruel trade."

Spicewell leaned forward in his chair. "It appears that you are knocking on some very well-guarded doors. Are you prepared to raise your sword against the king himself?"

Ela felt the blood drain from her body. "You think the king is behind this?"

"No, I don't. For one thing he's too young and I've heard no reports that he is involved in anything even slightly underhanded. He's pious and dutiful, and gossip even suggests that he's still a virgin."

Ela blinked. The very idea of discussing the king's bedchamber activities felt like high treason. "I've found him to be a thoughtful and intelligent young man, and I have high hopes for him as our king."

"He's a much different man than his father, God be praised."

"Indeed, yes." Ela had a sudden violent urge to cross herself. She obeyed it. Perhaps a troubled spirit walked abroad. "But you think one of the king's close friends or associates may be involved in this foul business?"

Spicewell tented his hands and peered at them. "If I thought it was just one of them—"

Ela stared. "You think more than one...?" A sudden thought occurred to her. A thought that appealed to her more than she dared to admit. "Is Hubert de Burgh involved?" She could already picture him twisting on the gallows, convicted of exploiting and abusing children, and took a most unholy pleasure at the prospect.

"De Burgh?" Spicewell exploded with laughter. "Good Lord, no. That man thinks of nothing but power—gaining it and increasing it. He'd never waste his time on activities that could endanger his hold over the king. The man has as much passion as my walking stick."

"Oh." Ela tried not to let her disappointment show. "Then who? Abbot Abelard de Rouen lives in the house behind St.

Michael and All Angels., but he's away in Rome for a meeting with His Holiness the Pope."

"Perhaps he went to Rome with a ship full of young children to be sold into the households of cardinals."

Ela's mouth dropped open. "You can't be serious."

"A life of celibacy can warp a man's desires into something sinful and cruel."

"Next you'll suggest that the pope himself—" She didn't like this train of thought and stilled her tongue.

"I've been on this earth many years and seen a lot in my practice as a man of the law. At this point there is almost nothing that would surprise me."

Ela felt horribly depleted. "You don't think it's someone in his household using the cover of the religious house to conceal their nefarious behavior?" She thought of the young African boy dressed in his finery like an exotic pet. She wished she could speak with him alone. Then she remembered that she'd tried.

"It's possible, but you know the old saying that if it walks like a duck and quacks like a duck…"

"We followed a monk named Brother Sebastian to the warehouse."

"So you have a monk entering a warehouse belonging to the king and you're wondering why the good sheriff of London is reluctant to break the doors down and seize him?"

Ela pondered this for a moment, then let out a sigh. "Of course the king would be unassailable in this instance. But it isn't him. Are men under holy orders exempt from prosecution?"

"Not entirely, but if the church closes ranks around them it will be impossible to bring them to justice."

"Then how can we stop them?" Her voice rose with a note of desperation.

Spicewell leaned back in his chair and peered at her down

the length of his slightly bulbous nose. "A man is only as good as his reputation. If word were to get out…"

"That a man of God was enslaving children." Ela frowned. "Who would believe it?"

"You might find that people already know the truth and were just waiting for someone else to blurt it abroad."

Ela took a moment to ponder this. "You think the sheriff might already know?"

Spicewell shrugged. "He might. And if he's a wise man he'd know there was little he could do about it. So he might choose to focus his energy on cases where there is justice to be sought and won."

"And stand idly by while Elsie Brice—a pure and innocent girl of eleven with her whole life ahead of her—is sold to the highest bidder and deflowered for the idle pleasure of sinful men—" She choked on her own words. "Well, God is my judge and I do not intend to stand aside while young children are exploited and ruined."

"These people are dangerous. I lost two of my best informants to them, as you know."

"And I two brave young guards." She frowned. "I won't just look away. I can't. Before I make any accusations I must know who is taking the children and what they are doing with them. But for now, the most important thing is to get the children back."

ELA DID NOT SHARE her plan with Spicewell. She left him thinking that she was going to ponder the matter for a few days. In truth, she'd done all the pondering she needed.

"We shall dress in dark clothing, to go unseen in the night." She paced across the floor of her mother's private upstairs parlor. Bill Talbot and two guards stood awkwardly against the paneled walls. She looked at the guards. "We shall bring three ladders that, when lashed together, will reach the high window."

The kitchen boy was hard at work on the ladders right now, binding staves to long poles. One thing Ela liked about London is that you could obtain the most obscure items with ease. The ladders he made would be lighter and easier to transport than any she could buy, and could be simply ditched into the river if necessary.

She'd tried to persuade Bill to stay home, but he'd refused. She was secretly glad. She appreciated his wisdom and moderating influence on her—at least when she had the good sense to listen to him.

"We'll wait until the bells have run for Matins. The streets should be near empty. We shall avoid the neighborhood of St. Michael and All Angels and head straight for the warehouse, taking care that no one—even in this household—sees us. Once there we shall lash the ladders together and raise them, and I—as the lightest—will go up them."

Naturally, there was a token protest at this, but Ela soon got them to agree. "I shall slip through the window and into the building, and Theo shall follow close behind me if necessary. Bill and Alun shall wait outside and watch."

"But surely the children, if they're in there, will be guarded."

"Perhaps, but I think not. We've now seen Brother Sebastian go there twice in a day, bringing a basket of what must be food. I think he's their watchman and that the children are secured with locks and chains rather than armed men. I pray they're still there."

She and Bill had checked—repeatedly—the old building near Westcheap, but there were no signs of recent use. The door remained barred and cobwebs now hung in the doorway. All signs pointed to the children being held in the warehouse by the river.

~

THEY WAITED until the Matins bells had stopped chiming and long enough for any night creatures heading to Mass to arrive inside the church and close the doors. Then they headed out onto the street.

Though she'd been tempted to dress as a man, Ela didn't do that. Perhaps the scandal from the one time she'd attempted it weighed too heavily on her. Instead she wore a simple dark blue tunic with no ornamentation and her hair tied back with no barbette or veil. She wore a short, dark cloak with a small hood that covered her hair and much of her face, and soft leather boots that made no sound. To climb the ladder she could tuck the hem of her skirt into the leather belt around her waist, which also held her knife.

Bill and the guards also dressed in plain, dark clothing bought at the market that afternoon. The moon shone bright enough for them to find their way along the streets. The guards carried the ladders, each taller than a man. Ela hoped that, lashed together, they'd be tall enough to reach the high window. If not, there was another high opening on the river side of the building to attempt.

The streets of London were never empty—or quiet. The raucous singsong of a drunk, the too-loud laughter of a woman of the night, the sudden splash of slops thrown from a high window—each quickened Ela's pulse as they hurried toward the dark river. The foul smells of the city seemed stronger at night and hung dismally in the air without the wind of her beloved castle mound to disperse them or the lush forest at Gomeldon to absorb them.

They passed few people, and those made a point of

shrinking into the shadows as they approached. Four tall, dark-dressed, purposeful figures in the night did not inspire friendly overtures. Although she'd told him to hide it, Ela could see the tip of Bill's long sword hanging beneath the hem of his cloak.

She smelled the river before she could see it, then it shone at the end of the alley before them. The warehouse rose up to their left, and she could make out the opening of the window about twenty feet up in the air.

One of the guards had bought rope to lash the ladders together, and the two men set to work on it.

"I can go up first," said Bill, in her ear.

"You're injured. I'll be fine. I'm the lightest." The plan was for her—once inside—to find her way down to the front door to let them in and to help the children out. One of the guards had brought something that looked like iron tongs, which could supposedly break even thick chain, and a bar to use for leverage if they needed to pry iron rings from the wooden walls.

The ladders reached handily to the window. A little too far, in fact. They propped the ladder against the wall, and Bill and one guard held it fast as they tried to persuade Ela they would be better suited to the climb. She shushed them quietly, tucked the front hem of her skirt into her belt and started up the ladder.

The slender rungs gave her pause, but they held her weight and her confidence grew as she climbed higher. *Don't look down.* She sensed the river to her right—a malodorous silver ribbon—and the men watching her intently from below, but she kept her focus on the window.

The ladder sagged toward the wooden wall of the building as she climbed higher. She reassured herself that two men held it steady at the bottom. She'd inspected its construction herself and knew it was sturdy.

At last she reached the window. But with the ladder being a span too tall, it didn't take her right to the sill, but past it. She'd have to take a sidestep off the ladder and into the unglazed window. It would be a leap of faith.

In the absence of a shutter, a piece of tattered cloth or leather hung inside the window and obscured her view. What if she heaved herself from the ladder and through the window, only to find it was barred or somehow blocked from the inside? She wasn't sure she'd be able to regain purchase on the tall, flimsy ladder.

Ela climbed until her foot was level with the bottom of the window opening. Her hand rested on the next-to-highest rung of the ladder.

Don't look down.

Her heart hammered for a second. Should she reach with her hand first or her foot? She found herself clinging to the staves of the ladder, fearful of the unknown.

This is better than riding into a rain of arrows. She'd likely faced more danger with each childbirth.

Keeping both hands firmly on the ladder, she stuck her left foot out toward the sill, which was only the distance of her foot away. Once the ball of her foot gained purchase on the sill, she took her left hand off the ladder and reached for the edge of the opening.

The ladder shuddered as her weight shifted, and she suppressed a shriek that rose in her throat. *This is it.* She'd have to hurl herself. There was no graceful way to manage the weight transfer from the bowing limbs of the ladder to the sturdier opening of the window.

What if the wood is rotten? It didn't feel rotten. It felt sturdy, and her toes poked the flap of fabric and hadn't hit anything hard. *What if there's no floor on the other side, and I fly in through the window, then plunge to my death?*

She intended to hang onto the window frame until she

could gauge what lay on the other side. The window was small enough that she'd have to fold herself in half to get through it. This would give her less control, but she had no choice.

Hail Mary, full of grace—Ela heaved herself from the ladder and toward the window opening. The small distance felt like a great chasm as her right hand flew toward her left and her right foot joined her left on the sill. The action pushed the ladder away and she heard it scrape against the wall as her fingers grasped the wood window frame and she heaved her weight into the opening.

CHAPTER 21

*E*la tried to halt herself on the sill, but the thrust of movement propelled her in through the window. She'd crunched up small enough to fit through the opening, and her folded legs wouldn't hold her steady on the sill.

Her left hand flew off the sill and she reached up to grab the curtain, which tore in her hand and fluttered down. Ela lost her footing on the sill and plunged forward into the dark opening, a scream rising in her throat.

But instead of her own scream, someone else's scream rose in the air as Ela came down hard on her shoulder on a wood floor.

She sprang to her feet, peering into the darkness. "Who's there?" She hoped it was lost children, not a band of brigands whose midst she'd fallen into.

No one replied. She heard some fumbling and scuffling in the dark. "Is Elsie Brice here?"

No answer.

"I come from Salisbury to bring her home to her family."

More silence, punctuated by shuffling and sniffing.

"Are you children in here?"

"Yes," said a boy's voice.

"Were you stolen from your parents?"

"Yes," said the same voice. "Some of us were."

Ela's heart swelled. She'd found the stolen children. But was she too late to bring Elsie back to her family? "Was Elsie Brice with you?"

"I'm here," said a very small voice.

"Praise be to God!" exclaimed Ela too loudly. "Your family will be overjoyed to see you again."

"They won't." said the same small voice. "My uncle sold me for a pound of silver. So he won't be happy to see me again." Her voice cracked.

Ela froze. "It's against the law to sell a child," she said. Was it? She wasn't even entirely sure. Money and children exchanged hands for apprenticeships and for labor, but surely this was different? "Regardless, we'll get you out of here now. How are you secured?" Her eyes still battled the darkness, and she couldn't see even the outline of a child.

"We're not tied up, but there's no way down," said a boy. "We're on the third floor of this warehouse and they remove the ladder after they leave us food."

She needed to bring the ladders in here. But how, if she couldn't get down to open the door? "Where is the opening for the ladder?" Perhaps she could lower herself down to the next floor.

"Over here," said a girl.

"All right. You stay right there and warn me when I'm close, so I won't fall into it." She felt her way along the floor. It smelled of new wood but was dusty and dirty. The room also reeked of filth, probably from slop buckets somewhere.

"You're close," said the girl. "It's a square hole in the floor."

Ela could already feel splinters from the floor—and likely

the window frame, too—in her fingertips and the palms of her hands. Hilda would have quite a time removing them once she was home safe—God willing.

The opening had raw cut edges of new wood. Ela peered down at the level below, which was even darker. She couldn't see where the next level began.

Looking up, she could at least make out the moonlit window opening she'd come through. She stood and walked back there, reassured at least that there was solid floor in between here and there. She stuck her head out the window. The men stared up at her from the street below, still holding the ladder.

"I need the ladder," she whispered as loudly as she could. They edged it over to the window opening, then pulled the base away far enough that the top of the ladder lowered and poked in through the window opening.

Ela grabbed hold of the top rungs and pulled it.

But it was too heavy and at the wrong angle and soon hit the ceiling. She probably needed only the top part of the ladder. "Is there a rope in here?" If she could lower the ladder, have the men cut off the top section, then pull it back up again—

"No. There's nothing in here. They don't want us to escape," said a girl.

"Who's the strongest among you? And who the tallest?" Children were agile. Perhaps between herself and them they could lower someone to open the door below.

"I'm the tallest," said a boy's voice, with the just-broken crack of a boy turning into a man. "And likely the strongest, too."

"If I hold your arms, do you think you can lower yourself to the floor below?"

"It'll be a jump, but I can do it."

Ela and the boy made their way gingerly toward the opening. Her eyes had adjusted enough to make out the shapes of the children—there were so many of them, eyes glittering in the blackness—and she could also see the large dark square hole in the floor where goods might be hoisted up here for storage.

Ela eased her way the edge and coaxed him to climb over. He hesitated, then lowered himself into the hole, hanging onto the edge by his hands. Ela took his wrists. She peered into the hole. What if there was another opening right under his feet and he'd fall all the way through to the ground floor, maybe breaking his neck in the process?

"Can you see the floor below you?" She asked.

"I can see the hole, so I must jump to the side of it."

"If I hold your wrists and lower you down, can you make it?"

"I think so."

Ela lay flat on the floor with her arms extended into the hole. "Children, two of you hold on to my feet." She felt small strong hands on her ankles. "What's your name?" she asked of the boy in the hole.

"Rafe, ma'am."

"Well, Rafe, I'm going to hold your wrists very tight, so when you let go of the edge we'll lower you down little lower. Are you ready?"

"Yes."

She gripped with all her might as he let go of the edge and his weight fell into her hands. He was a slight boy but still weighed several stones and his weight wrenched at her shoulders.

"Can you swing yourself to make sure you land on the floor?"

He stuck his legs out and generated some momentum,

while Ela gritted her teeth, gripped with all her might, and tried to ignore the floor biting into her chest.

"When I say 'three,' let go," said the boy. Ela was relieved that this boy could count.

"I will."

He was swinging himself in increasing arcs, challenging her ability to hold him. "One, two, three!" She let go and held her breath as he plunged into the darkness. She heard a thud as he hit the wood floor.

"Are you safe?"

"Yes," he gasped. He sounded winded.

"Can you peer down through the next hole to the floor below?"

"Yes." She could now just make him out, kneeling at the edge of the second hole. "I can see the ground."

She couldn't imagine how he could see anything in this lightless pit. It seemed the only open window was the one she'd come through. Maybe there were enough cracks in the walls to let some scant moonlight in down there.

"Can you jump down to it without help and open the door from the inside? My friends are there to help you all to safety." Ela wondered if she could manage to lower herself down after him. It was a long jump and—as a forty-year-old mother of eight—she wasn't as agile as a lithe twelve-year-old.

"I think so."

Ela realized the children behind her still held her ankles. She whispered that they could let go—she didn't want to distract the boy below—and eased herself creakily back onto her knees so she could peer down after him.

She watched the boy climb gingerly over the edge of the hole and lower himself into it, as he'd done before. This time he didn't swing back and forth, but simply dropped straight down. She didn't hear him land.

"Rafe? Can you hear me?" He didn't answer. Ela couldn't see him, but an image of his broken body—sprawled awkwardly on the packed dirt below—flew into her mind. One of the children behind her gasped. Another, more distant, began to cry. "Rafe."

"I'm fine," said a squeaky voice below. "Just winded. It's a big drop."

"Thanks be to God," breathed Ela. "Can you see the door to unlock it?"

"I can see it. It has bands of iron across it"

"Is there a latch?" Ela was used to doors being opened and closed for her by servants. She didn't have much opportunity to examine their workings.

"It's not latched on this side." She heard him rattling the door. "I think it's locked from the outside and there's no key."

They'd hardly have a warehouse that only locked from the inside, but she hoped that the interior of the door would have a way to unlock the door. "Hold on. Stay right there." She rose to her feet and hurried back to the window. Down on the street, Bill and the two guards stared up at her.

"Can you break the door down?" she said, as loud as she dared. "It won't open from the inside." Just because Sheriff le Duc had said it couldn't be done, didn't mean he was right.

Bill murmured some commands to the men, and they immediately set to the door. Ela prayed that they could cut through the wood around the lock or pry the whole door off its hinges. Naturally a warehouse would have sturdy doors like a castle to protect the precious cargo stored inside it from the city's thieves, which included skilled lockpicks and villains of all stripes.

She hurried back to the hole. "Rafe, they're trying to break the door down from the outside. See that you're out of the way when it falls, and tell them anything you can to help them."

She strained to hear a muttered exchange between Rafe and the men outside. They made thumping and sawing sounds enough to wake the dead. She prayed they'd get the door open in time to rescue the children.

Odd that their captors had left them unguarded, but this warehouse was a fortress indeed. There was no way to escape unaided. "How long have you been here?" she asked of the children.

Their answers varied. Some had been there since they'd been moved from the other building, others had arrived only a few days earlier.

"Who feeds you?"

"Usually the monk. There was another man with scary eyes, but he doesn't come any more." Vicus Morhees, probably.

"Does anyone else come here?"

"Yes. People come to pinch us and prod us like we're fruit in the market. Sometimes they buy a child and leave with them."

"Do you know who any of these people are?"

None of them did. "We're kept in the dark. We only see them by candlelight."

"So you wouldn't recognize any of them?"

"I'd recognize the monk," protested one boy. "He's that short. And he shuffles along in his long robe."

"It's just the one monk, the short one, or are there others?"

"There are others," said a girl. Ela couldn't see her in the dark, but she could tell she was as young as Edyth Wheaton. "I've been here the longest. Sometimes they take us places and dress us up. Then they bring us back here."

"Do men—do anything to you?"

None of them answered.

Ela strained her ears to listen to the sounds below. There was a fair amount of thumping and scraping coming from outside the door as the men worked to open it. It was only a matter of time before someone out on the streets would notice what was going on, and then what would happen? Would they alert the sheriff?

She wasn't sure how the sheriff would react to her breaking and entering into the king's warehouse. She'd proved that children were being held against their will. Surely that would be enough to justify her actions in any court of law?

"I hope to get you all back to your parents as soon as I can." She wanted to reassure herself as much as them.

"I don't have parents," said Elsie Brice. "They're both dead." Did Elsie know the role Ela had played in her becoming an orphan? Her heart clenched at the injustice that the Brice children must suffer.

"Me either," said a small boy. "My dad was killed by a bull and my mam died of the fever."

"So how did you come to be here?" He was close enough for Ela to reach out and take his hand. He snatched it back. Which reminded her that he had no reason to trust a strange adult. Elsie's words came back to her. "Did someone sell you?"

She could see him shaking his head in the dark. "I was begging in the town, and two men came along and threw me into a bag and put me on a cart."

"What town?"

"Canterbury," said the boy.

Ela frowned. "Where are the rest of you from?"

Their muttered answers confused her. They came from a variety of places, from small villages to large cathedral towns. Wondering how they all got here distracted her momentarily from the commotion below, which grew louder.

With a huge thud, the door flew in, bringing one of the guards sprawling with it. Ela peered down the hole. "Are you hurt?"

"I'm all right."

"Bill, I'm up on the top floor. We need the ladder. There's an opening between the floors. You'll have to break the ladder down into its parts to get it in here."

"There must be ladders in here, or how do they get up?" asked Bill. The guards searched the lower floor and found them lying up against a wall. It seemed an eternity of fumbling with ladders in the dark, then carefully guiding the children down, but eventually they were all out on the dark street.

The few people who saw them—a couple of tipsy sailors and a bearded beggar—clearly didn't want to get involved. Ela and the guards urged the children to keep quiet, and hurried them back to Alianore's house without speaking to anyone. She half expected some of them would try to peel off and run away, but none did.

Ela dreaded running into Brother Sebastian on the way back, but what would he do? He could hardly shout, "Those are my children you're stealing!"

BACK AT THE house the servants gathered to feed and bathe the children. Most were dressed in fairly new clothing, probably to better present them to prospective purchasers. Ela's sensibilities recoiled at the idea of people peering into the children's mouths or pinching their bottoms as if they were sheep or milk cows.

"Are we to summon the sheriff?" asked Bill at last. She could tell he'd been wanting to ask the question for a while.

"And tell him we forced entry into a warehouse he refused to break into? He didn't want me to find these children."

"True," said Bill. "He seemed unwilling to burst open a hornets' nest."

"Or he's being paid off and is therefore a sleeping partner in this enterprise. Until I know who's the keystone, I don't want to give him an opportunity to destroy evidence and avoid pursuing the matter."

"But what of the children?"

"We must find where each one came from and send them safely home. If we turn them over to the sheriff, there's no telling what could happen to them."

"But surely the people holding them will come looking for them?" Bill frowned. "I can only imagine they're very valuable cargo."

"Indeed, and when they do, we shall be ready. Alun is already dressed as a beggar and on his way to watch the alley to see who turns up to find the door broken in, and how they react." Alun seemed sharp witted as well as highly skilled with his weapons. He had a long dagger concealed beneath his ragged cloak and was ready for a fight. However, he'd been told to avoid one if at all possible, but to follow anyone who came. Her key objective was to discover the source of all this evil.

With the dawn, he reported, Brother Sebastian had arrived with his basket of food. He'd startled, dropping the basket at the sight of the broken door. He'd hurried away, lifting his cassock as he ran, and headed right back to Abbot de Rouen's house.

ALIANORE'S large house felt crowded with all the children in it. There were nine of them, including Elsie Brice. Hilda proved herself invaluable, soothing and caressing the scared younger ones, speaking bold talk to the older ones and making sure all were fed and settled.

Ela began the process of trying to discover each of their origins. The older ones mostly remembered the name of their village or at least the nearest town, but the three youngest didn't know. Their world was organized around such landmarks as "market street," "narrow lane" or "the old cross," which could be anywhere in England.

Most disturbing of all, four of them claimed to have been sold by their guardians—one boy sold by his own mother and father, who couldn't provide for him after being thrown off their lord's manor for poaching. "They said we'd all starve on the road when winter came," he said quietly. "And that with the money they got for me they could buy food until they found a place to settle. If you send me back and they have to give back the money, we'll all starve and they'll be angry with me."

Ela felt fury at the parents who'd told him this tale, true though it likely was. She was fairly sure she'd rather starve with her children under her care than sell them to strangers…but she tried to reserve judgement. Regardless, the boy had no home to go to—nor did Elsie Brice or the young orphan. What was to become of the ones who couldn't return home?

"YOU CAN'T EMPLOY them all, surely," murmured Bill softly, as they retired to the private parlor after supper.

"We'll be moving back into the castle this winter," she said confidently. "There's always a need for new staff."

"You expect to return there this year?"

"I intend to pay my tribute to the king before we return to Salisbury. I see no reason for delay."

"He'll have to inform de Hal that he needs to move and likely find him another posting."

"Even when he knows the man is a violent ruffian? I hardly think so."

Bill looked dubious. "De Burgh might have some say in the matter."

Ela released an unladylike snort. "True. He'll try to delay and obfuscate as long as possible to frustrate me, but he can't overturn the stated will of the king."

Bill was silent.

"He can't!" She was trying to convince herself as much as him. "But trust me, no time shall be wasted. I've sent word to my bankers to raise the funds, and when we return I'll begin the process of wringing the repayment from my various manors. It'll be quite a project." She leaned back in her chair. She enjoyed the business aspect of operating her manors and always had. Her husband had been wise to leave such matters in her hands from early in their marriage. "But that is a matter for another day. For now, we must flush Brother Sebastian out of his comfortable bush behind St. Michael and All Angels and find out who his master is."

"Perhaps he is the master?" suggested Bill.

"No." Ela shook her head. "He's a functionary, a go-between. If he was the master he wouldn't have dropped his basket and run, he would have rushed in to check the status of his investment." She sighed. "I'm beginning to suspect Abbot de Rouen himself may be the true head of this diseased body. I intend to put pressure on Brother Sebastian —it disgusts me to call him a brother—and see if I can wring the truth out of him."

"Surely such a thing should be done in a court of law?"

"Indeed it should, but as Master Spicewell has warned me, the church has its own laws, and they may be able to keep him out of the courts. I know the truth, however, so at least he will have a trial of sorts in the court of public opinion."

"I suppose if there were rumors of a monk or an abbot stealing children, the gossip would make it harder for him to do it in future."

"And hopefully the good men of the church would cut out the rotten flesh from St. Michael and All Angels and replace them with true servants of God."

"God willing," murmured Bill. He looked rather appalled by the whole idea. Or maybe that was his natural expression these days. "But how will you put pressure on Brother Sebastian?"

Ela straightened her shoulders. "I shall visit him tomorrow in the house and accuse him directly."

"He'll deny it."

"I shall then tell him that I have the children—and that they've identified him—and that I intend to tell the sheriff everything…unless he strikes a bargain with me. On striking the bargain he'll reveal and seal his guilt."

"And you won't tell the sheriff?" Bill looked confused.

"Not if that's part of our compact. I won't go back on my word. It's no great loss since—if you'll recall—I've already told the sheriff of him and his role and he showed no interest. So I'd merely pledge not to remind the sheriff of what he already knows and does not care one whit about."

Bill blinked. She could tell he didn't entirely understand her motivation, but she had a clear picture in her head. Since realizing she could never point the finger of accusation at de Burgh—and learning how hard it was to wrap the noose around the neck of a slippery miscreant like Morhees, who was skilled at directing the finger of blame to others—she aimed to be more creative in her methods of pursuit.

By the end of the day tomorrow she intended to have Brother Sebastian in her snare.

CHAPTER 22

"*D*on't be so pessimistic. Money always works." Ela reassured Bill quietly as they walked to Abbot de Rouen's house late the next morning."

"He did take it before, I suppose." It was a bright October morning, the sky almost painfully blue.

"And he doesn't know it was us that freed the children. He just knows they're gone." Ela felt optimistic. "All we need is to get in the door."

Bill blew out a long breath. He'd hinted that he was still injured and hoped he was adequate to the task of defending her life. She reminded him that her entire household had instructions to rush to the sheriff if she didn't return before the bells for Sext.

Ela walked through the delicate wrought-iron gate that pierced the wall in front of the abbot's door. She walked up the neat stone path and rang the bell hanging to the right of the door. The dooryard smelled of the rosemary and lavender planted along the walk, in contrast to the stink of the city.

A pimple-faced young monk with an untidy tonsure

opened the door. "We seek Brother Sebastian," said Ela with a smile. "We bring another donation to contribute to the glory of God and the beauty of St. Michael and All Angels."

He ushered them in, and Ela turned to shoot a smile at Bill as the monk guided them into the same parlor, with its big silver cross. The tang of stale incense stung her nostrils. The black-and-white marble floor beneath their feet gave Ela a rush of remembered fury at how she'd been treated in this house.

She looked forward to seeing Brother Sebastian squirm.

After some length of time, Brother Sebastian entered, looking wary. She hadn't announced her name, but perhaps he suspected it would be her.

"Good morrow and God's blessings, my lady," he said. He carried a book under his arm. "Won't you be seated?" He gestured to a sturdy wood chair. "I thought you might like to see this richly illustrated Psalter that the church recently acquired." He held the book out to her. Bill swept in and took it from his hands.

Ela sensed alarm in Bill's swift movements. "This book is too heavy for the countess to handle." Ela's first instinct was to protest that she wasn't a weakling, but she deferred to Bill's sensibilities and allowed him to place it gingerly on the table and to turn the pages for her.

Meanwhile, a young boy with blond hair entered with a jug of wine and three cups. Another boy, a redhead, unfolded a small stand to hold the wine and the cups. Bill turned some pages of the book, a nice enough Psalter, but nothing to exclaim over, while Brother Sebastian poured the wine and placed the three cups on the table, one at a time, in front of each of them.

Bill, still holding the book, remarked that it was fine and asked if they had an illustrated Gospel they might see, as the countess took a special interest in them. Ela fought the urge to stare at him in disbelief. What did he think he was doing?

"We do indeed." He turned to the redhead boy and ordered him to fetch a blue-bound book from the sacristy.

Ela watched, from the corner of her eye, as Bill swiftly exchanged her cup for Brother Sebastian's.

Startled, she struggled to stay focused on her task.

"Let us drink a toast to the future of St. Michael and All Angels," said Brother Sebastian. "Which is bright thanks to your generosity."

"Thanks be to God," replied Ela, raising her cup. She pretended to take a large swallow, complete with moving her throat, and she saw Bill do the same. They all watched each other like hawks stalking a mouse. "As you may know, my beloved husband, William Longespée, died this March. I would like to give a gift in his name so that he'll be remembered in the prayers of all men who worship here." Ela felt confident that William would fully approve of her employing his name in this ruse. "What do you think would be appropriate? Perhaps a fine cup for the altar?"

Brother Sebastian peered into his cup. Then up at her. He opened his mouth, then tried to clear his throat. A flash of panic widened his eyes. "I—" The word stuck in his throat. A gurgling sound then emerged that caused Ela to glance at Bill in alarm.

Panic flared in her heart. "Are you ill, Brother Sebastian?" she asked.

"I...I..." he glanced at the cup again, and suddenly spilled its contents out, splashing the hem of his robe and her gown, too. Then he peered into the cup. "I am poisoned!" he croaked out. He threw the cup down, and Ela picked it up. At the bottom of the silver interior she could see clinging grains of a powdery substance—soaked and discolored by the wine.

Ela drew in a breath. "My companion took the precaution

of exchanging your cup for mine. I was surprised by his action, but I see he's saved my life. You were trying to kill me."

She had no idea what poison he'd used. Would he take days to die, like her poor, suffering husband? Or would he be blue-lipped on the floor in moments? She couldn't waste time in gaining the information she needed. "Who is the master that commands the stealing and distribution of children?"

Brother Sebastian slumped in his chair, clutching at his throat as if it burned. "You're a witch!"

"I most assuredly am not." She felt shockingly calm. "You, however, have committed great crimes in the eyes of God and man by helping to steal these children from their parents and send them to a terrible fate."

The monk let out a whimper. His face turned gray. "I beg you, fetch a priest!"

"To give you last rites?" Ela rose to her feet, her nerves firing. "Indeed I shall and you shall have to make a full confession to receive your absolution." This rather horrible turn of events could work in her favor. She rushed to the door. "Fetch Father Dominic! Brother Sebastian is dying!"

Three small boys poked their heads around the corner, eyes wide with alarm. "Fetch him!" she repeated. "And don't delay!"

Brother Sebastian had slumped right off his chair and lay curled on the floor. Bill sat in his chair like a wooden figure. Perhaps he contemplated the fate of his own immortal soul under the circumstances.

"Bill, once again, you've saved my life. God be praised for your quick thinking and courage," she reassured him. She crossed herself and he followed suit then pointed out that they both knew better than to sip from any cup in this residence.

She heard a scuffle of feet in the passage outside and Father Dominic burst into the room, followed by several young boys and a tall, thin monk. "What happened?"

"He tried to poison me by putting something in my wine," she said quickly. "But Sir William Talbot had the wisdom to switch our cups so he has killed himself instead."

"How do I know that you didn't put the poison in his cup yourself?" Father Dominic's voice trembled.

"I suppose you don't. But, for now, he must confess all his sins in order to obtain entry to the Kingdom of God." The tall monk whispered orders to the boys, who ran away, then returned with two candles and a phial of oil.

Brother Sebastian clutched at the hem of Father Dominic's robe. "Please!" he rasped. "Help me!"

Father Dominic muttered an invitation to confession through stiff lips. His hands trembled, and his whole robe shook, as he bent over the dying monk. Ela glanced at Bill, who had his hand on the hilt of his sword as if he were ready for anything.

"Bless me father, for I have sinned—" gasped out Brother Sebastian. "I have sinned in thought, word and deed—" Then he launched into a litany of sins that made Ela's scalp crawl. He'd worked for years helping his master steal children, and his reward had been to spend time pleasuring himself with them in ways that caused bile to rise in her throat.

"Who is your master?" Ela interrupted. "Who is the foul fiend who commands such ill-use of children?"

Brother Sebastian gagged hard, hands at his throat and his face twisted with pain. She began to worry that he'd die before revealing the name she needed.

"Is it Abbot de Rouen?"

Father Dominic gasped and crossed himself. "Watch your tongue, woman!" he cried.

"This is not any woman, this is the Countess of Salisbury," protested Bill. Ela held up a hand for him to hush.

"It is… Abbot de Rouen," choked out the writhing monk. "He understood my special love for children—because he shared it himself." His eyes squeezed tight shut and he clutched his knees to his stomach. "We saved them from a life of poverty," he rasped. "And lifted them to a higher cause."

"Of being interfered with by disgusting perverts?" Ela couldn't hold her tongue. "May God forgive you because I cannot." She felt a sob rise in her throat. Thank God she finally had her answer, and in front of a roomful of witnesses. "Who else? Is Father Dominic involved?"

"No!" protested Father Dominic. "I know nothing of this."

Ela stared at him, trying to determine if he was lying.

Brother Sebastian rolled over onto his back, his face a mask of agony. "I'm dying!"

Father Dominic murmured words Ela had last heard when Bishop Poore uttered them over the hunched form of her dying husband. The priest applied oil to his eyes and mouth just as the bishop had done for dear William. Tears sprang into her eyes and blurred the scene and she found herself praying for William, who'd feared so greatly for the fate of his immortal soul.

When she blinked back her tears, Brother Sebastian lay still, his lips frozen in an odd pucker and his face ashen.

Father Dominic made the sign of the cross over him. "Lord Jesus Christ, receive the spirit of our departed brother."

After a moment of stunned silence, Bill rose to his feet. "We must summon the coroner."

255

"NO ONE LEAVE THIS ROOM," said Ela. "Until the coroner arrives." A servant was sent to fetch him.

Father Dominic's lips almost disappeared in his long mournful face. "You've killed him."

"Wait until the coroner arrives," said Ela. She didn't want to tell him what had happened because he might go remove all traces of poison from the dead monk's cell so as to better point the blame at them.

"On what authority?" asked Father Dominic, drawing himself up.

"On mine as Countess of Salisbury." She wished she could say, *and sheriff of Wiltshire*, but that would come soon enough. "Brother Sebastian is wanted for crimes against children, and Roger le Duc, the sheriff of London, is well aware of it. And don't pretend you're ignorant of this iniquity. This house is filled with young children."

"The church has a fine choir of young boys, as do many in this city."

"What of the African boy? And this young servant?" She pointed to the blond boy who'd brought their wine. He had the rose-cheeked beauty of a girl, and his blue eyes were wide with fear. "It seems unnatural for men of God to have young children as servants. In a religious house it's conventional to have the brothers serve each other."

"What do you know of a religious order?" scoffed Father Dominic.

"Much. My family founded the priory at Bradenstoke three generations ago, and we've maintain close relations with it since. My late husband charged me to found an order in his memory, and I also intend to found a holy order of sisters and join it myself. So the organization and management of a religious house is a subject close to my heart and one which I have studied for some time."

The priest looked more confused than ever. "I've only

been here a short while."

"As you told me previously. Have you met Abbot de Rouen?" Her curiosity was getting the better of her, though they really should wait for the coroner or the sheriff to arrive.

"I met him, yes. Before he left for Rome."

"Did he strike you as a holy man? A pious servant of God?"

Father Dominic blinked. A muscle worked in his jaw. "I was not fortunate enough to become intimate with him."

"Your answer speaks volumes," replied Ela.

IT SEEMED an eternity before the coroner finally arrived. The two child servants sat on the floor, their backs against the wall. Father Dominic stood stiff as a board in his cassock, his face gray-white against his dark hair and his bony fingers working the wooden cross around his neck in moments of distraction.

Bill, calm and watchful as always, remained a soothing presence. Ela always preferred action to quiet waiting—a failing she regularly prayed over—and had to school herself to be patient. She even suggested that they say some prayers over the lifeless body of Brother Sebastian, who was—after all—still a child of God even as he was a monster who preyed on children. Father Dominic led them in a few disconsolate prayers and looked as relieved as she was to hear the clatter of hooves on the cobbles outside.

Two of the sheriff's men burst in before the coroner, Theobald Crux, entered the room, panting slightly, his white hair disordered. His eyes fixed immediately on Ela. She suspected that different words hovered on his tongue, but when his mouth opened, he said "My lady," with a slight bow.

Ela rose, "God be with you, Master Crux." She drew a deep breath. "We came here to offer a donation to the church, and Brother Sebastian offered us each a cup of wine. On a hunch, my companion, Sir William Talbot, exchanged Brother Sebastian's cup with the one intended for me while his back was turned. The results are as you see."

She looked down at the contorted form of the monk where he lay on the floor, his robe gathered up around his knees, exposing his short, hairy calves.

"He died of poisoning?" Crux knelt over the body and lifted one of Brother Sebastian's eyelids to peer at his eyeball.

"To all appearances. When he poured out his wine on the floor"—she pointed to the splash that decorated her hem —"there were grains of...some substance remaining in the dregs." She pointed to the cup. Crux rose creakily, and peered into it. He sniffed it and frowned.

"It must have been a very fast-acting poison," said Ela. "He felt its effects from the first sip."

Father Dominic took a step forward. "For all I know, he was poisoned by these people here." He spoke tremulously, clearly not sure where his interests lay.

Crux looked at him. "Who are you?"

"I am the priest charged with guiding the flock of St. Michael and All Angels in Abbot de Rouen's absence."

"I took the precaution of keeping everyone in this room while we waited for you," said Ela to Crux. "So that one of your men could search Brother Sebastian's room for poison. I didn't want an accomplice to go remove evidence before you arrived."

Crux gave a signal to one of his men and spoke to Father Dominic. "Have your servant show us his room and show proof that it is indeed his room."

Father Dominic ordered the blond boy to lead him. Ela

took reassurance in the fact that the child would have no motivation to lie about whose room they entered.

Crux looked at Bill, who winced involuntarily, possibly from the pain of his injuries which likely were aggravated by sitting so long. "What made you exchange the cups?"

Bill cleared his throat. "I suspected that Brother Sebastian knew the Countess of Salisbury had uncovered his ring of child thieves and that she'd identified him as part of it. I thought that she placed herself in danger coming here."

"Then why did you come here?" asked Crux of Ela. His white brows lowered over sharp, dark eyes.

"To find the truth," said Ela. "We saw Brother Sebastian taking food to the warehouse where the children were imprisoned. I informed the sheriff of this already."

Crux looked confused. Clearly the sheriff had not mentioned the matter to him.

"I had asked the sheriff to gain entry to the warehouse and free the children, but he was unwilling to force the door. I'm afraid I decided to take matters into my own hands, and the rescued children are now at my mother's house."

Crux's eyes widened.

"Brother Sebastian played a role in this gang of child thieves, but I knew there must be a head to this diseased body. Brother Sebastian's confession—witnessed by Father Dominic—revealed that fiend to be none other than Abbot de Rouen himself."

Crux stared from Ela to Father Dominic and back. His expression remained blank.

Fear flared in Ela's heart. Theobald Crux was undoubtedly a man with many years of experience. Had those years sharpened his tools in the quest for justice, or blunted them for use against the powerful institutions that ran this city—and this country?

"Just because he bears the title of abbot does not mean he

is a true servant of God," protested Ela, before Crux had a chance to respond. "As he made his final confession, Brother Sebastian described the foul ways that de Rouen and himself, and countless others, used these children and many others over the course of some years."

Crux looked at Father Dominic. "What ways were these?"

Father Dominic swayed slightly, as if in a wind. Ela saw his throat bob. "He did describe…uh…intimacies…" His voice tailed off as if his throat were swallowing itself.

"Intimacies of a…" Crux glanced at Ela. "Of a sexual nature?"

"Yes," rasped Father Dominic. "I assure you that I played no role whatsoever in these activities. If they even existed. Which I doubt." His voice gained strength as it rose on this final note of protest. "As I've mentioned, I came to London only recently, from Norwich."

Crux examined the body, then closed both eyes in a practiced gesture of his fingertips. He rose creakily to his feet and peered at Bill Talbot. "You'd like me to believe that you came here expecting to be poisoned?"

"Expecting the countess to be poisoned. We'd already discussed that neither of us should eat or drink anything within these walls."

"So, since you didn't intend for either the countess or yourself to drink this wine, by giving it to Brother Sebastian you have effectively murdered him." The word *murdered* rang off the carved stone of the great fireplace.

"It was Brother Sebastian who intended to commit murder. Sir William only intended to save me from poisoning," cut in Ela. "He had no way of knowing for certain if I'd drink it or not."

Bill stood gallantly still, looking ready for a blow on the chin. Ela's heart swelled with tenderness for him. Even injured and in daily pain, he remained her resolute defender.

"Sir William Talbot bears no responsibility for anything beyond protecting me from harm, which he's bravely done since I was a girl."

"Perhaps you could explain why you expected Brother Sebastian to poison your mistress?" Crux peered at Bill.

Bill launched into an account of the events of the past weeks: the disappearance of Edyth Wheaton from Salisbury and their efforts to seek her; the information Ela had received from Spicewell's informants and their subsequent pursuit; Ela's kidnapping; the death of Vicus Morhees and the subsequent slaying of her two guards and the discovery of the children in the warehouse. "It's possible that Brother Sebastian knew the countess was involved in the removal of the children."

"Then why would he let her into the house?" asked Crux, looking doubtful.

"Most likely because he saw an opportunity to be rid of me," replied Ela. "Though I did promise a large donation to St. Michael and All Angels, and I intend to uphold that promise." She paused. "Though naturally I wish the donation to assist in their efforts to celebrate the glory of God, not to further the enslavement of young children for sinful purposes."

"Quite," muttered Crux. "I must speak with the sheriff about this. My men shall remove the body." He looked from Father Dominic to Ela to Bill, possibly wishing he could reasonably arrest at least one of them. "There is the matter of the poison."

Ela looked at the door. The young boy had not returned with Crux's men. "Shall we help you look for the poison?"

"Absolutely not." He harrumphed. "Please return to your home and await word from either myself or the sheriff. This is an investigation of murder. Neither you or Sir William may leave the City of London until this matter is resolved."

CHAPTER 23

The children kept Ela occupied and the household bustling. Some of the children agitated to return home, but Ela reminded them that they would need to testify about their captors to the sheriff. Instead she helped them compose letters to their worried families, and hired messengers to deliver them without delay, with instructions to read them aloud in case the recipients weren't lettered.

The sheriff didn't arrive until the next day. He rode up with two men and a world-weary expression on his face.

"You understand that I can't arrest an abbot," he said, after the polite preliminaries. "Especially not one that is currently in Rome."

"Men of God are not above the laws of man," protested Ela. She'd expected this line of evasion. "Right now, today, Abelard de Rouen might be interfering with young children. The children eating their bread in my kitchen said that three of their number went with him to Rome. Those unfortunate souls have no doubt already been sold into the households of other degenerates. Do you think it's fair they should be forced into a life of sin and suffering in a foreign land, never to see their loved ones again?"

Her voice rose as passion filled her, but she couldn't bear for le Duc to think this was just another "unfortunate matter" that they would have to ignore because it trampled on the toes of powerful men.

Le Duc had the decency to look sheepish for a moment before his brows lowered into a stern expression. "You could be accused of breaking and entering for forcing your way into that warehouse."

"To rescue innocent children!"

"You could also be accused—at least Sir William Talbot could be—of killing Brother Sebastian by giving him a cup of poisoned wine."

"Sir William had no way of knowing that wine was poisoned."

"The coroner said that he switched his cup with yours."

"On suspicion that it *might* be poisoned. If Brother Sebastian hadn't poisoned it himself, he would still be walking among us. He sealed his own fate."

"And conveniently confessed his crimes with a roomful of witnesses. You almost couldn't have planned it better." Le Duc looked down the length of his nose.

"He certainly incriminated the abbot." Ela inhaled. "Look to your conscience. Can you sleep at night knowing that a fiend is stealing children and pressing them into slavery?"

Le Duc looked vaguely uncomfortable, but did not dignify her question with a reply. "I understand that you'll soon be sheriff of Wiltshire," he said, after a pause.

"Indeed." She lifted her chin. "I trust that I'll serve the people of Wiltshire to the best of my abilities. I certainly intend to prosecute all villains to the fullest extent of the law, regardless of their wealth or connections."

"I sincerely hope that your worthy ideals are not soon

bruised by convention." His wry expression contradicted his words. "The fact remains that the person managing the day-to-day activities, Brother Sebastian, is now dead, as is Vicus Morhees, who was some kind of procurer for them. The abbot is beyond our reach, so, as far as I am concerned the case is closed."

Ela struggled to keep her expression calm. "Did you interview the children in the household? They may know of other members of the order who are involved."

"And who will be untouchable behind the invisible rood screens of church hierarchy."

Ela tried to control her fury. His nonchalant attitude irked her as much as his dismissive words. "Our good King Henry is a worthy and pious man. I'm sure he'll be deeply shaken by this flowering of evil in a church so close to his palace at Westminster." She paused and peered right into le Duc's eyes. "I shall write to him at once, and we shall see if he finds this matter so easy to ignore."

The tiniest hint of alarm lit the darkness of le Duc's eyes.

"Perhaps I could talk to the children and try to learn more about the people involved," he said slowly. "Then if events are as you describe I could write to Rome and inform the pope that one of his abbots has wandered too far from the fold and needs to be disciplined."

Ela allowed a tiny smile to cross her lips. "The children could meet with you in this parlor. Would you like to see them one at a time or as a group?"

"One at a time, to start with."

THE SHERIFF and one of his men spent most of the afternoon deposing each of the children. They learned damning information about Abbot de Rouen, who had personally undressed and groped several of the children before leaving on his pilgrimage to Rome. Their stories were so consistent that le Duc could hardly dismiss them as childish fancy.

They also learn details of the depravity of Brother Sebastian, who would do disgusting things to the children, then exhort them to pray for absolution from their sins. Their accounts implicated the late and unlamented Vicus Morhees and eight or nine other individuals in the London area in criminal activities related to stealing or imprisoning or abusing the children.

Ela stayed in the background, encouraging the children to be truthful, even if the truth was difficult. Some were glad to tell, others so distressed and ashamed that they could barely get the words out. She assured them that what had happened to them was none of their fault and they had committed no sin.

The abbot and his tonsured henchman, however…

At last the children were sent to the kitchen to eat a meat stew and le Duc donned his leather gloves in the front hallway, ready to leave.

"How will you proceed?" Ela quietly blocked the doorway as she asked her question.

Le Duc's face was grave. "A terrible crime was committed against these children."

"And countless others. This has been going on for years."

Le Duc cleared his throat. "I intend to write to the pope and inform him of the abbot's ungodly activities. I will also tell him about Brother Sebastian and the other brothers mentioned and suggest that the entire order undergo a severe housecleaning."

"I'm glad to hear it." Ela wanted to cheer aloud but managed to restrain herself. "What action do you expect the pope to take?"

"I expect him to order an inquisition into the abbot's

behavior. Given the large number of witnesses and the number of killings associated with this criminal activity, I do not imagine that even Rome will be able to sweep this aside. I fully anticipate that the abbot will be excommunicated and likely hanged for his crimes."

Ela didn't enjoy planning an execution even when the culprit was guilty as sin itself. In this instance she did feel that the earth would be rid of a foul scourge in the person of Abbot de Rouen, who'd used his power and his "holy pilgrimages" to transport enslaved and abused children throughout Europe and beyond.

"And can you take steps to shut down the overseas channels by which these children are placed in foreign hands?"

Le Duc frowned. "I can reach out to the authorities in Bruges. That seems to be where the last shipment of children went. From there, who knows where they ended up."

"God willing, they will all be returned safe home to England," said Ela.

"The world is a bottomless cesspit of crime, my lady." Le Duc looked tired beyond his characteristic world-weary expression. "The trafficking of children has doubtless gone on since the beginning of time and shall continue until Judgment Day, but rest assured I will do what I can to fight against it here and now."

"God go with you, Sheriff le Duc." She lowered her voice. "Your position as sheriff of London is no doubt a delicate balancing act between prosecuting criminals and maintaining the favor of the powerful—without which you would not long hold your position. I shall endeavor to learn from your experience and temper my idealism with wisdom."

"God go with you, my lady," he said, with a small bow. Unwritten words hung in the air…. *Because you'll need Him.*

A SWIFT INVESTIGATION into the Abbot's channels of transport led to the arrest of another tonsured procurer in Bruges, who in turn pointed to a Parisian order infected with the disease of abusing and selling children. In time the conspiracy and its chain of arrests led all the way to Venice and from there to Rome. A new abbot was appointed to command St. Michael and All Angels, and Ela prayed he would be just and kind with the children already there.

Ela heard of these events by letter, since she returned immediately to Gomeldon. Most of the children were returned to their homes, except for three who either didn't know where their home was or didn't want to go there for fear of being sold again.

Ela offered Elsie Brice a job in her household as a temporary assistant to Hilda, whose pregnancy sometimes caused her to be too ill to tend to Ela's needs. Once she had an idea of Elsie's aptitudes, she could find her a more permanent position. Elsie did not broach the question of Ela having any role in her parents' deaths—perhaps she knew little of the whole disturbing affair—and Ela did not intend to bring it up. She did, however, send word to Elsie's siblings that their sister was returned safe to Salisbury and that they could visit her when they were able.

Before leaving for Gomeldon, Ela arranged for her bankers to make full payment to the king. She had Spicewell review all the contracts to make sure the payment of her "fine" would obtain the fealty she required—full possession of the castle and the role of high sheriff of Wiltshire.

As expected she could not seize either immediately. De Hal had no doubt paid a sizable sum to obtain the castle and the position, and whoever had pocketed the money—de Burgh, perhaps—no doubt had to scramble to find him a new, suitable position without alerting the king to his dealings.

Ultimately it was agreed that she should be installed in the castle by Whitsuntide of following year. In the meantime, she vowed to review the management of her estates and pour herself into plans for the two monasteries she'd pledged to found, one in her husband's name and one in her own.

CHAPTER 24

*B*y a quirk of circumstance—or the will of Heaven —Ela took possession of Fernlees in trust for Hilda's baby on the same day that Abbot de Rouen arrived in London in chains. The disgraced cleric was imprisoned in the White Tower to await his trial. A messenger galloped to Salisbury with the news.

Arriving at Gomeldon midmorning of the following day, the rider had to gallop onward to Fernlees to find Ela, who'd taken Hilda to visit the manor that would soon be home to her and her child. Ela received the news of the abbot's imprisonment with gratitude and urged the messenger to head back to Gomeldon to take rest and food.

"Everyone is where they should be," exclaimed Hilda, as she picked her way across the weedy courtyard at Fernlees. She walked halfway to the house, beaming, then turned back. "Elsie, would you bring my cloak? There's a chill in the air."

Ela, stunned, wasn't sure whether to scold Hilda for acting like a little lady of the manor or to encourage it. She suspected Hilda was only mimicking her own imperious behavior. Except that she hadn't realized how imperious she must sound until she heard her words issuing from her maid's mouth.

Elsie brought the cloak without a word of complaint—the girl rarely spoke—and put it on Hilda's shoulders. Hilda's head-turning beauty, a dangerous liability in a poor servant girl, would serve her in good stead as a young lady of property in search of a husband.

Even her pregnancy could be somehow reinvented as a sworn engagement tragically broken by the cruel murder of her fiancé. It was hardly unknown in these fast-moving times for a girl to share her virtue with her lover before marriage. And her child's natural father had once been a knight of the realm, even if he'd come to them in much reduced circumstances.

Hilda tested the handle on the door. "It's locked."

"I have the key," said Ela. She produced it and let Hilda open the door of her new home.

The lock required a good deal of rattling and produced a rain of rust. Hilda's smile fell from her face as the door creaked open to reveal a filthy clay tile floor, cobwebs hanging from the low-beamed ceiling and a large rat scurrying into the ash-filled hearth. "It needs cleaning," said Ela, with what she hoped was a reassuring tone.

"Will I have to clean it?" asked Hilda, plaintive.

"Who better? Elsie can help. And I'll send a lad to help with the hard scrubbing and the weeding."

Hilda took a tentative step forward. The house had sat empty for months and had no doubt been neglected even while still in use. An unpleasant odor hung in the air. At least Drogo Blount couldn't see the sad state of his old family home.

"It's very large," said Hilda as she peered around the corner into the hall. A scarred table with two benches sat at the far end. Ancient and weighty it was about the only thing that hadn't been removed—likely sold—by the manor's previous occupants. Even the fire irons were gone.

Ela sighed. Did she need to furnish this house for Hilda and her baby? Once you held out a helping hand to lift someone up it started a chain of responsibilities that never seemed to end. But no doubt she could find some sticks of furniture about her manors and have them brought here to give the young family a start.

Though Fernlees dwarfed the country cottage Hilda had grown up in, it would be a comfortable home once a fire burned in the grate and the rat was banished back to the woods.

"We must tour the fields and forest and assess the best way to wring an income from the property," said Ela brightly. She wanted to get outside and away from the stale atmosphere of dead rat. "For you'll need money to repair the thatch and replaster the wattle and buy clothes and food for yourself and your baby."

God willing, Ela could find a husband to help Hilda manage the estate. The girl had proved herself kind and willing, but she did not have a head for business. Ela had tried to teach her to manage the kitchen accounts and found it tiring work.

Hilda had already run upstairs to see the bedrooms. "Oh, there's a view over the meadow from this one. It shall be mine!" she exclaimed cheerfully. "And I shall put the cradle in this corner, away from the drafts."

Ela followed Hilda upstairs, with Elsie trailing silently behind her. The spring had reappeared in Hilda's step, and she dashed from room to room. "I shall have seven children in all, and they can share a room, two and two!"

Ela smiled. "May God bless you with all the children you desire. They are the greatest joy in life."

Hilda bustled into the next room. "Don't your children

miss you when you're so busy solving crimes and catching criminals?"

Ela stopped in her tracks. Was this censure? Or genuine curiosity?

And was it perhaps her own guilt that made her look to Hilda's motive for asking it?

"No doubt your mother was often busy with her tasks—milking a cow or spinning wool or weaving a basket—but she was there for you all the same."

"Oh, yes. I didn't mean to criticize. And where would poor dear Elsie be if you didn't put the needs of others ahead of your own?"

Ela glanced at Elsie. Who looked swiftly down at the floor. The poor girl had not yet recovered from her ordeal. Worse yet, her aunt and uncle had sold her into it and she had no true home to return to.

On instinct Ela took hold of the girl by her upper arms. "The Lord has big plans for you, Elsie. He brought you into my life when I need you most." She laid a kiss on the girl's smooth, pale forehead. "Sibel, my faithful lady's maid of many years, abandoned me for a husband, and now Hilda, her niece, will soon be busy with her child. Who would take care of me if you weren't here?"

Elsie did her best to manage a crooked smile, but Ela could tell that tears hovered behind it. "I thank you, my lady, for your kindness," she stammered, in her country accent. "I'll do my best to repay it."

"You owe me no debt, Elsie." Ela squeezed her arms. "Wait until we move to the castle. You'll be rushed off your feet."

"It's almost half a mile from one side of the hall to the other," said Hilda with a grin. "Sibel said she was up and down stairs all day there."

"That's hardly true," protested Ela, surprised that Sibel would have said such a thing to her family. Then she realized she'd grown defensive about what was no doubt a well-meaning jest. "Well, perhaps there is a grain of truth to it. It was built to accommodate a large family and half of Wiltshire at the same time."

She kept hoping to see a glimmer of something—anything—in Elsie's big brown eyes, but it was not to be. Ela lifted her hands away and wrung them together for a moment. "Hilda, make a tally in your mind of the tasks to be done. As mistress of Fernlees it's your duty to plan the work and make sure it gets done."

"When will I move here?"

"Not until the floor is mopped, that's for certain." Ela didn't want to answer that question. Should she wait until the girl was safely delivered of her baby and secure in her claim to the manor? Or should she move in early with—perhaps—a sister or another aunt to help care for her in her confinement?

So many questions. And Ela still didn't know exactly when she could move back to the castle. Her comfortable feather bed at Gomeldon itched her like a hair shirt. She craved the bracing morning air of the windy castle mound and the flurry of public affairs in her great hall.

"What's in this room?" Elsie tugged at the handle of the door at the end of the hall. It had a simple pull handle with no lock, but firmly resisted her efforts to open it.

"I'm sure it's just another bedchamber," said Ela, ready to be quit of this untidy place, which had a rank smell of disuse. "Likely the wood has expanded and it's stuck. One of the lads can free it for you."

"It's not stuck, it's nailed shut. Look!" She pointed to wooden blocks nailed into place at the top and bottom.

"How odd." Ela's walked over and peered at it. "Why would anyone do that?"

"Maybe this is where Morhees kept his treasure?" said

Hilda in a rush of excitement. "You said he was like a pirate. They usually have a treasure chest hidden somewhere."

"Only in tall tales, my dear." Ela frowned. "But now I'm curious." She drew the knife from her belt, slid the blade under the block and wiggled it slowly to lever the block up from the floor, pulling the nail with it. It sprang free, sending her backward, where she almost knocked Hilda off her feet.

She stood on an old chair to perform the same operation on the upper block, and as the long nail and its block fell to the floor, the door creaked open.

"Ew! What is that smell?" Hilda's hands flew to her nose. There was indeed a fearful smell—like that which pervaded the rest of the house but a thousand times worse now that it was released by the open door.

The smell of death.

Ela's breath caught in her throat. Elsie retched, the first sound she'd made in ages.

"I think we should go," said Hilda tremulously.

But Ela pushed the door open to reveal a dark room, the sole window shuttered from the inside. Her hand pressed to her mouth, she hurried to the window and unlatched the shutter. Light poured in, revealing the room to be cluttered with battered pieces of old furniture and a rolled tapestry with visible moth damage on the exposed underside.

On the far side of the room she saw a familiar sight. The wood trunk belonging to the late Jacobus Pinchbeck. The one that contained his ledgers—coded and inscrutable—and his various accounts. He'd been found dead, crushed by his own cartwheels, and his son Osbert had taken over his business, only to be duped out of it by the vile Vicus Morhees.

Ela's stomach shriveled. *Something—someone—is inside that trunk.* And she was almost certain who.

Still pressing one hand to her nose in a vain attempt to keep out the odor of death, she forced the blade of her knife into the lock. It took some doing, but eventually she was able to break the mechanism. The heavy lid seemed weighed down by all the cares of the world. "Help me, Hilda." Ela struggled to lift it. Hilda, who had shrunk back into the doorway, came reluctantly forward and peeled a hand away from her face to help lift it.

Hilda screamed and sprang back when the contents came into view. Ela, still holding one hand to cover her nose and mouth, was forced to snatch her hand back to stop it being crushed as the lid fell.

She heard Hilda's panicked feet on the stairs, and Elsie's hurried after them. Deciding that their wisdom exceeded hers, she followed them down the stairs and out into the open air.

"Oh, my blessed saints," squeaked Hilda. "There's a dead body in there! Horrible and purple with great holes for eyes."

Elsie bent double over a clump of wild St. John's wort and emptied her stomach.

"I'm sorry you had to see that." Ela laid a hand on Elsie's back and offered her handkerchief for the girl to wipe her mouth. "But I know who it is. We must call the coroner."

"Who is it?" Hilda gazed fiercely at the house. "Who's dead in my child's house?"

"I fear it's Osbert Pinchbeck, a former inhabitant of the house. Vicus Morhees told us he'd gone abroad, but he was sealed up in that room the whole time."

Hilda stared at her. "He's the man that had Drogo arrested for poaching! Osbert Pinchbeck wanted to get my beloved hanged for trying to feed himself in his time of need." She spat his name like a curse. "If it wasn't for you he would have seen Drogo hang."

"That is indeed true." She wanted to scold Hilda for calling Drogo her beloved. "I also thought it was unfair." In retrospect, inviting the lascivious Drogo—charming rogue though he was—into her home had unleashed a tidal wave of trouble.

"Pinchbeck deserves to rot in there."

"The Lord is our final judge, Hilda."

"He shall be judged harshly." She pursed her pretty mouth.

"So shall we all."

ELA TOOK the girls home to Gomeldon, then returned to Fernlees to meet the coroner. Haughton's bay palfrey stood tied up outside when she arrived back there with a single armed escort.

Ela found herself humming with anticipation as she entered the door. She'd missed her almost daily interactions with the gruff coroner. "Sir Giles?" She called up the stairs.

"My lady Ela!" He emerged from the unlocked room, his voice as filled with cheer as her heart. "It's good to see you again, though perhaps not under these circumstances."

"Poor dead Osbert Pinchbeck was here under our noses—quite literally—the whole time."

"Indeed," said Giles Haughton, from the top of the stairs. "Morhees must have encouraged him to spread the news of a sojourn abroad so that no one would question his disappearance. Then he strangled him."

"You can tell?" Ela braced herself for a return upstairs. The smell had been largely kept out of the rest of the house by the tight-fitting locked door. Now the foul odor of death permeated the entire space. But as sheriff, she couldn't be squeamish about a dead body. Even one that had been pickling in its own juices for many weeks.

"The ruined skin of his neck still bears ligature marks. He was strangled with something thin, like a leather whip end."

Ela crossed herself as she entered the room. "May God rest his soul."

"Unlikely, since he apparently killed his own father, with goading from the double-crossing Vicus Morhees."

"Who is undoubtedly sweating in the sewers of hell himself."

"Morhees is dead?" Haughton's eyebrows rose.

Ela blinked. "It's been some time since we spoke. He fell afoul of his evil bedfellows in the child abduction ring. He was the link back to Salisbury and the reason that Edyth Wheaton and Elsie Brice were taken. Though Elsie Brice was sold by her aunt and uncle, poor thing. Such a thing shouldn't be legal, though my lawyer informs me that it's not explicitly forbidden."

"There would be little point in locking up Elsie's uncle and aunt and turning the rest of the children out on the road to starve."

"True, though you know I would never do that."

The familiar teasing glow lit his eyes. "You would find them all a place in your household?"

She should be offended at his mockery, but she just smiled. "I shall have room for more helpers. Perhaps you haven't heard? My household will soon be growing."

The sparkle left his eyes. "You are to marry?"

"No!" Ela stared at him for a moment. Then laughed. "I am to take up residence at the castle again, as sheriff of Wiltshire."

Haughton stared back at her, clearly astonished. He looked as if he didn't believe her, or he thought her touched in the head.

"I've made an arrangement with the king," she explained, somewhat affronted by his disbelief. "It's all settled."

"Congratulations," He made a small bow. "My lady sheriff. I shall be pleased to see you return to the castle. I tire of de

Hal's antics. He seems more interested in gaining property for himself and his cronies than in maintaining the rule of law and order."

"Fear not, he'll be gone by next Whitsun."

Haughton beamed. "It will be a tonic to all Salisbury to see you restored to your rightful family home."

"And to myself as well. I look forward to having many more conversations with you in close proximity to a moldering corpse." She cast a glance at the box. She noticed for the first time that the wood down near the floor was stained darker than the rest, no doubt from the liquid produced during the putrefaction process.

"Your strong stomach is a testament to you. De Hal would have excused himself some time since," said Haughton with a grin.

"I've raised eight children, which will strengthen the stomach of almost anyone."

"Yet, God be praised, your heart is not hardened to the ills of the world like a battle-weary soldier's might be."

"And I hope it never shall be. A sheriff should not be concerned only with matters of property and maintaining the king's peace. An orphaned peasant girl is as much a child of God as the king himself and deserves the same protections from the cruelty of men. It's intolerable that a holy order should provide the channels to transport young children throughout Europe and beyond. And worse, that men who pledged themselves to serve God were interfering with them for their own indecent purposes."

Haughton sighed. "It's not the first time I've heard of such."

Ela looked at him. "You know of others? How has no one put a stop to them?"

Haughton cleared his throat and glanced over at the box, where the stinking remains of Osbert Pinchbeck festered.

"The church is more powerful than any man, even the king. To step on a bishop's robe is to tread on the tail of a deadly snake."

Ela struggled to compose her thoughts and drew in a deep breath. "While I fear God, I do not fear the mortal men that sully the sanctified ground of his holy church. If they do wrong they shall fear his wrath and mine too." She paused. "But I shall think twice before asking you to step on a viper's tail."

"For you, my lady, I shall grab the serpent behind its head, should the need arise."

His deadly serious tone made her laugh even as his words warmed her heart. "Let's hope that will not be necessary."

He sighed, and a wry smile tugged at his mouth. "With you, my lady, anything is possible."

THE END

AUTHOR'S NOTE

Simon de Hal is a historical figure who did become sheriff of Wiltshire shortly after the death of Ela's husband, William Longespée. It suited my artistic purposes to have him be less than stellar in the role, but when I researched him it soon turned out that he was an absolute supervillain. There are records of multiple lawsuits filed by his lawyers laying claim to other people's property. The letter from the burgesses of Scarborough is lengthy and describes such violence and intimidation at the hands of de Hal's men that local people were afraid to bring their goods to market. Ela must have been horrified when her beloved castle was handed over to such a man in the wake of her husband's death.

Henry III's Fine Rolls reveal that Ela did indeed pay a fine of £500—a great sum—to regain shrievalty of Salisbury castle and take up the role of sheriff of Wiltshire in 1227. Later she had to pay another fine of £200 to keep them. Talk about a racket! It's hard to imagine the level of chutzpah that must have been required for her, a forty-year-old widow with young children at home, to demand this degree of power from the king—especially considering that Hubert de Burgh was the young king's closest advisor. As is mentioned in book 1, Ela had coldly turned down a marriage offer from de Burgh's nephew Raimund, observing his family's low social status compared to her own (and the fact that her husband, though missing, was still alive). This must have keenly insulted de Burgh, who was arguably the most powerful man in the land and was by then married to Margaret, the daughter of King William I of Scotland. Given that contemporary chronicler Roger of Wendover himself accused de Burgh of poisoning William Longespée, it must have taken tremendous courage and self-confidence for Ela to stride into de Burgh's royal sphere and make her demands. I can only imagine that she showed the same bravery and daring in the role of sheriff. I look forward to imagining her exploits in that role in future books.

If you have questions or comments, please get in touch at jglewis@stoneheartpress.com.

Cover image includes: detail from Codex Manesse, ca. 1300, Heidelberg University Library; decorative detail from Beatus of Liébana, Fecundus Codex of 1047, Biblioteca Nacional de España; detail with Longespée coat of arms from Matthew Parris, *Historia Anglorum,* ca. 1250, British Museum.

Printed in Great Britain
by Amazon

77894918R00171